THE LOST DRESSES OF ITALY

THE LOST DRESSES OF ITALY

A NOVEL

M. A. McLaughlin

alcove
press

Copyright © 2024 by M. A. McLaughlin

Published in the United States by Alcove Press, an imprint of The Quick Brown Fox & Company LLC.

Alcove Press and its logo are trademarks of The Quick Brown Fox & Company LLC.

Library of Congress Catalog-in-Publication data available upon request.

ISBN (trade paperback): 978-1-63910-564-9
ISBN (ebook): 978-1-63910-565-6

Cover design by Lynn Andreozzi

Printed in the United States.

www.alcovepress.com

Alcove Press
34 West 27th St., 10th Floor
New York, NY 10001

First Edition: February 2024

10 9 8 7 6 5 4 3 2 1

Dedicated to my dear husband, Jim

"Il percorso verso il paradiso inizia all'inferno—The path to heaven begins in hell."

—Dante Alighieri

PROLOGUE

Verona, Italy
April 1945

I couldn't wait much longer; it was too dangerous to remain in the empty streets of Verona at such a late hour. Vile things happened to those who lingered alone in the dark, the kinds of unspeakable acts that people only hinted at in hushed tones for weeks afterwards—and never quite forgot.

Glancing up and down the Via Salerno, I watched as the night shadows crept along the street with spidery tentacles, moving along from building to building as if hunting for lost souls. My hands grew clammy at the chill, black silence.

But I stood my ground, flattened against the palazzo wall behind me, trying to blend into the hard stone against my back while I waited anxiously for my buyer to arrive; he'd promised on the phone to bring enough lire to purchase what I had to sell: a valuable Renaissance emerald. The stone had been attached to a basket pendant of woven yellow gold which I had already melted down, and now I needed to dispose of the jewel. After some haggling, we had eventually agreed on a sum and a meeting time; he said he would wear a white rose in his lapel so I'd recognize him. The color of purity and innocence, though our transaction was neither since I was a thief and he was a criminal.

Granted, I shouldn't have taken the jewel, but these were desperate times, and those I loved needed food and shelter. Once they were taken care of, I would make certain the partisans received the rest of the proceeds.

We all simply wanted to survive the war and were holding our collective breath as if in the moment between the thunder and the rain; perhaps when the skies finally opened, they would wash away all of our sins. At least, I fervently wished that would be true.

If I lived to see it . . .

Everyone was terrified the end would not come soon enough.

No lights appeared in the windows along the street—just empty, dim portals, behind which people huddled, hesitant to switch on even a single lamp for fear it would draw attention to their homes. It was safer that way because, after midnight, the last remnants of German soldiers would come out and pick through the rubble, helping themselves to any scraps of food or clothing. Their Führer's surrender was all but certain, but a few loyalists remained in parts of the city, hiding in the ruins of bombed buildings, not willing to accept defeat in spite of their hunger and misery. They were starving, and I knew their despair only too well; but I also hated them enough to kill over this jewel. I touched the pistol tucked into my belt. I had used it before, and I would again.

If they knew what I possessed, they would surely try to shoot me first.

Then it began to drizzle, just a light mist—hardly a redemptive cleansing, but enough to blur the harsh reality of the ruins that lay around me: the crumbling palazzos and unevenly pitted streets took on a hazy glow. And the smell of decay turned to a pleasant scent of moss and cedar.

Allowing my thoughts to drift away for a few moments, I could see the Via Salerno in my mind's eye on a bright summer's day, with the vividly colored palazzos of my boyhood: shutters thrown open and flowering vines across the doorways. Vibrant and alive. And all along the avenue, I could watch people talking and laughing as they strolled with their children during the early evening passeggiata. Sunbeams streaming down with the radiant joy of peace and prosperity.

A flash of lightning streaked across the sky, and my vision from the past faded abruptly into a view of the dim wreckage of the present. I closed my eyes for a few brief seconds to summon those beautiful memories of the past again, but I still couldn't block out what lay before me.

Yet, in my heart, I believed those idyllic days would return. I knew it. And I would walk in the light of hope again, perhaps even with my own wife and family. A daughter with the smiling eyes of my recently deceased mother, and a son with the sweet demeanor of my long-gone father. Anything would be possible once this damned war ended. I had to cling to that image of the future . . .

A quick, light step on the cobblestones caught my attention, and I froze in place, curling my fingers around the weapon. I could feel my heart beating faster as I squinted in the mist to make out who was approaching, but I couldn't see anyone yet. As the steps grew closer, I felt my breath coming in shallow, quick gasps. Squaring my shoulders, I gritted my teeth in resolve. I would see this through and show everyone that I had coraggio.

A figure finally appeared, wearing a large, hooded coat that hid his face. Then I spied the white rose in his lapel and I exhaled in relief, letting go of the gun as I reached for the jewel in my trouser pocket.

"Buona notte," I said, moving out of the shadows as he approached.

He stopped in front of me and slipped down the hood.

I blinked in surprise. "What are *you* doing here? It's too risky to be outside at night—"

"I want the emerald. You should not have taken it and set up this transaction on your own; we were supposed to do it together. Remember?"

"I knew if I told you, you would want to hold out for more money, but we can't wait. People need to eat, and the partisans need ammunition." Holding my ground, I kept the stone in a tight clasp. "Where is the buyer?"

"When I overheard you on the phone talking with him, I found out who it was and decided to pay him a visit in person. I was even able to negotiate a higher price, with certain incentives." A deadly flatness accompanied the last word. "He is waiting at the Castelvecchio—for *me*."

I drew back. "Did you reveal partisan names?"

"Not exactly."

I didn't believe it.

"Just give me the emerald, Tonio, and you can simply walk away. I'll even share a small amount of the profits with you."

More lies.

"You know I can't do that." Another jagged line of silent lightning lit up the night. "I have to complete this task because so many people need what this money can provide for them, and we can't be selfish with so many lives at stake. We have fought too long and hard to turn into mercenaries now. But if you've been double-dealing with my buyer, I will find someone else to purchase it because there are only too many men who will pay well to own something this valuable. I don't want to discuss this any further because I have to finish my task, so you need to move aside—now." When there was no reaction, I lunged forward and, suddenly, felt a sharp, thin blade pierce the flesh on my side. A stiletto. I gasped at the burning pain for a few moments and then pressed my hand against the wound. When I looked down, my fingers were covered in blood.

Dio mio.

I fell to my knees, dropping the jewel, and it flipped over and over, finally landing just out of my grasp.

"I'm sorry, but you gave me no choice. Truly, I wish it could have been otherwise."

My attacker retrieved the gem, pulled up the coat's hood, and started to withdraw, but not before casting the rose into the rain-soaked gutter next to me, its petals floating on the water's surface like wings of an angel.

But I faced the devil.

"After what we've been though, I'm begging you to send someone to help me—per carita!"

"It's too late."

Then I was alone again.

Moaning in agony, my eyes stung with tears as I clutched the wound, but the bleeding wouldn't stop. I struggled to stand again, but my legs began to shake as if I were facing a strong and violent wind, and I collapsed fully onto the cobblestones. *I couldn't die this way—not after everything that I'd endured.*

"*Aiutami! Aiutami!*" I shouted to anyone who might hear, propping myself up with one elbow.

I heard a window open and then close again. But no one came to help; they were too afraid.

Just then my arm gave out, causing me to fall flat onto my stomach, and I began to pray for God's mercy and grace.

Padre nostro, che sei nei cieli, sia santificato il tuo nome . . .

Gradually, everything seemed to turn calm and numb, with only the gentle patter of the rain on my back. I managed to twist my face toward the sky, thinking I could see my Mama's sweet face gazing down at me in love and pity as she murmured my name: *Tonio.*

As I felt her reach for me from the heavens above, I realized that my dream of the future was rapidly fading away. No wife. No children. Niente.

Only Mama.

At least she would be waiting for me—with Papa.

As I stretched my fingers toward the rose to give to her, I touched its silken petals and drew my last breath.

CHAPTER 1

MARIANNE

"Come back to me, who wait and watch for you:—
Or come not yet, for it is over then . . ."

(*Monna Innominata*, Sonnet I)

Verona, Italy
October 1947

How do you begin anew when all of the beauty in the world has disappeared? Even two years after the war had ended, it seemed an impossible task. Every sunrise cast its light on the crumbled dreams of what we had lost, and every sunset spread across the horizon with a sigh that yet another day had passed without a change of heart. Yet the future somehow still beckoned, ever elusive, in the next moment's breath, with a whispered promise of hope.

But who could say for certain when it would happen?

All we could do was cling to the possibility of a new life . . .

So I had traveled all the way from Boston to Verona to take on the task of helping a colleague and friend who had struggled through the horrors of war and was trying to revive her life and her country through the artistry of the past. My dear Rufina Rovelli, classmate from my student days at the College of Art and Design in Massachusetts, had contacted me a month ago about mounting an exhibit of Victorian dresses; it would be a part of the many new initiatives to restart the fashion industry, which had been all but destroyed. She had studied industrial design, not fashion curating, and was out of her depth. At first I had resisted Rufina's persistent appeals, not wanting to open the emotional doors connected to people and places from my past, which I had firmly shut. It was too painful. Instead, I had found contentment by being constantly busy with work at the college; but, ultimately, the pull of our friendship was too strong. I couldn't ignore her requests since she had been my closest and most cherished ally when I was a freshman and, later, novice curator trying to find her place in the world. *Rufina.* Her name meant "the woman with red hair," and she had the sassy unconventionality to match her wild mane, but she was also kindness itself.

And she seemed to bring out those same qualities in everyone she met—including me.

Perhaps she and Italy would help me find those lost keys to the doors that had sealed up my soul.

Forse.

I had flown into Rome's Ciampino Airport yesterday and boarded the train for Verona, though I was afraid to see how much the war had ravaged the country since my last visit a decade ago. On this exact rail route with Rufina in 1937, the last time I'd visited, I had spent most of my time absorbing the same dreamy landscape dotted with hilltop villages, fascinated by how the sky shifted between green and ochre like a silken fabric of undulating colors under the sunlight. Now, as then, I couldn't take my eyes from the breathtaking views and, at first glance, it did not appear as bad as I had anticipated.

The usual signs of harvest season were everywhere—leaves scattered in thick layers across the ground and a slight mist hovering around the valleys.

Yet, as I peered closer, the towns still bore the wounds of war, only half healed. Some buildings still stood with all four walls but vacant spaces within where the roof and windows had once been visible. Around them lay decayed piles of rubble. Roads scarred by deep holes. Abandoned, blown-out cars rusted into skeletal, twisted frames.

All of it waiting to be fully brought back to life.

My own vacant image in the window glass wavered over the scenery: dark eyes with pale skin and pale lips, an angular chin, and thick, inky-colored hair cut into a bob that barely brushed my shoulders. No expression except for a blank stare. I, too, was waiting.

If it ever happened.

Sighing, I glanced away from the window and took in my fellow travelers: a nicely attired young woman scolding her two little girls in rapid-fire Italian as they kept poking at each other, and an older man who was doing his best to ignore them as he read the latest *La Stampa* headline. None of us spoke to each other, but their furtive glances in my direction gave me the feeling of being immediately identified as a stranger in their country.

Someone who didn't quite belong but wasn't a threat, just acknowledged as different from the normal passengers.

An aging, slightly stooped conductor approached, asking for my passport and ticket, and I handed him both.

He looked at the documents carefully, then me. "Signora Marianne Baxter?"

"Sì." I said nothing more. Even though the war had ended over two years ago, I knew they were still looking for Nazi agents and Italian traitors.

Apparently satisfied that I was neither, he moved on to the hassled mother.

I checked my watch. We would arrive in Verona, the "Painted City" of *Romeo and Juliet* with its aching beauty and ancient history, by late afternoon, and it could not come soon enough. Not having journeyed overseas in years, I felt bone-weary and wanted nothing more than to lay my head on a soft pillow and sleep for an entire day. Still . . . my curiosity about what awaited me would not let me rest fully until I actually saw the garments that Rufina had found. In her letter, she had listed the discovery in a matter-of-fact manner:

> *One blue poplin walking dress, one summer silk evening dress, and one day dress of figured India muslin. All impeccably preserved, except the last one, which has some damage to the skirt and neckline.*

But her mundane tone belied what I knew was barely controlled elation about the discovery.

It was a miracle to find so many nineteenth-century pieces in one place. The thrifty women of that era tended to refashion clothing, often altering items from generation to generation, until the fabric grew too thin and worn to assemble into yet another dress. Then they would be discarded or cut into rags. Sometimes a wedding dress or a very expensive designer piece would survive intact, with only minor wear; but finding three well-preserved gowns was remarkable, especially in a city that had seen so much destruction during the Allied bombings.

Certainly, in the scheme of world events, it appeared a trivial find; but, to a costume historian like me, it was thrilling. A textile dream come true, which allowed me to peer through a portal into the life of a once living and breathing woman. A chance to connect with something tangible after the wearer was long gone. I could already imagine myself brushing the fabric nap and feeling the threads of each meticulously sewn seam, through my gloves, of course. Even from brief contact, the natural oils from human skin could damage antique fabric.

In contrast, as I smoothed down my own black striped A-line dress, I grimaced at the mass-produced cotton under my fingertips, so different from the handwoven materials of the past. Like most curators, I could never afford the kind of garments I worked with since they were reserved for only the very wealthy. Certainly, a far cry from my middle-class Midwest roots where my chemistry teacher parents counted every penny to buy discounted apparel; but they kept their jobs during the Depression and managed to keep the three of us fed as well as clothed. And they scrimped and saved to send me to college, even though they never quite approved—or understood—my chosen path.

Their hearts beat to the hum of a bubbling test tube in their lab, whereas mine followed the song of a sewing machine, repairing some long-lost piece of fabric. Two different worlds. And, as an only child, I always felt like the odd one out who was never understood, only accepted. Like a chemical reaction that couldn't be explained.

But from the moment I first saw my mother unpack a box of old garments that belonged to my aunt, I was enthralled. It was a few days after my tenth birthday, and I thought when the mailman delivered the package, it might've been a late present. But it turned out to be so much more than that, rather the gift of a lifetime: blouses, dresses, and even a pair of blue leather T-strap shoes—all from the twenties. I took each piece of clothing up to my room, laid them out on the bed, and saw my future unfold in front of me with absolute certainty.

I had found my calling.

But it was a lonely one, until I went to college and bonded with fellow students who'd chosen the same path, almost a second family—not that I didn't try to bring my parents into this new reality.

Once, on a semester break, I had brought home a fashion book that Rufina had bought for me at a secondhand store in Cambridge; it contained a picture of a Schiaparelli scarf and, as I waxed poetic about it, I saw puzzlement flash across my mother's face before she managed a slight smile. She tried to connect with my passion for its unique style and craft. Over and over. But it was a challenge.

However, a year later, my parents gave me a Schiaparelli scarf for Christmas: a coral, geometrically patterned sliver of silk. I don't know how they found one—or afforded it—yet for that and their love, I would always be grateful to them. They had let me pursue my dream. They were nearing the end of theirs with looming retirement, but that wouldn't be for a few years yet. For now, their beloved lab still beckoned.

Even as antique clothing called out to me.

I wore the scarf in their honor today; it was tied loosely around my throat with one end tossed over my shoulder and, as always, I felt transformed by its elegance.

Just then, the carriage jerked to a halt, and I realized we had arrived at the Porta Nuova—the main station in Verona. Excitement flared inside of me as I stood up, grabbed my worn leather suitcase, and quickly followed the other passengers out of the carriage and down the steps to the platform. It had been so long since I had seen Rufina that I wondered if I would recognize her, until I spied her red hair standing out like a scarlet beacon as she hurried toward me. When she drew near, arms outstretched, words weren't necessary; we simply embraced each other tightly, and I caught the scent of her signature L'Heure Bleue perfume, chic and slightly exotic. After a long moment, she pulled back, searching my face with her sparkling eyes.

"Mia cara vecchia amica," she exclaimed.

"My dear old friend," I echoed, scanning her heart-shaped face, framed by a short, curly cut, more French than Italian, but she had worked in Paris, marketing her family firm's exquisite silks before the war, and taken on the high style of Parisian couture. "Always so glamorous."

"Hardly. You wouldn't have recognized me a year ago when food was so scarce." She reached for my suitcase, but I shook my head as I noticed the hollows under her cheekbones and slight downward tilt to her mouth. Tiny reminders of darker days. But then she flashed a row of even white teeth at me and the shadows disappeared. "Flowers bloom even in the cracked and broken stones."

"So true." How often I wished I'd mastered her buoyant attitude, but I'd come to expect less, not more, from life.

"La Bella Figura . . . it's the only way." She linked her arm through mine and drew me toward the station at the far end of the tracks. "You look the same, Marianne. Just a bit older, but we have to expect that, don't we?"

"I suppose so—not that we have to like it." I rolled my eyes in reluctant agreement, catching sight of a young man smiling in my direction as he leaned against a stone pillar. I'd forgotten the open and frank way men appreciated women in Italy and, somehow, it felt oddly refreshing after the stream of politely averted glances at home. No one seemed to know how to act or what to say once I became a widow. They would simply murmur condolences and move on quickly before the conversation became too awkward.

"Still, being a 'woman of a certain age' does have some benefits. I can wear my Schiaparelli scarf with everything and be damned."

Rufina laughed. "It makes being in our thirties almost worth it."

"*Almost.*" We moved past my admirer and entered the crowded, brightly lit interior of the station; it smelled of fresh paint, and I was surprised by the sleek, almost utilitarian look of its long, rectangular windows and square-domed roof. A far cry from its former incarnation as a lavishly decorated Belle Epoque structure.

"The stazione was reduced to rubble, so they decided to create a new one with a completely different look; I'm still not sure if I like it or not," Rufina said, reading my mind as we kept pace with the throng of hurrying travelers. "So much of the city was damaged by the bombings . . . bridges blown up, basilicas torn apart; it's taken quite a bit of time to rebuild, even partially." She shook her head, then gave my arm a squeeze. "Luckily, much of the Centro Storico survived—"

"What about your family home—the Villa di Luce?"

"It had only minor structural damage to the roof." She placed a hand over her heart in a gesture of gratitude.

"That's a relief." I had many happy memories of her Veronese residence on the quiet Piazza dei Signori, with its warmth and genteel wealth. Filled with antique furniture upholstered in velvet, cabinets with gold-edged china, and soft beige Persian carpets on the floors, the villa maintained all the inviting comforts that reflected the boundless hospitality of Rufina's parents. Nothing stood out as purely ornamental. Even the baby grand piano in the salon was used for nightly entertainment as her mama played her favorite Scarlatti sonatas. And I always stayed in the large, airy bedchamber on the floor above, which overlooked the lush courtyard filled with violets and lilies.

The images danced in my thoughts with a tantalizing glimpse of days gone by. Slightly melancholy in their sweetness of Rufina and I in our early twenties—blithe and carefree. Before the rise of Fascism. Before the war. Before the end of all of our illusions about life.

"I live there alone now since my parents passed away . . . in too many quiet, echoing rooms." Her voice caught in her throat. "I just clatter around, half expecting to see Mama sitting at the piano or Papa reading in his study. But I suppose it was fortunate in some ways that they died from influenza before the war and didn't live to see what happened to their beloved city. It would have crushed their souls."

"A small mercy, but I know you miss them dearly," I murmured as we exited and lined up for a taxi along with several young women chattering away in Italian. "Nothing replaces family."

"Sì." Rufina adjusted her hat and managed a little smile. "At any rate, I have plenty of space for you to stay at the villa with me while you work on the exhibition. I know I badgered you to take on this task, but I think you need to reclaim your life's purpose: to make antique clothing come alive again and connect the joy of your discoveries with others. It isn't good to keep yourself isolated from everyone now that you're a widow." She paused and bit her lip. "I was very sorry to hear about Paul. I know you must still mourn him."

I simply nodded.

Paul. My funny, sweet husband whom I'd also met in design school. Our friendship had turned to love slowly, gradually, from an initially awkward meeting when he bumped into me at a student gallery show, then into the realization that I couldn't imagine my life without him. A gifted photographer, his poor eyesight had ironically kept him out of the war—until the end, when our country began to draft every man who could stand on his own two feet, including someone like Paul who knew only how to handle a camera, not a rifle. But he had wanted more than anything to defend his country at all costs. He didn't last six weeks, and I was left, like so many women, alone and desolate.

Unlike Rufina, I hadn't moved on from my loss. The shadow of his presence remained a part of me, in a hidden corner where people kept their deepest feelings and hopeless longings.

I wish you were here, Paul. You would love it.

In the early days of our marriage, we had talked many times about visiting Verona together, so Paul could snap a picture of the famous Ponte di Pietra during sunrise, but he kept putting off the trip since he had begun to exhibit his work extensively. I had started to teach at the college and would visit Rufina alone during summer semester breaks, until the mid-1930s when the dark curtain began to fall over Italy, and Paul persuaded me it was growing too dangerous to travel there. My trips ceased before his ever began.

Then it was too late.

A loud, honking sound jolted me back to the present as a ramshackle taxi rolled up haltingly, and a portly, middle-aged man heaved out of the driver's seat. Head bent down, he blocked the rest of the waiting passengers, motioned for us to climb in the back seat, and then tossed my luggage in the trunk. In minutes, we pulled away, leaving the young women standing there, faces drawn tight with annoyance. One of them flashed a rude hand gesture at us. Rufina ignored her, whispering to me that the driver had picked us first because he could tell I was an American. "We are indebted to your country because the English wanted to punish us for the war, and we were starving, cut off from the rest of the world. No industries. Little food.

Almost no clothing to wear. It was awful. Then your people helped us and money flowed in . . . they even sent cotton and wool to start up our textile factories in Milan again. We were so grateful."

"It's only what you deserved. What would be the point of inflicting more pain on everyone?" I glanced in the rearview mirror and thought I saw the driver's craggy face soften slightly in response; then he became riveted on steering the vehicle through the crowd.

Rufina nodded. "Not everyone sees it that way."

"Then they are being as cruel as the ones who caused the suffering in the first place."

We fell silent as the taxi chugged past the Roman arena positioned in the center of the city. Surprisingly, most of it was still standing. Some of its walls had been shelled and tumbled down in jagged, stony waves, but the basic structure remained as it had for almost two thousand years. A miracle. I had attended a midsummer opera there once, sitting on the ancient marble rows of seats, listening to Verdi's music echo around the arena with perfect precision. Moving and poignant.

Rufina began to hum an aria from *Tosca* now, and my mouth curved upwards at her sweet mezzo-soprano notes. "Will there ever be another opera season there?" I asked.

"Of course. Music will *always* return. The Veronese have seen so many difficult times, from the fall of Rome, to the struggles between the emperors and the popes, to the horror of the Fascisti, but we have survived and will carry on. The good times and the bad times; they ebb and flow."

Unless you drown in them . . .

The taxi darted in and out of the traffic around the arena and then headed down the Corso Cavour, a winding street of yellow and terra-cotta buildings covered in faded murals. "Rufina, if you don't mind, can we stop and look at the dresses before I settle in at your villa? I'm exhausted from the trip but too keyed up to sleep without seeing them first."

"I had already planned on it," she said with a knowing smile. "They are at the Fondazione Museo Menigatti, a museum in the oldest part of the city and only a few blocks away from my home. It's located in a palazzo that once belonged to a powerful Veronese family, the Menigattis, who fell on hard times as their line died out near the turn of the century. Fortunately, the last descendant set up a trust and turned it into a museum before he died and, except during the wartime, it's been open ever since then for the public to see the beautiful contents—"

"How did the dresses end up at the Fondazione?" I asked.

"It was an astonishing piece of luck during the renovation of an upstairs room a few months ago." As she turned to me, her face kindled in excitement. "Even though the palazzo was relatively unharmed by the Allied bombing, it sat empty and neglected the last few years; then the top floor took some water damage from the recent summer rains, so the direttore decided to repair the wallpaper in one of the front rooms. As he worked on it, he realized it had been plastered over a false wall, and behind it was a small dressing room that contained one item: a Victorian trunk. It must have been left there almost a hundred years ago. Can you believe that?"

I sat back in stunned silence. "And no one knew about it?"

"Apparently not. The palazzo has over twenty rooms and, while the first two floors were converted to exhibit areas, the top level has been used mostly for storage of uncatalogued items. The Menigattis lived there for almost five centuries, so the house was filled with art and furniture collections that couldn't all be on display at the same time. I have to say, it's a magnificent setting for such beautiful pieces."

The taxi slowed to a crawl as we approached the busy Piazza delle Erbe. I recognized its open-air market centered in the middle of the square, with tented booths selling everything from fresh cheese to jewelry. As we passed a man selling handblown glass, I remembered how I had bought Paul a keychain with a Murano glass pocket compass which I told him would always lead him home. He took it with him when he was deployed to Germany, and the War Office sent it back to me in the mail after his death, with the dial cracked and the needle fixed into the east/west position. Frozen in time from a Berlin battlefield. I kept it with me because it was one of the last things that Paul had ever touched, my link to his final moments on this earth.

Our driver rammed on the brakes. "Andare avanti!" he yelled at a young couple slowly strolling along the crosswalk, so engrossed in each other that they didn't even look up. When they eventually reached the other side of the street, the driver muttered, "Che palle." *What a pain.* Then he pressed down the gas pedal, and we jerked forward again.

So much for appreciating amore in the city of Romeo and Juliet. How ironic to be in the setting of Shakespeare's play about the most famous, passionate couple in literature, with no lover, no husband. That part of my life is over.

I heard Rufina give the address to our driver in Italian, and he stiffened in response, keeping a tight grip on the steering wheel as the road narrowed to one lane. We passed under an archway, famous for the ancient piece of whalebone suspended from the top that looked like a large fishhook.

"Still hanging there after almost four hundred years." Rufina pointed at it with a thread of amusement in her voice. "And I suppose it will be forever, waiting for an honest person to walk underneath, unless the legend was wrong and it's all just superstition."

"Let's hope for the latter because surely it would have fallen on *us*, being such frank and forthright women." I raised my hands in mock resignation. "Good thing, too, because I'd hate to see this old taxi take any more dings; it's barely running as it is."

She stifled a chuckle. "I've missed your sense of humor, Marianne. There hasn't been much to laugh about for a very long time, but we will find the happiness of our younger days again as we work together on this exhibition; it will remind everyone that the force to create something eternal is stronger than that to destroy."

At her words, I felt a flicker of hope that it was true, and that my part in this discovery would have some deeper meaning, not just for me, but for everyone else who was seeking something positive to hold onto during the days ahead. We all needed that more than anything right now.

The taxi made a sharp left turn, and I braced myself against the car door as Rufina slammed up against me.

"Piano. Piano," she exclaimed, straightening herself again.

The driver responded in a low voice as he kept going, but I caught only a few phrases: Misterioso. Fantasmi del passato. Anime perdute.

I shivered as I murmured the words in English: *Eerie. Ghosts of the past. Lost souls.*

"I see you haven't forgotten your Italian." Rufina leaned in closer and whispered, "He thinks the street is haunted and doesn't want to linger too long."

"Why? Did something happen here?" Curiously, I scanned the various palazzos along the quiet Via Salerno in a gracefully unfolding fan of connected residences. Mostly three-storied Renaissance-style structures with flat roofs and earth-toned exteriors, they seemed in decent repair, with only the occasional crooked shutter or chipped paint. Then the street curved toward the Adige River and ended in front of a palazzo that stood apart from the others. Slightly smaller than the rest, it had a Gothic façade, with ornately carved Moorish window casings and a shadowy fresco painted across the front. Washed out and faint, the scenes had a dreamy quality, softly colored in a coppery gold, like a picture slightly out of focus. Hardly sinister.

I spied the small brass plaque on the front wall: Fondazione Museo Menigatti.

Rufina lowered her voice. "One night, near the end of the war, a young man was stabbed here. His body wasn't found until the next morning when the direttore arrived to open the museum and saw him sprawled across the steps. Just horrible." She shuddered visibly.

"The Germans?"

"People like to think so, but some of us believe it was a local assassin because a stiletto was found the next day in a nearby garbage can; it was the kind of weapon made in Maniago with a stag-horn handle. Particularly deadly. But because the armistice was declared soon after, no one wanted to investigate what really happened just in case it had been an Italian. Everyone was anxious to move on and forget all about it."

"But what's wrong with knowing the truth? We have to *remember* what came before to make peace with what comes after," I said, meeting the hard stare of the driver in the rearview mirror, his eyes narrowed and mouth tight-lipped. *Was he warning me?* Then he blinked and switched his gaze forward again as he brought the taxi to an abrupt stop. Quickly, he slid out of the vehicle, retrieved my luggage from the trunk, and set it on the sidewalk. As we climbed out and attempted to pay him, he waved us off and sped away.

I picked up my suitcase, coughing through the cloud of exhaust that trailed in the taxi's wake. "He certainly didn't waste any time making a quick exit."

Rufina shrugged. "I'm hoping when the dress exhibit is unveiled as part of the museum's grand reopening, it will wipe away all of the bad memories that people connected to the place."

"It *will*," I echoed, trying to sound more confident than I actually felt; just standing in the spot where a murder had occurred made me intensely uneasy.

After Rufina pushed open the massive front door, we strolled into a cold, airless atrium with dusty marble floors and Roman-style pillars. Toward the back of the high-domed space, a half-restored curved staircase arched upwards with a carved wood banister that was missing several slats. *Shabby grandeur.* It would take some work to make it an appealing backdrop for a dress exhibit.

"Just leave your suitcase here; it's quite safe." She nudged me forward. "The trunk is in a room on the second floor."

As we began to tackle the stairs, I scanned the paintings that lined the walls on our way up, mostly sacred art. Portraits of the Madonna, images of basilicas, landscapes of holy sites— all lushly composed in vibrant, rich detail and what I'd expect in an aristocratic family's collection. But when we reached the landing, one piece stood out that was totally different from the rest: a modernist painting of an armless figure with the head of a mannequin, surrounded by overlapping colors at odd angles. *Strangely compelling.*

While I remained, absorbing the canvas, Rufina kept ascending the stairs. When she realized I had stopped, she turned around, clutching the banister. "Come on, Marianne, the diret-tore is waiting for us. You'll have plenty of time to look at the *L'uomo senza Braccia* later."

"The Man without Arms," I murmured. "Intriguing . . ."

"I see you're admiring our Futurist painting," a deep male voice said from above. "Not everyone appreciates its . . . uniqueness."

Tilting my head up, I saw a tall man standing at the top of the staircase. He was dressed in a white shirt and cuffed tweed pants, his arms folded. As he stared down at me, I took in his dark hair, combed back and threaded with thin streaks of gray, aquiline nose, and classically Italian features—quite handsome were it not for the flinty edge in his eyes and the faint jagged scar along his jawline.

Rufina rushed the rest of the way up to meet him, greeting him as the direttore and explaining nervously that our unexpected appearance was due to my eagerness to examine the trunk's contents.

While she was talking, he kept his gaze fixed on me. "So, you're the fashion designer from America?" In spite of his slight sarcasm, his English had that charming Italian way of stressing the last syllable of each word.

"I'm a costume *curator*," I corrected him. Even after over a decade in the field, it still irked me when people assumed I was a dressmaker or, worse, a hobbyist who played around with clothing like a little girl with her dolls. "In fact, similar to you, I study, preserve, and arrange historical artifacts, except that my work is with textiles. But garments also show truths about our past as a society. How people lived and what made them special. Clothes have meaning just like any other relic or objet d'art, like a Roman mosaic from Pompeii." I paused. "I'd be happy to talk about it more at length with you sometime."

"Brava, *signora*." He clapped slowly. "Thank you for lesson in antiquities *and* the invitation, but I'm too busy right now with the museum's inaugural exhibits to discuss women's . . . apparel. To be honest, I agreed to this Victorian dress display at Rufina's request and, while I don't question the significance of antique clothing, I can't be distracted from my work. Just now, I was designing a custom mounting of several eighteenth-century paintings with my small group of volunteers when you simply showed up, costing me precious time to meet with you. I'm permitting the interruption today, but if you decide to take on this project, you will be largely on your own, as the more crucial exhibits are my primary concern."

"I'm prepared to do that since this is an important job as well," I countered as I slowly made my way to where he and Rufina waited for me. "The sooner I see the dresses, the sooner I can get to work." My voice turned matter-of-fact as I stood on the same level with him.

A few inches taller, he regarded me with the polite detachment of a man who had seen too much and kept his emotions under strict control, but, still, there seemed to be a flicker of interest in his dark eyes. "Then I shall allow you to view them immediately."

"First, if I may make the formal introductions," Rufina cleared her throat. "Marianne Baxter, this is the director of the museum, Alessandro Forni."

I smiled and held out my hand; he did neither.

So we were not to be friends.

Instead, he pivoted on his heel and motioned us to follow him down the carpeted hallway, decorated with massive paintings of various battlefields. *How fitting considering that Italy had seen war from coast to coast.* "The Fondazione is set to reopen in three weeks, which means you will need to evaluate and prepare the clothing for the exhibition by then."

"Are you joking, signor?" I quickened my pace to keep up with him. "It will take that long just to lay out each dress under a magnifying glass to assess the textures and threads; fragile fabrics can disintegrate if not handled properly. And I don't even know exactly what condition the garments are in. Not to mention, I'll need help to create mannequins to fit the specific shape and size of the individual dress, which is not a quick process—"

"As I just mentioned, I have few resources to share, so if you're not up to the task, then perhaps you can suggest someone else who is?" He left the question open-ended as we rounded a corner and stopped in front of a set of closed, wooden double doors at the end of the hallway.

"No," Rufina protested in a firm voice. "There is no one like Marianne when it comes to costume display; it must be her because a second-rate exhibit could affect ticket sales and future donations. Not to mention, if we bring in a lesser talent, the dresses could be irrevocably damaged, and we can't allow that. It wouldn't be just a loss of antique artifacts, but the loss of an opportunity to illuminate, through her clothing, a woman's life who is long gone. That would be tragic." She pushed me forward with a firm hand. "I have full confidence in my friend."

Alessandro reached for the crystal doorknob and waited. "It's her choice."

Clenching my jaw, I struggled with my decision. It would be a hellish grind to mount an exhibit with almost no assistance in less than a month. An impossible undertaking. And yet . . . I could feel something beyond this threshold drawing me inside like an unseen presence, whispering and beckoning. My fingers itched to touch the fabrics that awaited me and to connect with the woman who had once worn them.

Taking in a deep breath, I raised my chin. "I'll do it."

"Va bene." He pushed open the doors and then stood back.

I gasped at the stunning beauty of the meticulously renovated, all-white room, bare of contents, except for a few tables and the trunk. Floors of ivory marble and a ceiling of textured alabaster, the room glowed like an opaque beacon from all sides. *Delicato.* And it would make a perfect setting for a dress exhibit, because nothing would distract from the color of the dresses. A blank canvas.

In contrast, the old brown leather trunk stood out in tattered discord with the room's blanched perfection, its dented tin inserts askew and dusty lid propped open. The front had a piece of decayed wood in the center with the initials *CR* carved on it, presumably the owner. As I drew closer and inhaled the scent of rose and lavender that emanated from it, my pulse skittered, intoxicated by the smell of another time.

As I slowly moved toward the object, Alessandro held out a pair of cotton gloves. "They might be a bit large."

Taking them from him, I slipped the gloves on and noted a small gap at the end of each fingertip. Definitely too big. But they would do for now, until I could unpack my own specially designed cotton ones. I had learned early in my career that glove fit was so important when handling fragile fabrics.

"I'll leave you to it then," Alessandro said as he strode toward the door. Then he added: "We'll talk later about scheduling your days at the museum and which areas are restricted; I have specific rules about the times people are allowed in the Fondazione and where they can go during this restoration period."

After he exited, I turned to Rufina with an accusatory glare. "You might have warned me that I'd be working with someone who is less than welcoming, to say the least."

"I was afraid you'd turn me down." She offered a sheepish grin. "He can be exacting, but his skill in overseeing an exhibit is renowned. A true passion for art and artifacts, in spite of his irritating manner. And there are reasons why he is so ill-tempered . . ." Her voice trailed off and she averted her eyes.

"Such as?"

Rufina fastened her glance on me again, direct and pointed. "Alessandro was the one who found the boy who'd been stabbed in front of the palazzo, and, even worse, it was his younger cousin, Tonio."

"How awful—" I broke off with a grimace and a twinge of guilt that I had judged him so quickly. "He must've been devastated."

"Of course . . . but he kept his feelings to himself. It seemed a little unusual, even during wartime, not to mourn publicly. But he simply went about the business of burying Tonio three days later, without a service, and no masses said in his honor. Everyone was surprised. Then, afterwards, he threw himself completely into his work, becoming cold and withdrawn. Something had changed inside of him . . . Perhaps if he could've expressed his grief, it might have been different, but he would not speak of it, not even to me, and I grew up with him in Verona."

His hard-edged expression rose up in my mind . . . only now it made sense. "I'll try to be more tolerant."

Nodding, she led me the rest of the way toward the trunk.

Holding my breath as we moved closer, I finally stood in front of it, gazing down at its contents, neatly folded garments within the frayed brocade interior. With my fingertips, I lifted the blue poplin walking dress on top and noted that a layer of white silk separated it from the one beneath it, preserving them from each other.

I exhaled in relief.

No color bleed.

As I unfolded the elaborate sleeves, two sheets of yellowed parchment slid out from under one of them and floated down onto the carpet. Carefully, I scooped them up, trying not to further damage the crumbling, irregular edges; they looked to be very old—probably from the same time as the dresses. "Did you see these papers?"

She shook her head. "I only barely touched each garment to identify the style and fabric before you arrived and saw nothing

more than some torn neckline trim and a slight tear in the skirt
of one dress."

I scanned the neatly penned lines of faded ink as I placed the
pages in order, noting the first one had a bold scrawl in a different handwriting across the top: *Fata Morgana*.

"A phantom image," I whispered.

"What?" Rufina pressed in an urgent voice as she peered
over my shoulder, trying to read the document.

"Someone left this letter in the trunk, and it's written in
English." Blinking in confusion as I scanned the rest of the top
page, I clasped it a fraction tighter in my gloved hand, mindful
that the antique paper could be crushed by an overly tense grip.
Even with such gentle handling, though, a small corner of the
bottom sheet fell away. "It was tucked inside the bell-like part of
the poplin sleeve."

"How odd."

A ripple of excitement passed over me. *I'm holding a hidden
piece of history connected to the garments in my hands.*

"Maybe the letter was written by the woman who owned
the dresses, explaining why she left them here." Rufina offered,
then cleared her throat with audible impatience. "For God's
sake, what does it say?"

Taking a moment to compose myself, I began to read aloud
its contents . . .

Gabriele Pasquale Giuseppe Rossetti
London
10 April 1854

My dearest Christina,

*If you are reading this, my dear daughter, then I am gone from
this world, and you have found the hidden compartment in my*

precious box where I left this note for you, along with a pendant and a volume of Dante's poetry. Always the clever girl.

I have lived a long life, so do not mourn me. But I do have one request: I would like you to return the Dante book to Verona in my homeland. I know you have not had an opportunity to travel abroad, but at some point, I also know that your brother, William, will take you to Italy and you will finally see the country where your ancestors were born and died.

The book belongs in the Biblioteca Capitolare from where it was taken; I should have never brought it with me to England.

I paid the price many times over since my obsession over Dante has impoverished our family, but that is my sin and I shall also pay for it in the next world. I cannot go back in time and change what happened; all I have is the here and now and the vain hope that you will see this note one day and know what happened so long ago.

As you are aware, I left Italy as a young man because I knew I would die if I stayed in Naples as a university student.

It might not have come swiftly, but the assassin would have eventually found me. And it would come unexpectedly, probably on some afternoon when the sun was setting over the Adriatic Sea in vivid gold and red streaks across the horizon. But it would happen.

I knew what fate awaited me after I wrote pamphlets and poems against King Ferdinand; all of my creative passions had fused into the great cause of freedom for Italy, and I could not resist. I had joined with other students in secret meetings, scattered and disorganized at first but, eventually, unified as part of the Carbonari with a single purpose to overthrow the king. I should have been more temperate, working in the shadows of the ancient marbles and bronzes of the Capodimonte Museum in Naples instead of writing verse about the rivoluzione, but

I never could hold my tongue when it came to challenging the power of a tyrant.

I could not be silent.

So I made the decision to go into exile.

As I remember what happened on that journey and dwell on my impending final journey to the afterlife, I think of my father, Niccolo, whom you never knew, my dear. He was a blacksmith who spoke little but had a boundless love of his family. I can still see him, head bent as he fashioned ironworks, pounding his hammer in powerful strokes, shaping the objects into practical objects like horseshoes and candleholders. Simple yet beauteous forms born out of fire. He had a craftsman's patience and an artist's hand. This hand-carved box belonged to his father, and Papa gave it to me before he died, showing me its secret compartment, should I ever need to use it.

I became a poet because of his encouragement, a most fortunate choice since, under a death sentence from the king in Naples, it was my poetry which caught the eye of a British admiral's wife, who arranged for me to be smuggled out of Italy at the Castel dell'Ovo under the cover of a moonless night.

My role in the rebellion ended then and there.

But I want you, Christina, to know what happened that evening because it is important.

My rescuers left me at the castle and went to collect my friends and comrades at arms: Fabiano with his easy-going temper and way with women; and Giovanni, quiet and calculating, who seemed to view life as a sinister puzzle. We had all sworn loyalty to each other, so I could not depart without them. Or Peppina, my first love.

But events did not unfold as planned . . .

Leaning against the castle's stone walls, clutching Papa's box that held my cherished belongings, I felt the minutes pass slowly as if time had stretched a web around this fortress that jutted into the sea. The British ship lay offshore and had sent a boat to the beach for us.

As I waited, I imagined Peppina in my mind's eye with her black eyes and wild curls; she had drawn me to her from the moment she crossed my path in the woods outside Naples, appearing like a fiery dream of beauty and sweet passion. A servant girl, but I loved her—heart and soul. Ever loyal, she supported my risky activities with the Carbonari and never once questioned that our lives might be at risk, even when the polizia brought her in for questioning, and she pretended to have severed all ties with me after our son, Niccolo, died. The child conceived in love and named in memory of my father, but because it meant "people of victory," a child of this land.

Fabiano and Giovanni returned—alone. They explained that Peppina never showed up at the statue of San Domenico where they were to meet.

But I refused to leave without her.

When the rowboat to take us away drew near, I glanced upward, toward the dim outline of Mount Vesuvius, which loomed over Naples with its ever-present threat of eruption. Beautiful and dangerous. Always reminding me that life could shift in unexpected ways, as all my carefully laid-out plans were evaporating before my very eyes. The soldiers threw up a rope, and motioned us to tie it off and climb down. But I could not do it.

Then Fabiano and Giovanni forced me into the boat, while I protested violently. At that moment, the police appeared and fired on us, and the rowers pulled us away from the castle.

As the boat glided over the surf, I watched the shore grow more and more distant, blurring the outlines of Naples into a formless image of city and sky. But as the moonlight bathed the beach in its soft light, I saw Peppina standing there, motionless.

I demanded that we return, but no one listened. Believe me, my daughter, I wanted to go back for her with every fiber of my being.

Fabiano said we could arrange for another boat once we reached Malta and were under British protection, but even if that happened, she would never forget that we left her. I saw her despair and knew that I had failed. Although she later joined us in Malta, she never forgave me.

I lost her love forever . . . and, tragically, the revolution collapsed shortly thereafter.

Peppina and I drifted apart, with her wanting to go back to Italy and re-create what we had together and my looking to make my way in a new country. I could not persuade her to my way of thinking. Gradually, she grew more and more despondent, until she finally threw herself off a cliff. I was devastated. Then I found she had left me a farewell note with the Dante book and the pendant as tokens of those wild years that we shared together, and it assuaged my guilt somewhat. Peppina explained that she acquired them during our time in Naples and intended to sell them for a small sum to help finance the rivoluzione, but after the rebellion ended, she simply kept them. I could tell the book was stolen from the library in Verona because it bears the Biblioteca Capitolare stamp, but I do not know the origin of the pendant. So many years have passed, it hardly matters.

After Peppina's death, I withdrew from my friends and departed from Malta as soon as I could arrange passage, telling only Fabiano about her note because he was the one who angrily broke the news of her suicide to me. I thought if he saw she had gifted those cherished items to me, he would not hold me completely to blame, but I am not sure I succeeded. Truthfully, I deserved his contempt.

And thus, I left my boyhood companions and all that I knew, hiding Peppina's gifts in the secret compartment of Papa's box, hoping to put those memories behind me.

The rest of my story you know only too well, Christina. I found my way to London and married your mother, the second great love of my life, and had my beautiful children, including you. Never doubt that I cherished all of you so dearly.

You gave me more joy than I deserved.

But as death approaches, I have been haunted by what occurred in my youth, trying to make sense of the intricate pattern of events which led me here as an exile and atone for my transgressions, especially keeping the stolen Dante book. I could not bear to part with it because it began my fascination with his poetry, but that was selfish and wrong. If you can honor my request to take it to Verona, I shall rest in peace.

As for the pendant, it seems appropriate to leave it to you, my own beloved daughter, since you possess the same fiercely loving nature as Peppina.

Your Mama may have suspected some of this story, but I could never bring myself to speak openly about my first love. I hate to ask you to keep such a secret from the rest of your siblings, especially your brother, Dante Gabriel, but he is afflicted enough by the burden of his artistic brilliance. As for William and Maria, it is also for the best that they do not know because I do not want them to think badly of me after my death.

As always,
Your loving Papa,
Gabriele Rossetti

Lowering the letter slightly, I noted a parenthetical at the bottom of the page written in the same angular script as the Fata Morgana phrase: *Papa's last letter to me.* I glanced up in astonishment, first at Rufina, then at the *CR* initials on the nameplate, trying to make sense of Gabriele's request and how they connected with the contents of the trunk. "Is it possible these dresses belonged to the poet, Christina Rossetti? I recognized her name only because she was connected with the Pre-Raphaelites whose art and fabric I studied in design school, but I know nothing about her."

"Neither do I."

"So how did an Englishwoman's clothing end up in Verona, hidden away in a trunk for almost a century?"

Rufina shrugged.

Holding up the letter again, I recited the two words on the front page once more for my friend to hear:

Fata Morgana.

CHAPTER 2

CHRISTINA

"I wish I could remember that first day,
First hour, first moment of your meeting me . . ."
(*Monna Innominata*, Sonnet II)

Albany Street, London, England
10 May 1865

There always seemed to be two warring factions inside of me: the proper British lady who managed the household, took care of her parents, and went to church on Sunday; and the fiery, passionate woman driven by her Italian ancestors who embraced an inner world of hidden desires and private longings. The clash of these polar opposites came out through my poetry—images of refined females in lace dresses who dreamed of exotic creatures. I had lived such a mundane life in so many ways but, inside, dwelled in sensual places that had an edge of the forbidden. It was as if I heard a music that no one else could discern . . . notes that traveled on silent, elusive winds. But I followed where they led, no matter what.

If only in words.

As much as my mother tried to tame me, I *was* the daughter of Gabriele Rossetti, beloved teacher and revolutionary who filled our London house with émigrés and artists, and as the youngest of their four children, somehow both constrained and indulged by everyone, I felt my nature more divided than the rest. My siblings, Maria and William, were the "calms," and Dante Gabriel and I were the "storms," but I, Christina, now seemed to be both, and it had made my life a rocking boat on shifting seas, navigating my way between two points on the compass, each one urging me on in different directions.

And it seemed like more and more I was choosing the safe port, secure but dull.

In the fourth decade of my life, I suppose it was inevitable that the world began to close in on that part of me that wanted to sail out onto the open seas and experience all that life had to offer. Freedom. Travel. Adventure. I craved it all—and more. The sensual delights of a great love. How I wanted to experience that, too. But did I have the courage to live that kind of life when society demanded that I subdue all of my inclinations within the delicate bounds of convention? If only I could take the wheel and pilot my own ship . . .

"Christina, you have been staring out that window for almost half an hour," Mama pointed out in a gentle voice. "You must finish your tea and buttered toast."

Slowly, I turned and took in the picture of my family chatting amicably at the breakfast table. All so dear to me. Mama in her black crepe dress, still mourning Papa's death after ten years; her olive skin was remarkably smooth and unlined, though her hair had turned the color of pale silver. Maria, my oldest sister and the most Italian-looking of all of us: dark curls, brown eyes, and boldly etched features that belied her quiet, pious demeanor.

William, the reliable one with his kind face and shy nature, always taking care of the family to make certain we did not fall further from genteel poverty. And Dante Gabriel. Brilliant and handsome, with an intense, heavy-lidded gaze and goatee beard, he had the soul of a poet and the eye of an artist, along with the erratic nature that accompanied such imaginative heights. He lived recklessly, but I understood the impulses that drove him to paint his visions on canvas after canvas and spin webs of beauty in sonnet after sonnet. The powerful emotions demanded form and expression, as they did from me as well.

My father had named him after the great Italian poet and scholarly preoccupation of his life, Dante Alighieri, believing no doubt that, if he did so, my brother would follow in his literary footsteps. And Papa's wish had come true. Dante Gabriel's star ascended high in the sky, the blazing light and founding member of the Pre-Raphaelite Brotherhood, young men who had wanted to illuminate a new way to write and paint with a dreamy sensualism as they worshipped feminine beauty with their brushes and brashness. My brother was their undisputed leader.

Certainly, I could not compete with his magnetism and poetic skills even if I had wanted to attempt it, but I was as deeply devoted to my own poetry, especially since my first collection, *Goblin Market*, received a fair amount of critical success, though, admittedly, some of it was due to Dante Gabriel's lush illustrations. Still, I had dipped my toes in the literary world and found the waters warm and inviting.

He looked over and smiled at me now as if he knew what I was thinking as he leaned down to feed Mama's longhaired lapdog. My verse might not have the power and scope of his work, but it spoke its own truth.

Unutterable in person . . . until the lines were carved on the page.

My heart was like a singing bird.

My words. My poem.

"I believe she is watching for her would-be fiancé, Charles, by keeping a close eye on the street and counting the hours until he arrives," Dante Gabriel teased as he dropped the last piece of meat in the dog's mouth, then patted her on the head. "But poor, dear Charlie is probably caught up in his latest translation of the New Testament and has lost all sense of time in the ancient world of saints and sinners."

Charles Bagot Cayley, the man who wanted to marry me.

"In fact, he may be wandering the streets as if he were in . . . Purgatory," Dante Gabriel added with a wink.

"Unlikely." Leveling a pointed stare at him, I moved toward the large oak table that stood in the center of our dining room where everyone had gathered, a small space, but decorated vividly with my brother's paintings of dreamy religious and Arthurian myths. "At least he can *tell* time. You would be late for your own funeral." Not surprisingly, Dante Gabriel had sent a note that he would be joining us that morning from his residence at Tudor House in Chelsea, though we had then waited over an hour for him to appear and begin breakfast. Typical. He hated rising early.

"Only if it were held before noon, and none of my friends would show up to grieve my passing either." He trailed a mock tear down his cheek.

Maria laughed.

Mama held up a slim hand with her widow's ring of three dark stones—peace, love, and grief. "I am sure Christina was simply lost in her own thoughts about our upcoming trip since we leave in barely a week . . . first Milan, then Verona and Brescia, in the country of your dear, departed father. He would be so happy to know we are finally going to travel to Italy." She paused, taking a sip of tea. "I am sorry that you are not to accompany us, Dante Gabriel and Maria."

"I would like nothing more, but my duties at the All Saints Sisterhood are consuming most of my time at present," Maria said. "We are starting a school for orphan girls, and I shall be teaching them about humility and devotion to God. As Mama always says, 'the less we live for things outward, the stronger burns our inward life.' It is my calling to guide them along the spiritual path."

So true, I added silently, especially since she intended to take her vows as a novice in the Anglican faith. In some ways, I envied her faith and conviction. But I had little inclination to live in the society of women behind the nunnery walls.

"You put me to shame, dear Maria, because I have no excuse, except that I am too lazy to pack." Dante Gabriel leaned back in his chair, propping his arm behind his head. "But our estimable brother, William, more than makes up for my deficiencies and will shepherd Mama and Christina through the foreign lands."

"I will most assuredly attend to my family flock." William smiled through his full beard, which offset his bald head. *A good man.* That is what everyone termed him. If he was a bit pedantic at times, we all overlooked it because he could always be counted on to do the right thing.

I seated myself next to Maria as she poured my tea in Mama's beloved blue willow china decorated with delicate wildflowers. A gift from her own English mother. As I took it from my sister, I stared down at the light-colored liquid and grimaced. We could afford only a small amount of tea each month and had to make it last, but this serving had been a reheat of yesterday's morning and afternoon brews, weak and tepid. I took only a tiny sip.

"Not to your liking?" Dante Gabriel raised a brow. "If you want a more full-bodied refreshment, I shall be receiving

Ruskin later at my studio in Tudor House, and he always brings his favorite Ceylonese black."

Of course. Ruskin always wanted the best in life and could afford it. A powerful art critic, he had befriended my brother a few years ago, made sure he had good press after every exhibit, and engaged commissions when he grew short of funds. Having such a patron was every artist's dream—and nightmare, because everything came at a price, and Ruskin liked nothing better than to make "suggestions" to Dante Gabriel about making his art more commercial.

"I should like to come," Maria cut in swiftly, her face lit with an eagerness somewhat at odds with her spiritual nature. But we had all noticed her recent attachment to Mr. Ruskin after a particularly lively dinner here a few months ago when he had shared some of his critiques of the recent architecture at Regent's Park. I often wondered if they might form a more full-bodied connection, but it seemed unlikely now that her path to the nunnery seemed all but certain.

"As would I," William added.

Dante Gabriel gave a nod of assent, then focused on me. "What about you, Christina? You can even bring along Charlie, if you like. I find him quite pleasant in an abstract sort of way, with his nose always buried in a book as he rambles about."

"The complete opposite of you?" I posed, drawing up the image of my suitor next to my brother: Charles with his crumpled shirt and spectacles sliding down his nose, and Dante Gabriel with his dashing elegance and sly humor. The contrast could not be more striking. I was fond of Charles, and still considering whether or not to marry him, but in my heart, I wished he had more of the fiery streak that ran through my family; it would make life more interesting and my decision much easier. Certainly, I admired his stability and kindness, but was *esteem* enough to propel me into marriage?

"Indeed, but I aspire to his self-discipline." Dante Gabriel stared at one of his paintings from years ago which hung on the wall next to Papa's two small sketches of the Italian countryside: *The Girlhood of Mary Virgin*. We had all sat for him—Mama, our servant, Williams, and I—in a portrait that depicted me as Mary, being taught embroidery by Mama as Williams picked fruit outside an ivy-covered window. A scene of domesticity with a holy tinge. Of course, I had pretended since I hated needlework. It was Dante Gabriel's first major oil piece, but it received only lukewarm reviews, and it had distressed him hugely at the time. "If I had only applied myself as an art student at the Royal Academy, I might have mastered the skills of line and color more fully . . . but I was young and impatient."

My glance followed his, but I found the portrait somewhat charming in that it enshrined our family setting from our youth, when everything lay before us as an empty slate, playing together and learning together in the city; spending summers at Holmer Green with our grandfather, Gaetano; nurturing our creativity as we experimented with art and poetry. Now, so much had already been written, the good and bad, and what was to come was rather predictable.

"We were all restless then," William chimed in, buttering his bread. "But I believe the lessons of life alter our perspectives of what is possible, so Charles's natural prudence should fit in with Christina's newly evolved calmness nicely."

More like oppression . . . I have had to restrain my "storms" for so long that I scarcely know myself.

Maria and Mama murmured in agreement, but I said nothing. Had they ever really understood me?

As for Charles's proposal, I contemplated marrying him not to embrace caution, but to escape the fate of an unmarried woman in an age when a "spinster" was considered little more than a failure at the very least. A creature to be belittled and criticized. After one broken engagement to another man when I was only nineteen, I felt as if I were descending deeper into that role with every year that passed and, now in my thirties, I welcomed my engagement as a chance to break free, so my heart would be like that singing bird, stretching her wings.

A woman could not find real liberty in poetry alone.

"I am truly fortunate," I finally said quietly, not believing the words even as I spoke them.

"'Because the birthday of my life / Is come, my love is come to me,'" Dante Gabriel quoted from one of my own poems. *He knew.*

Mama beamed at me. "The thought of your marriage brings such joy to me, knowing you will be happy . . . and I shall have a grandchild after all. Truly, I have so longed for a little one to spoil—"

Dante Gabriel shoved his chair back so violently that it slammed against the wall. Then he strode out of the room without another word.

"Mama, how could you?" I demanded, rising quickly to follow him. As I moved toward the doorway, I heard William trying to soothe my mother as he switched into Italian, telling her not to blame herself for the slip of the tongue. Non e colpa tua. Mama began to cry, apologizing for her insensitivity.

As I emerged from the dining room, I spied Dante Gabriel in the foyer, leaning against the wall with his shoulders hunched and head down. He picked at the ivory buttons on his waistcoat, muttering to himself.

"She did not mean to upset you," I said, touching his arm in reassurance. "Her mind is not as sharp as it once was, and she blurts out whatever pops into her thoughts . . ."

"No, Mama still blames me for Lizzie's death." He uttered the words bitterly as if he spat out an unripe fruit. Much as

Dante Gabriel tried, he could not forget the death of his wife. None of us could. "I should not have left her alone that night; she had been so sad, talking about our stillborn daughter as if she had died only the day before and not a year. I could not find a way to console her, much as I tried. My poor, dear Lizzie."

Lizzie. Elizabeth Siddal.

Beautiful, with her flame-red hair and delicate features, she had drifted into Dante Gabriel's life first as his model, then as his first love, intense and all-consuming. He painted her over and over, as if trying to exorcise the haunting obsession that her beauty had over him. But it was never enough to quell its power. And, sadly, the real woman disappeared somewhere in his fantasies, and she grew tired of waiting for him to propose to her. By the time they finally married, she had become disillusioned, and ill health had settled in, causing her to grow thinner and thinner, a shadow of the "stunner" who had once entranced my brother; his courting of her had been a pilgrim's progress that ended badly.

> *Too late for love, too late for joy*
> *Too late, too late!*
> *You tarried too long at the gate.*

I mourned her loss, even though I never really knew her, nor fathomed how to behave in her company. She rarely spoke, but she did not need to because men would simply stare at her like a sacred icon casting spells in silent allure. I was somewhat envious. Although I had always been called pretty, with my dark hair and large eyes, I had never inspired worship of that sort. Then again, the more her beauty inspired, the less real she became, and I did not want to be a man's dream. It was just another cage of illusion.

"If only I had not gone to teach that night, but I did . . . and by the time I returned home, she was unconscious." He raised his head, and I saw the same wild expression in his eyes that I had seen so many times before. "The doctor could do nothing."

We avoided stating the reason why: Lizzie had overdosed on laudanum.

As Dante Gabriel continued relating the desperate events of that night, I slipped an arm around him, simply listening, as I had done so many times before. It was as if he had to narrate the story over and over, like the Ancient Mariner, to purge his soul and find an end to his guilt. His words came slowly, haltingly, without emotion at first, then more and more intense as he spun out his narrative of the events that I had heard so many times before, including the shock of finding her unconscious on the floor and his desperate attempts to bring her back to the living. Then the overwhelming grief afterwards.

My tormented brother. If only I could take away his pain.

Toward the end of his retelling, his voice cracked with emotion, and I murmured soothing phrases as I stroked his hair. No matter how many times he told his tale or painted her from memory as his Beata Beatrix, he would never be able to forgive himself. So I let him simply bare his soul.

When he finished, he exhaled with an audible breath of finality.

The tragic story was done—for now.

Unfortunately, I knew that no sense of redemption would follow; the grief and guilt would well up again and demand release.

"Will the sorrow ever go away, Christina?" he asked, staring beyond me into some great, yawning space of darkness.

"No, but it lessens over time, if you let it."

"I . . . I cannot." He touched his forehead to mine as we had done as children when we had been banished by Mama to our nursery for temper tantrums. A symbolic bond of two siblings, two poets, two restless spirits in an often cruel universe. "Do you remember when we played card games as children?" he reminded me in a lighter tone. "Your favorite suit was diamonds, brilliant and sparking."

"And yours was hearts because of your loving nature."

"Perhaps too much so. It has not made for a comfortable life to be guided always by what stirs my passions, but it does seem to make for good art . . . or at least I would like to think so." He drew back, a glint of humor touching his face once more. "One could never accuse me of not putting my heart *and* soul into my paintings."

"Never," I agreed, patting his shoulders. "Now you must apologize to Mama or she will obsess about it all afternoon until she has worked herself into a state."

"Of course." He turned away, then halted without looking back. "I did love her, you know. Lizzie, I mean. I was not the best husband, but I tried in my own way to be the man she wanted. I wish I could have done things differently . . ." He paused, then made his way into the dining room, his footsteps heavy and slow.

Exhaling deeply, I sank onto a rickety little accent chair and felt a sense of calm settle over me again as I heard Dante Gabriel's melodic voice drift out in an appeasing tone as he begged our Mama's pardon: *Perdonami, Mama.*

Eventually, my mother stopped weeping.

Of course, she would forgive him. How could she not? His genius drove him hard, and his tragic marriage tipped him near the edge of sanity at times, but he always had us. Our family.

We would never let him descend into madness, because we loved him too much to let him squander what was left of his future with paintings not yet finished and poems not yet written. Surely, he had good fortune ahead, perhaps even a new love.

And what about me?

Soon I might have a husband and maybe children of my own—as well as, most certainly, a new volume of poetry published next year, *The Prince's Progress.* I had worked on the verses for almost two years, and it contained some of my favorite pieces about love and longing and waiting.

> *Somewhere or other there must surely be*
> *The face not seen, the voice not heard,*
> *The heart that not yet—never yet—ah me!*
> *Made answer to my word . . .*

So I suppose I did have a future of sorts, even if Charles were not exactly the heart that *made answer to my word*; at least I would possess a measure of independence. For so many years I had taken care of Papa and now Mama, the types of duties that Dante Gabriel and William never had to assume but were relegated to the women of a family. I did not resent my brothers, but I certainly envied their freedom to choose how their coming days would unfold. I had but two choices: single or married.

I had missed my chance at wedded bliss almost two decades ago and, if I did this time, I would likely receive no more offers of marriage.

I would be trapped.

Forever part of a family without a life wholly my own.

Glancing across the foyer, I stared at the large photograph of us—sans William—in the garden of Dante Gabriel's house in Chelsea. One of his friends, Mr. Dodgson, had taken it two years ago, capturing the familial scene of Dante Gabriel playing chess with Mama while Maria and I looked on with varied degrees of pretended interest. I scrutinized my image as if I were a stranger seeing the photograph for the first time. Positioned near the group, I stood sideways, still slim, though not exactly in the first flush of youth. My face was reflected in profile with a pointed chin and dark hair pulled back in a neat chignon—no sagging jawline yet. Unfortunately, the black and white portrait did not capture my hazel eyes from my half-English mother or the slightly dusky skin of my pure Italian father, reflecting the contrast of two cultures and what I thought were my best features.

But would anyone else besides Charles be intrigued?

Probably not.

Laughing at my own foolishness, I rose again and smoothed down the folds of my ecru cotton dress. *I have to make a decision; it is not fair to Charles to keep him waiting for an answer.* After we returned from Italy, I would agree to marry him, write my poetry, and find solace in good causes. There was no point in "waiting at the gate" any longer.

Then the grandfather clock chimed with ten strokes, and I took a quick glimpse at the tall mahogany case that had belonged to Mama's mother, decorated with a hand-painted sun face gazing down at a moon-like dial. With a start, I realized that I had barely fifteen minutes to make my appointment at Highgate Penitentiary run by the Sisters of Mercy Convent where I volunteered several days a week. If I hurried, I might be able to arrive in time to meet the new donor, Giovanni Pecora, who had contacted me a few days ago. He had apparently met my Aunt Charlotte and heard about my work at the penitentiary; fortunately, he had been intrigued enough to offer a donation to our halfway house for "fallen women," to use the popular phrase, though I hated the term. They were women who often had been pushed into a life of vice, rather than taken a voluntary plunge into immorality. But, regardless of how anyone referred to it, we would welcome the funds.

Reaching for my lace-trimmed summer bonnet that hung on a nearby brass hook, I called out to my family to tell them I was leaving and would return by teatime.

Before Mama could respond, I let myself out the front door and rushed down Albany Street toward the park. The sun shone brightly in a rare blue sky with a balmy morning breeze, which seemed a happy respite from the normal London rain in June. Small groups of young ladies in white dresses strolled by arm in arm, nodding at me with pleasant smiles, and a few carriages rolled along with older female passengers in brightly colored silks. Those with wealth rode; those with modest resources walked. But I did not mind.

As I hurried past the red brick row houses, I rehearsed my upcoming conversation. Signor Pecora had hinted in his note that he was still considering the actual amount he would give to the halfway house, hopefully enough to train at least a dozen women to a new and respectable profession where they would be able to support themselves. Dressmaking. Factory work. Domestic service. Hardly luxurious, but at least a start on a new road to self-respect. Some of the other ladies who volunteered at the Sisters of Mercy came armed with their spiritual mission to redeem the "lost" women, but I was more concerned with offering food, shelter, and medicine. And Signor Pecora's financial gift would go a long way to providing all of these necessities.

Truly, a welcome gift.

Striding along the last two blocks, I arrived, breathless and flustered, at the entrance to the building, adorned by only a small brass plaque on the right side engraved with the name of the convent. The door swung open and I beheld Evelyn Ashford, our efficient director; she did not look pleased. "You are late, Christina." She pointed at a small watch pinned to her black dress with its high neck and long sleeves—the volunteers' uniform, which I had not had time to don this morning. In truth, it was somewhat severe for my Italian nature, so I often "forgot" to wear it. Evelyn scanned my summery frock with a critical eye, but she said nothing.

"I apologize for my tardiness, but my brother had a distressful episode this morning," I said, stepping into the small foyer. Unlike the dark exterior, the inside of the building had whitewashed walls and bright red and beige tiles that looked like a chessboard of patterned tones. "It will not happen again." I slipped off my bonnet and hung it on a nearby hook.

Evelyn gave no response. Like most of London, she knew all about Dante Gabriel's marital woes and deep grief over the loss of his wife, since there had been a public inquest over her death, resulting, thankfully, in a verdict of "accidental overdose" of laudanum. But the damage was done, because his personal life with Lizzie became the subject of widespread gossip and speculation. Not that Evelyn ever said anything to me; she was too discreet. About a decade older than I, Evelyn had pale, translucent skin and blond hair, now fading gradually from yellow into silver; but she kept her features so carefully controlled that most people thought her to be much older. I knew very little about her, other than that she had come from a well-heeled family and performed her duties with military precision as an Associate of the Sisterhood, preferring (somewhat surprisingly) not to become a nun.

"Mr. Pecora is already waiting for you in the parlor." She gestured toward the French doors at the far end of the foyer, which led to a formal room reserved for special benefactors. "His donation would be most appreciated now since we have received quite a few new arrivals. It would be unfortunate if we had to start turning women away . . ."

Meeting her eyes in some alarm, I nodded. In this matter, we were in complete agreement: the halfway house *must* remain open to all women who sought our help. "I will do everything I can to make certain Signor Pecora understands the urgency of our needs. *He* contacted me, so I trust that means I will not have to work too hard to convince him."

"I hope so," she echoed my mixed feelings.

Moving toward the doors, I took a few moments to compose myself, then I pushed them open to greet our visitor. He stood near the large bookcase, staring at the thick volumes of history and geography which we used to teach our residents. As I strolled forward, he turned, and I took in his distinguished air, which echoed my father's generation: well-groomed beard and attired in a perfectly fitted dark suit and polished shoes. His skin, bronzed by wind and sun, seemed stretched over his aging face, taut over the elegant ridge of his cheekbones. Slightly bent, he carried a cane with an ornate gold handle.

"Buongiorno, Signorina Rossetti." Giving a small bow, he shook my hand. "Thank you for agreeing to meet me this morning."

"It is my pleasure."

"And mine." He scanned my face intently, as if searching for something lost and now found. "Especially when I know you must be preoccupied with preparations for your upcoming trip."

I drew back for a moment, until I realized that Aunt Charlotte must have shared this news with him. "My aunt seems to have blathered on about my life."

"Only in the most charming way," he hastily assured me. "I traveled here from Italy for business and met her at a cultural event, a gathering of Italian art lovers who also want to raise funds for various London charities. As we were conversing about Titian and Tintoretto, she mentioned your work on behalf of women in need, and that you were about to journey to my home country of Italy."

"Indeed, yes. My brother, William, is escorting our Mama and me around the northern regions." Relaxing again, I added some of the local sights that we were going to visit, including Milan and Lake Como. "I assume you know the area well?"

He nodded. "I live in Verona, only a short distance away."

"Really? How remarkable, because we intend to travel there as well." My interest sparked. "My father always spoke so affectionately of his home country and never lost that sense of being Italian." An understatement, of course. Papa had talked incessantly of his boyhood growing up in Vasto, the hillside city on the coast, the ancient alleyways where he wandered as a boy and the golden beaches on the Adriatic where his father taught him to swim. I had listened to his tales many, many times and never grew tired of them. "Perhaps you have heard of him—Gabriele Rossetti?"

"Who has not?" His glance became more animated. "Actually, it was one of the reasons I was most eager to meet you: in truth, I knew Gabriele well since I, too, grew up in Vasto. Mi amico. We were boyhood friends, you see, and spent many a day playing in the piazza with the other boys from the town. Later, as young men, we attended the University of Naples, and Gabriele made me believe in the Risorgimento, the unification of Italy, which has finally happened, now Garibaldi has led our country to freedom. Your father's dream became a reality. I could have simply sent a check to your worthy cause, but when I heard your name, I knew I had to pay my respects to my boyhood friend's daughter. He possessed honor and courage, and I came here today to share my memories of him and, of course, to tell you that I shall contribute to your worthy cause."

My spirits soared in delight at both prospects. "We are so grateful for your charity toward the convent, and I am especially appreciative of your kind words about my father, even though he died almost a decade ago. I do not believe he ever mentioned you, but I know he would be so pleased that you have such praise for him."

A shadow of regret passed over his features. "I wish that I could have attended his funeral and shared them with everyone who knew him only in England. But I was traveling in East Africa, and word of his death did not reach me until weeks after his demise. At that point, I figured it was better to simply mourn him in my heart, but make no mistake, his death was a loss to the world and many of us who knew him felt it deeply, though we may not have put it in words."

Ah, the unspoken grief . . .

He struck a chord in my being, knowing that eulogizing a life like Papa's could never truly capture the complexities of his past. But I fervently hoped Signor Pecora's recollections could fill in some of the blanks that my father had never shared with me. I slid onto the chair and folded my hands in quiet anticipation. "I am most eager to hear your tales, sir."

His face broke into a smile that glowed with lightness as he pulled the other chair close and seated himself. "I promise that you shall not be disappointed, signorina, for our lives played out in the most astonishing ways, and our fortunes rose and fell many times. There were three of us who grew to manhood in Vasto on the coast of Abruzzo—Fabiano, Gabriele, and me. We had little money, but Vasto was so idyllic, especially in the summer when wildflowers covered the land with such a blanket of color that nothing felt of any consequence in the face of such natural beauty . . ."

"Who was Fabiano?" I queried, puzzled since Papa had also neglected to mention him as well. How many more details from his youth had my father left out?

"He was the baker's son who lived near your father's house, as did my family, who were fishermen," Mr. Pecora explained. "Very convenient since we always had Fabiano's fresh bread to go with the seafood my own father caught. In spite of our hardships, our close-knit town sustained all of us. I would have probably lived and died there, if not for Gabriele. He wanted more than the blacksmith's trade with his love of literature, and was clever enough to be accepted at the University of Naples. Then he pushed us to do the same, so we all became students together—until the rivoluzione broke out, and we had to choose sides. Of course, we followed Gabriele into his secret meetings and plots against King Ferdinand. It was a perilous venture, and we all paid dearly for it when the king placed a death sentence on us; we would have been executed if we had not escaped to Malta."

I found myself leaning forward as I grew more and more intrigued. "Papa mentioned that he fled to Malta, but not that his two friends accompanied him."

He gazed down briefly at his hands, bent and gnarled with age. "We made a pact to tell no one; it was safer that way because spies were everywhere, even in Malta. But it was not long after we arrived there that the revolution ended. We found ourselves rudderless, without a sense of where the political winds would drive us, and our brotherhood gradually dissolved. Gabriele emigrated to London and Fabiano disappeared. Later, I found safe passage to northern Italy and settled in Verona."

"All of you gave up everthing for the revolution and were left with nothing," I murmured.

"It was worth it." He placed a hand over his heart solemnly. "But I hope Gabriele at least managed to keep the treasured box his father had given to him."

Sitting back in my chair, I had a flash of one of Papa's prized possessions. "Do you mean the one with an ivory carving of the three Muses on the lid?"

"Ah, yes . . . you know it, then?"

I nodded. "It sat in his study for the longest time, then he gave it to me shortly before he died. He kept his favorite verses inside, mostly ones he wrote himself in Italy—I think."

"Of course, his beloved poems about freedom and liberty." Signor Pecora sighed. "They inspired us, but sadly, after our dreams dissolved, we went our separate ways. Perhaps that is why Gabriele never told you about us, because, in the end, he did not want to dwell on how the revolution and . . . other circumstances split us apart."

Reaching over, I touched his arm and he glanced up. "You should have written to him, because I know he would have corresponded and received you as a dear friend. Our house was always filled with Italian émigrés, men who had lived hard—some even committed crimes—but Papa made a place for every one of them at our table, no matter what had brought them to our door."

"I would like to think so." Mr. Pecora patted my hand.

"Truly, I *know* it. Papa loved every exile as a brother." Though it did seem odd that he had never mentioned either one of his old friends. "What about Fabiano's fate?"

He shrugged. "I have no idea, but I fear the worst since he had neither your father's connections nor my shrewdness."

Secretly, I shared his concern because Papa had told us the situation on Malta had been dire: informants of the king everywhere . . . men shot, women strangled, and children left as orphans. "I suppose we are lucky to sit here and talk about the past from the safety of this time and place, thanks to the bravery of men like Papa and yourself."

"Grazie mille." He gave my hand a last squeeze. "Few people are willing to hear an old man's stories, even my own son."

"You have a family?"

"Only my son and I now, since my wife, Delfina, died last year." Sadness threaded through his voice like an autumn breeze blowing lifeless leaves to the ground; he was the last of a generation who had seen the winds of revolution actually change his country. "Actually, he is in Milano right now."

"Maybe we can meet when we visit in a week or so, if he is still there. Will you have returned to Italy by then as well?"

"Sì, and I would be honored to introduce you to him . . ."

We fell silent, an awkward pause between two strangers who had shared more than they had possibly intended, but still, a tentative bond had been formed.

Just then, a soft knock at the door broke the silence, followed by the appearance of Sarah, one of our newest residents, an auburn-haired, slightly freckled young girl barely out of her teenage years. "Miss Rossetti, would you like me to begin preparing lunch?"

"Yes, please. I will join you in the kitchen shortly, but first I want to give Signor Pecora a tour." No doubt, Evelyn had sent her to give me an opportunity for a graceful exit, but I found myself not wanting to end our conversation. He had brought Papa to life again, and I was reluctant to let that go.

She gave a curtsy and left.

"Is she typical of the ladies you help here?" he queried.

I nodded.

"So young to have lived through such hard times . . ." Rising slowly as he clutched his cane, he reached into his jacket pocket and gave me a folded check. "Unfortunately, I cannot stay to be shown around, but I trust in the importance of your work here. Please accept this donation in honor of what Gabriele once meant to me."

"Thank you so much." I rose and shook his hand. "I hope we shall connect again in Milan since my family and I would enjoy hearing more of your stories; we may even be able to figure out what actually happened to Fabiano."

"Indeed. I shall look forward to it." He handed me his card, and we spent a few more minutes exchanging pleasantries before I showed him out.

After I closed the door, I unfolded the check . . . and gasped. Instantly, Evelyn appeared and peeped over my shoulder.

"Praise the Lord," Evelyn exclaimed as she caught sight of the number.

I spun around and presented it to her in triumph.

Clasping it between her hands in a motion of gratitude, she closed her eyes briefly. "This will keep our doors open for the rest of the year, a miracle when our funds had dwindled to almost nothing. I shall send Signor Pecora a note of appreciation immediately."

"And I will also thank Aunt Charlotte for mentioning our need to him; she is the one who set it all into motion—so fortunate."

"Our prayers have been answered." She folded the check again and tucked it into her sleeve. Then she turned to me and said, "Now, we must go back to work." All business again, she headed toward the kitchen, but I remained in place, savoring the moment of happiness over our new benefactor who had not only given us such charity but who had also brought me the gift of Papa's presence as well.

My focus drifted back to Papa . . . and how he would reminisce by the fireside about his home country, often with visitors who had shadowy backgrounds, like Sangiovanni—an exile who boasted that he had killed a man in a knife fight, but he always remembered to bring me a sweet when he showed up for dinner.

"Christina?"

"Coming." I followed in Evelyn's wake, but my thoughts returned to Mr. Pecora and Fabiano. I still found it unusual that Papa had not mentioned them when he not only freely discussed other Italian revolutionaries, like Sangiovanni, but also invited them to our home. Vowing to ask Mama if she knew about Papa's boyhood friends, I cleared my mind as I entered the kitchen and saw Sarah, her blue eyes wide and anxious, sitting near a large pile of potatoes that needed to be peeled. Slipping on an apron, I picked up the paring knife . . .

Two hours later, I helped serve lunch in the dining room that had once been a storage area with papered-over windows and stained walls. But Evelyn had renovated it into a light and airy space, now filled with the chatter of a dozen women. Most of them had been referred here by nuns in a nearby convent; all young, they had been hard-bitten and wary when they first showed up. Often left in London alleyways as children, they had to survive in one of the few ways a penniless woman could, by selling their bodies. A brutal life.

Much as my own family could be quite . . . complicated, they would never abandon me to such a fate. So how could it be wrong to give women without loving relatives a second chance? True compassion came from the spirit of forgiveness, not punishment.

I had learned that from Papa as well.

"Miss Christina, I can finish up serving on my own, if you would like take a break after doing most of the cooking," Sarah said as she set out a large meat pie as the main course.

"No, I do not need—" I broke off, shifting my thoughts to something that Mr. Pecora had shared: the box. Papa's keepsake from Italy. After he had died, I had shoved it in the back of my wardrobe and forgotten all about it—until now. All of a sudden, it seemed significant. "Actually, I do have an errand that I need to do, but it should not take long . . . if you are certain that you can handle the rest of lunch."

She gave a firm nod.

Before she could change her mind, I retreated to the kitchen, removed my apron, and retrieved my bonnet, then let myself out the back door. Evelyn would not like my spur-of-the-moment exit, but with any luck, I would return before she even realized that I was gone. As I emerged into daylight, I looked upward and noted heavy clouds had gathered in the previously sunny skies, and a light drizzle had begun to fall. Typical London weather, changing by the hour. With a little shiver, I hastened along the cobblestones and made a quick turn onto High Street, catching sight of a tall man disappearing around the next corner. Otherwise, I was alone. Quickly, I moved along, arriving home right before the sky opened into a hard rain.

Once inside, I shook out the raindrops from my dress, calling for Mama, but she did not answer, nor did my siblings or the servants. I waited for a few moments, then smiled to myself as it sank in that the house was empty.

My activities would be undisturbed.

I scrambled up the stairs to my second-floor bedroom, a large, square space that held an old four-poster bed, wardrobe with matching vanity dresser, writing desk, and a lone window that faced east over another terraced row of brick dwellings. The Albany Street home was the nicest house we had ever rented in London, in spite of its lack of a decent view of anything besides other similar dwellings. Still, I liked the privacy of being able to compose my poetry with the sunlight streaming in during the early morning hours . . . quiet and solitary, before the rest of the family and servants stirred.

At present, my room was in disarray, with a half-packed travel trunk on the carpet and brand-new clothing strewn on the bed.

Never having made a trip outside of England, I had no suitable apparel for a continental trip, so my Aunt Charlotte had several dresses made for me, colorful silks and poplins, quite unlike my normal palate of inexpensive gray and black frocks that passed for day and evening occasions. I loved the vivid fabrics.

Opening my wardrobe, I hunted around through the rest of my clothing and bonnets until I found Papa's box on a shelf in the back. As I slowly pulled it out, I spent a few minutes scanning its exterior as if I had never seen it before. About the size of a silverware chest, it was surprisingly light, with carefully pieced wood in the shape of books that lined up evenly along the sides, and an ivory carving of the three ancient Greek Muses on the lid. The lovely adored deities of song, dance, and memory. So pretty, and a fitting container for Papa's favorite poetic creations. The box was never far from him until his dying day when he gave it to me, but, oddly, he never told me or the rest of the family anything about it, other than that his father had passed it on to him and, later, he had brought it with him from Italy. After his death, I had looked inside and found a few of his old poems. Nothing remarkable.

So I stored it in my closet and forgot all about it.

Opening the lid for the second time in ten years, I spied Papa's poems still nestled in the blue velvet interior. Unfolding each piece of verse, I scanned the lines, which covered Papa's favorite topics of liberty and brotherhood. Then I lifted the box above my head to see if anything was attached to the bottom. Again, nothing remarkable.

Lowering it, I stared at the Muses in puzzlement, then traced my fingers along the front edge, as if they were gliding across the spines of real books. About midway, I felt a small click and one of the little volumes popped out, revealing a hidden space. Curious, I peered into the cavity and saw a small volume tucked inside, along with a yellow-gold pendant in the form of a woven basket with tiny enamel leaves and a square green stone in the center. I took in a sharp breath of surprise. Had Papa hidden them in there?

And did he mean for only *me* to find them, not Dante Gabriel or William or Maria?

I plucked out the necklace and book, setting the box on the bed as I strolled toward the window. First, I held up the piece of jewelry and contemplated the pendant; the stone appeared to be made of cheap green glass. *Pretty, but hardly valuable.* Then I examined the book's quarter leather cover attached to exposed beechwood boards and spied a small label glued to the spine with the title, *La Divina Commedia, Brescia, 1487.* It was a very old Italian version of Dante's great poem, perhaps even one of the first hand-printed volumes, and in surprisingly good condition. *How remarkable.* As I opened it carefully, I noticed Papa's annotations were scattered throughout the pages, partially faded but still visible nonetheless. When I reached the halfway point, a wax-sealed note slipped out. Quickly, I caught it before it fell to the carpet, broke the seal, and unfolded the pages. My eyes widened as I realized it was a letter from Papa, dated the day before he died.

Then I absorbed the first sentence: *If you are reading this, my dear daughter, then I am gone from this world, and you have found the hidden compartment in my precious box where I left this note for you . . .*

My body stiffened in shock as I realized these words were the last ones that my dear father had written to me. Slowly and carefully, I continued to scan the letter's contents, hearing Papa's voice in my mind as I recited each line to myself . . .

"I dream of you to wake; would that I might
Dream of you and not wake but slumber on . . ."
(*Monna Innominata*, Sonnet III)

*

June 5, 1842, Milan
"On Women Poets"

"La loro persecuzione a un istinto, un diritto, una missione, perché essi sono creati importuni, come altri nascono poeti, artisti, comici, o saltimbanchi. Guai a chi volesse opporsi all'esercizio della loro facoltà; tanto varrebbe comandare alla pioggia che non bagni, ed al sole che non abbrucci."

Society is wrong to persecute an instinct, a right, a mission, because they are so important to those who are born poets and artists . . . Woe to those who wish to oppose the expression of their talents; it would be like trying to command the rain not to bathe us, and the sun not to embrace us.

Il Corriere delle Dame
(di Mode, Letteratura e Teatri)
Ladies' Courier
(of Fashion, Literature, and Theater)

CHAPTER 3

MARIANNE

"I lov'd you first; but afterwards your love
Outsoaring mine, sang such a loftier song . . ."
(*Monna Innominata*, Sonnet IV)

Verona, Italy
October 1947

I saw Rufina cross herself when I said the words, *Fata Morgana*, aloud, and I raised my brows in puzzlement.

"Do you know what that phrase means to an Italian?" she asked, keeping her eyes riveted on the parchment sheets in my hand. "It doesn't denote only a 'phantom mirage,' but the harbinger of a coming tragedy. My mother used to talk about seeing one when she visited her aunt in Genoa as a girl; it was an image of a floating, inverted ship that she saw at sunset along the shoreline and, not long after that, the aunt died of a sudden heart attack. Others have spied them at sea and say they are . . . a warning that bad storms are approaching." She closed her eyes briefly. "I've never seen Fata Morgana, nor do I want to."

"I don't believe in such things; they're simply optical illusions. I've had friends who sailed off the North Shore in Boston and seen that kind of mirage; it's merely a trick of light," I assured her, somewhat surprised at the shift in Rufina's mood. It was very unlike her usually sunny nature. "More probably, Christina Rossetti scribbled the comment as a poetic addendum to her father's letter. In English, the Fata Morgana also refers to 'Morgan le Fay,' an enchantress from the Arthurian legends. Maybe Christina is connecting the ancient legend to Peppina—the charmer from her father's past who haunted him as part of his lost youth. I doubt if it means anything sinister." My reasoning sounded plausible, yet, as I said it, I felt a twinge of doubt. Morgan le Fay was also depicted in literature as a siren who drove men mad with unattainable desire. *Was Christina referring to something beyond her mythic figure . . . like an elusive love?*

Rufina drew in her lower lip and chewed on it for a few moments. "I suppose so, but don't you find it . . . unusual?"

"Of course, but thanks to your friend, Alessandro, I don't have the leisure to think about it since I'm on a tight timeline to prepare these dresses to be exhibited. I can't become too distracted by *it* or the woman's life who might have penned the words, even if she was a famous poet. I need to know only enough to make the pieces come alive again to tell their story."

"But her life is part of that tale, isn't it?"

As I glanced down at the trunk's contents, I paused, knowing I couldn't disagree. Every dress absorbed the weight and feel of the woman's body who once wore it: an imprint of her existence. No matter how many times I worked with antique clothing, I never quite grew used to that first moment I handled a garment, feeling the texture of the fabric and inhaling the scent of a living, breathing person who once wore it. And there was always something, a tiny stain or a frayed hem, that spoke to a specific event long forgotten and often impossible to know.

Taking in a deep breath, I exhaled slowly. "Certainly, the more we learn about Christina, the better, and she left us a record in her father's letter of why she came to Italy—that's a start, I suppose, but I need to see the dresses laid out before I decide anything else." I set the letter on a small bench. "If you could give me a hand, we can set them on the tables."

"You're not too tired?" She pulled out a pair of gloves from her purse and slipped them on.

"Exhausted, but I can collapse later."

Carefully, we lifted each dress out of the trunk, one by one, unfolding them and gently spreading the material flat on each table. I marveled at their state of preservation and refined loveliness. A powder-blue poplin day dress, a summer silk evening gown of Pomona green—both pristine—and a slightly flawed, figured Indian muslin with a floral print. *So stunningly elegant.* Miraculously, the colors hadn't faded at all, but glowed with the vividness of a rainbow arching across the sky.

"These pieces are hardly a 'phantom mirage,'" I murmured as I moved from one table to the next one, straightening a sleeve or smoothing down a skirt. "I've never seen such an extraordinary collection."

"Nor have I." Rufina stood in front of the blue poplin frock that had been placed on top. "This one seems shorter than the other ones, especially in the front part of the skirt."

I moved to stand next to her, scanning the length of the garment, from the hem gathered up in the front with a velvet bow, to the tiny rosebuds stitched along the modest neckline. "It was probably a walking dress; they had shorter hems, so women could stroll around without a train gathering dirt behind them, a little practicality in such a confining style."

"I couldn't have managed more than a few steps in that outfit, whatever its length." Rufina shifted from foot to foot, pretending to lose her balance, and I laughed, relieved that she had regained some of her normal lighthearted air.

"The dress was hardly the problem," I added pointing at the voluminous skirt. "She would've been wearing a crinoline underneath the skirt to make the fabric billow out . . . it was a structured hoop petticoat that fastened around the waist like a cage to puff out the folds and create that balloon-like effect in the lower part of the dress. It would've been made of horsehair and linen thread with several starched petticoats. Awkward and bulky."

"It sounds hideously uncomfortable," Rufina echoed, frowning. "Not to mention, probably very heavy."

I nodded with a grimace.

"So, what do you think? Considering the state of their condition, will you have enough time to not only mount the exhibit but maybe even re-create Christina Rossetti's time in Italy?" she posed.

"Normally, we'd need about three months lead time to launch it, but with the right type of forms and mounts, along with research to fill in some background about her, I can probably come up with a visual theme to organize the exhibit . . . and finish it." Rubbing my forehead, I felt a wave of fatigue wash over me, and not just from the strain of the journey. I hadn't done this kind of work in years, especially with such meager postwar resources. "For certain, I'll need to be more informed about Christina than what's in her father's letter. What do you know about her?"

Rufina picked up the old document and studied it for a few long moments. "Not a great deal . . . I'm a clothing manufacturer, not a scrittore. All I remember from studying English literature in my early school days is that she was a Victorian poet who wrote in English and Italian and had a famous artist brother, Dante Gabriel. I wasn't even aware that she had traveled to Italy. But her father is another matter; every Italian knows his name." She looked up. "Gabriele Rossetti is almost a national hero in Italy. He was a poet and revolutionary during the early days of the Carbonari rebellion, but had a death sentence put on his head and then escaped to London, where he lived out the rest of his life. Sadly, he never saw the Risorgimento. Much of what is in this letter bears out his actual exploits, especially the escape from Naples. That story has been retold many times."

"What about the two friends he mentions? Or Peppina?"

She raised her hands, palms up. "I've never heard of them."

"No matter," I said absently, as a sudden vision rose up in my mind of mannequins positioned around the room in various positions . . . with Gabriele's letter in a glass case at the center. "But I think I might have a possible theme: 'The Daughter of a Native Son.'"

"'La Figlia di un Figlio Nativo,'" she translated as her mouth curved into a smile. "Brilliant!"

"We could include some of his poetry and hers, showing how she traveled here at his behest to connect with the country of his birth. Love and heroism. It might be inspiring for people to hear right now with the war still so fresh in their minds. Perhaps we could even include some Pre-Raphaelite artwork, especially any paintings her brother did of her with Italian themes." My thoughts were racing ahead, as my vision took on more detail with flashes of color and strategically placed lighting. "You still have connections with galleries in London, don't you?"

"Just one, but the owner is well versed in the art world; he would be able to put me in touch with someone who specializes in that kind of Victorian art," she enthused. "I'll ring him today. What else do you need?"

I gave short laugh. "Mannequins, underpinnings, board mounts—the list is endless. I'll have to set up my notebook and create a time line, including everything necessary to start, but I'm going to need an assistant. I can't do this alone . . ."

"I've already thought of that, and since I'm tied up at the family factory, I begged Alessandro for his younger brother, Nico, to be assigned to us; he already does odd jobs at the Fondazione, so it wouldn't cost anything to have him work part-time on our exhibit or divert any of Alessandro's volunteers. I haven't heard back yet, but I'm hopeful." Before I could respond, she added hastily, "Don't worry, Nico is quite pleasant."

I shifted a long, low glance of skepticism in her direction.

"Trust me, you'll like him." She winked. "Very easygoing and easy on the eyes, too. Molto bello."

I turned away. "Not interested."

No more intimate entanglements with men; it makes losing them all the more difficult.

In that instant, I recalled how Paul's quirky attractiveness seemed imprinted on my heart from the first time Rufina introduced him as a fellow student and local photographer; he was standing outside the Boston Museum of Fine Arts with his camera in hand, snapping pictures of a piece of outdoor sculpture being debuted. When he swung the lens in my direction and took my photo, I was momentarily caught off guard.

Then, as I watched him lower the camera, I felt captivated by his even features, offset by a slight stubble and disheveled hair. Artistic and unpretentious. It was an irresistible combination. He told me later that his mainline Bostonian family had hoped he'd study law or engineering, but he followed his own muse and became a photographer. We had both managed to disappoint our families, and that bonded us right from the beginning. Following our hearts in our careers had led us to each other.

And we were happy together . . .

"Marianne?" Rufina's voice jolted me out of my reverie. "You just turned as pale as a sheet; it's time for you to rest. We can start on your list tomorrow."

As I came fully back to the present, I found myself lingering over the dresses that lay around me. "If I'm going to put some substance into this exhibit, I'll need you to help me get a sense of Christina as a poet and a woman. What kind of verse did she write? What was her relationship with her family? Did she ever marry and have children? All of those personal details affect the way I interpret her clothing."

"I suppose we can start with the poetry." She rubbed her chin meditatively. "Our local public library is functioning again and, even though many books were destroyed, they saved most of the nineteenth-century volumes, which might include an edition of her verse. I'll see what I can do. And there might be a literature scholar at the University of Padua who could fill in some of the details about her life."

"Excellent. I can start preparing the dresses while we fill in the unknowns about our mysterious poetess." Tracing the waistband of the walking dress, I was pleased to feel its tightness, which meant the material hadn't started to thin or fray. "It doesn't look like the fabrics are too fragile, but manipulating them onto mannequins can place stress on the seams, so I'll need to thoroughly examine each piece before we even start to think about exhibiting them." In spite of my fatigue, I began to grow excited at the thought of seeing the dresses take on a three-dimensional appearance. Then I glanced around the tables and frowned.

"Is there something wrong?"

"Not exactly, but something just occurred to me. Aside from the curiosity of how the trunk ended up hidden behind a wall, I can't help but wonder why there was nothing else in it besides the dresses. A Victorian lady would have had chemises, undergarments, accessories, and the like. So it appears as if *only* these garments were placed in the trunk—with the letter. Why?"

Rufina paused. "Perhaps this piece of luggage was misplaced or . . . stolen from part of a larger set?"

"Or she deliberately left the trunk behind?" My frown deepened. "Though I can't imagine discarding such beautiful clothing, especially during an era when fabrics were so costly that women would repurpose them when fashions changed. These dresses would've been worth quite a bit of money—"

"Thus, worth stealing?" Rufina finished for me with a note of impatience. "But we're not going to solve that one today. I'm going to look for Nico, so he can drive us home before you fall over from tiredness."

As if on cue, a man wearing a paint-splattered apron appeared in the doorway. Slim and dark-haired, he introduced himself in English with a wide smile, a refreshingly younger, more aimable version of Alessandro. "I apologize for my appearance, signora, but my brother has me working on restoring the main gallery." He untied his apron and then left it neatly folded outside of the room before he entered, explaining that Rufina had told him to be careful not to damage the dresses.

"Grazie, they are quite old," I said gratefully, avoiding Rufina's glance. I knew she was already trying to play matchmaker, just as she had with Paul.

"Alessandro just told me that I'd be working with you over the next few weeks." He walked slowly around the tables, taking in the various garments with a slightly inquisitive expression.

"I've never helped to put ladies' dresses on display before, but I'm willing to learn."

Rufina flashed a wide grin in my direction, then mouthed silently, *I told you so.*

She then explained briefly to Nico what we had planned so far in terms of the exhibit. "But we can talk about your duties tomorrow. Could you please bring the car around, and I'll show you where we left the suitcase."

"Sì." He gave a brief nod before pivoting toward the door.

"We'll meet you downstairs in five minutes, and don't forget the letter," she tossed over her shoulder as she followed him out.

"Lettera?" I heard Nico ask her as they exited, but I couldn't catch her explanation as they retreated down the hallway.

Finally alone, I stood very still, absorbing the hushed silence of the past that emanated from the dresses. They would take on a new life once they were mounted and installed, but for now, they were simply deflated echoes from a previous time, remnants of spirited joy and sparkling dreams. Faded and long gone. Still, I loved this moment . . . the space between the promise and the possible. I would let the dresses speak to me as I learned about Christina's life, and they would eventually show me the way to bring her alive again, if only for a short time.

I touched the waistband of the walking dress again, lightly tracing two embroidered rose buds on the right side, pleased to see the colors of the petals still held a bright pink hue. Then, as I fingered the neatly sewn pleats of the skirt below, I felt a . . . pocket. Not surprising, since many Victorian dresses of this period had them as convenient places to keep a handkerchief or smelling salts. But, as I peered closer, the pocket appeared to be basted shut with large, loose stitches, as if done hastily and clumsily. Startlingly different from the exquisite work in the rest of the dress. Intrigued, I carefully shifted the skirt folds aside to examine the pocket, and I spied the top part still gaped open, revealing a little corner of pale green silk fabric.

My heart beat a little faster as I gave it a little tug, causing the piece to slip out like a soft sigh.

Holding the slightly padded silk square up to the window, I realized it was a fabric postcard, one side hand-painted with the scene of two sailboats floating gracefully on a lake with the caption: Lago di Como. Had Christina visited Lake Como and bought this postcard? It looked to be more of a souvenir, perhaps from a visit there? Certainly, it was not suitable for the mail. Turning it over, there was a single sentence written in black ink with Christina's slanted handwriting: *I met him here and first heard the nightingale sing* . . .

Taken aback, I read it over several times, wondering who might've caused her to hear the bird's melody of beauty and passion.

A car horn blared outside, and I almost dropped the postcard. Then I heard Rufina shout my name from the street below. Not quite sure what to do, I wrapped the postcard in a piece of white silk from the trunk and placed it atop Gabriele Rossetti's letter, gazing at them for a few seconds. Had Christina found a lover in Italy? Certainly, the place meant something so significant to her that she had hidden a souvenir of her trip to Lago di Como in the dress. I just didn't know what it was yet . . . but I would find out.

★　★　★

The car trip to Rufina's Villa di Luce was mercifully short. Sagging in fatigue en route, I registered only brief images of narrow streets and dilapidated buildings, with an occasional palazzo that seemed partially restored to its former glory, freshly painted and with potted flowers at the doorway. A few pedestrians walked their dogs and waved as we drove by, but I could barely keep my eyes open at that point to notice much else. When we arrived, sadly, my friend's once-lovely home looked tattered and decrepit, with a crooked roof, peeling exterior, and missing window shutters.

Nico stopped the car and began to unload my suitcase while Rufina hustled me inside, ushering me up the creaking stairs to my former bedroom on the second floor. But it, too, looked worse for wear. Bare walls and floors. I shivered at the chill and noted there was little furniture in the chamber, except for an old mirrored dresser and a four-poster bed of carved wood; flannel pajamas were set out neatly on top of the bedspread.

"I think we're still about the same size." Rufina switched on an ancient-looking radiator, but it spewed out only a few feeble whiffs of heat. After kicking it a few times to no avail, she walked over to the large window and pulled the heavy brocade curtains shut, blocking out the afternoon sunlight. "Why don't you take a nap, and we can chat later tonight?"

"But my luggage—"

"Not to worry, I'll take care of it." Her tone brooked no argument as she gave me a quick hug and then let herself out of the room.

As the tiredness set in, I placed the letter on the dresser, catching sight of my reflection in the mirror: hair tangled, features drawn and haggard. *It had been a long day.* Stepping back, I slumped onto the bed, sinking into the thin mattress, its hard and lumpy coil springs poking up against my thighs. But I was too worn out to care. As if in a trance, I slipped out of my clothes, donned the pajamas, and crept under the covers. Settling my head on the pillow, I caught sight of the faded fresco of smiling angels on the ceiling above as I closed my eyes . . .

I awoke with a start, not sure where I was at first. Then, as my eyes gradually focused on the dreary bedroom, it all came rushing back: the train ride to Verona, the trunk filled with stunning Victorian dresses, and the short drive to Rufina's villa. It all seemed a blur, except for the garments. They were real. And I wanted to learn everything about them, as well as their owner, Christina Rossetti.

My stomach fluttered in excitement—and hunger. It had been almost a full day since I last ate anything.

Throwing back the covers, I slipped out of bed and opened the curtains, squinting in the bright midday sun. *I must've slept through the entire night and next morning. No wonder I was ravenous.*

Glancing around the room, I noticed my suitcase had been left at the foot of the bed, and my clothing hung on a cast-iron clothes rack with the shoes lined up below. Even my toiletry bag had been unpacked and set on the dresser's marble top. I closed my eyes briefly in silent gratitude to Rufina.

As I reached for the bag, I noticed a frayed leather book lay next to the letter. *The Poetry of Christina Rossetti.*

How had Rufina found a copy so quickly? As always, I marveled at her resourcefulness. I picked it up and noticed an ornate silver bookmark with her family's crest had been inserted to mark a particular spot. Quickly flipping the book open to that page, I immediately blinked as I noticed the title of the designated poem, "Fata Morgana," written decades after her father penned the letter we found in the trunk. After Christina had written that phrase on Gabriele's last request of her, had his relationship with Peppina haunted *her* for all of those years?

A blue-eyed phantom far before
Is laughing, leaping toward the sun:

Like lead I chase it evermore,
I pant and run.

It breaks the sunlight bound on bound:
Goes singing as it leaps along
To sheep-bells with a dreamy sound
A dreamy song.

I laugh, it is so brisk and gay;
It is so far before, I weep:
I hope I shall lie down some day,
Lie down and sleep.

I reread the poem, slower this time, letting the phrases with their long vowels and soft rhymes waft through my mind like a murmuring whisper: *I chase it evermore . . . A dreamy song . . . It is so far before, I weep.* A lyric of such love and longing, yet also very personal. No, this poem was not about her father's lover but her own "phantom" that led her "toward the sun" but always seemed to just beyond her grasp? Perhaps the man she had met at Lake Como? If so, what had happened to keep them apart?

All I had were questions and more questions.

A sharp rap on the door interrupted my thoughts. Then it opened a fraction and Rufina tilted her head inside. "So, you're finally awake."

"You shouldn't have let me sleep that long," I protested. "There are so many things that have to be done for the exhibit, and I'm anxious to start . . . but first, I have to know how in the world you found that poem so quickly." I held up the book in disbelief. "It's been only a day since our discovery."

She laughed. "No, *first* you need some sustenance. I picked up your favorite cream-filled cornettos and made coffee—"

"I'll be down in ten minutes," I cut in quickly as another hunger pang hit. "And thank you—truly."

"Prego."

I beat a hasty retreat into the tiny en suite bathroom and managed to maneuver a hand-held shower in the tiled corner niche; the water trickled out in a lukewarm stream, but it was enough to feel revived again. After I toweled off, I kept the rest of my routine brief, with a quick hair comb and lipstick before I donned a gray sweater and black, high-waisted pants. And the Schiaparelli scarf. As I fastened it in a loose knot over my shoulder, I retrieved Christina's postcard and the book of her poetry, leaving Gabriele's letter on the dresser. I could hardly wait to hear what Rufina made of it all.

Letting myself out of the bedroom, I made my way down the stairs and followed the coffee aroma toward the kitchen located in the back of the villa. Smallish, with old-fashioned appliances and a stone floor, it still charmed, with a few pieces of blue and white china stacked on open shelves and a hanging rack of dull copper pans. *A family kitchen.* I could almost smell the risotto Milanese that Rufina's mother had made for me one evening, with its blend of olive oil, rice, saffron, and shallots; we ate a la famiglia by candlelight, drinking wine, talking and laughing for hours. But as I entered now, Rufina sat alone at the table in her slightly worn navy striped jacket and skirt with no other adornment except a small cameo pin on her lapel. It felt lifeless. I took the chair across from her and set the book down, avoiding the obvious topic of how much her fortunes had changed as she pushed a cup of coffee and plate of pastry toward me.

"A bit different from your last visit, isn't it?" She absently traced a deep groove in the oak tabletop.

"Quieter, but still a . . . home."

Looking up with a twist to her mouth, she said, "You probably noticed much of the furniture and my family's treasured possessions are gone."

Considering my words carefully, I took a deep swallow of the coffee, strong and pungent, then replaced the china cup in its saucer. "It's certainly less . . . cluttered."

"Marianne, you're so diplomatic," she reached over and squeezed my hand.

"What happened to everything?"

She leaned back, glancing around the room with a sigh. "Some of it was stolen, some of it was destroyed—it's what happens during a war, leaving only shadows where paintings once hung or a chest once stood. Then again, I'm fortunate that the villa survived intact." Her eyes came to rest on me. "I still have a home."

"Yes, you do." *Whereas I feel adrift . . . not sure where I belong.*

"And . . . I have the chance to begin again and create a new vision around me. A fresh start." Her voice turned upbeat on the last two words. "Which brings me to another item that I wanted to share with you. To be honest, part of the reason I wanted this exhibit to be successful is I thought it might attract some of the wealthy Milanese vendors to invest in our Verona businesses and, more personally, I could try to persuade them to buy fabrics made in my family's factory. Right now, I'm struggling to make ends meet. We're producing the same quality material we did before the war, but no one seems to want to buy it. A popular antique clothing show could turn things around."

"Oh, Rufina, I'm happy to do whatever I can to keep your factory going," I assured her warmly. "It's been in your family for three generations, and after managing to reopen after the war, you don't want to fail now. It would be heart-wrenching."

"And . . . I would probably lose this place." elbows on the table and raised the cup to her mout. keeping it going as it is."

"We won't let that happen," I said in a firm voice. ...en willing to be cordial to your boss for the sake of the exhibit." His face rose up in my mind with the cold, congested expression I'd seen yesterday, but in retrospect it seemed more like a mask concealing his true nature. "What's his story?"

"Not all that different from the rest of us." Rufina fastened her glance on me. "He started out full of promise and big dreams. His parents died of influenza when he was barely out of university and struggling to establish himself as an artist in Rome, and he had to abandon his ambitions, return to Verona, and take on the responsibility of raising Nico while managing the family properties. Eventually, he became direttore of the Fondazione and faced incredible pressure during the war years to join the Fascisti, but he steadfastly refused, even to the point of having his family estate seized by them and being reduced to near poverty with Nico. Instead of giving in, he did everything he could to protect his brother from being swept up in their madness. It's rumored that Alessandro helped the partisans and concealed precious artwork from the Germans, but I can't say for certain; even now, no one admits to having participated in some of their activities because no one wants to think about it anymore. Still, being associated with the partisans was incredibly dangerous, which may be why his cousin was murdered—a retaliation against Alessandro. Who knows? If so, it could explain why he didn't want the killing investigated." She propped her elbows on the table and held her cup in front of her. "In many ways, men had a tougher time than women when it came to their allegiances. But Alessandro's loyalty was always to his brother first."

"Is there no one else left in his family? A wife?"

"Sì—Isabella. But she divorced him when he gave up the high life in Rome, and . . . no, I've already said too much." She halted with a shake of her head, replacing the cup in the saucer. "There's no point in rehashing old gossip, especially when it touches on private things between a couple."

So there was an ex-wife? What else was in his past?

"I suppose we all possess secrets," I pointed out as I nibbled on the cornetto, savoring the creamy pistachio filling that tasted like cherries drenched in chocolate, as I contemplated the twists and turns in Alessandro's life. "And the older we are, the more we have to conceal."

She smiled. "But you wanted to know how I found the poem. It was surprisingly simple. After you went to bed yesterday, I called the public library and they found one volume in the antique books section, so after I picked up the pastries this morning, I stopped by to check it out. When I scanned the contents, I immediately noticed the "Fata Morgana" poem, all about chasing a phantom of love and passion. Do you think the verse connects to the same phrase on her father's letter?"

It cannot be a coincidence.

"See what you think after you read the message on this postcard . . . I found it in the walking dress pocket which had been sewn shut."

She blinked. "Hidden inside?"

I nodded.

Retrieving the rectangular piece of fabric from the book, I passed it to Rufina and watched her expression of mild curiosity shift into astonishment as she took in the bucolic scene on the front, then flipped it over to read the words on the back: *I met him here and first heard the nightingale sing . . .*

"That's Christina's handwriting, so it seems like she might've had a romantic 'connection' with someone at Lake Como,"

Rufina spoke slowly as if she were verbally piecing together missing parts of a puzzle. "The nightingale is the bird of the night that lovers hear together . . . until the sun rises—"

"And they have to part ways," I finished for her. "It's a rather melancholy image, sweet and sad."

She turned the postcard over to reveal the sailboat scene. "At least Christina might have heard its melody, if only for a short time."

"But who was this man?" I wondered aloud.

"I have no idea, but we might be able to figure it out once we know more about her." Rufina broke her cornetto into two pieces, causing the fluffy cream to spill out onto the plate. "I also called the University of Padua this morning just before you woke, and they gave me the name of a Victorian poetry expert who's a visiting professor from England: Dr. Rupert Harrison. I left a message with the literature department's secretary to say you'd like to speak with him and, hopefully, he can supply some information about Christina and her time in Italy. But if you want to meet in person, I'll have to ask Nico to take you to Padua since it's about a two-hour drive and I can't take an entire day off from the factory."

"Perfect . . . I'm happy to have him, as my *driver*, of course." I raised my brows for emphasis. "Nothing more."

"You might change your mind," she teased, pushing the postcard in my direction. "It looks like even Christina succumbed to Italy's charms."

"I'm immune to that kind of persuasion." I popped the last bite of my cornetto in my mouth, dabbed my mouth with a linen napkin, and stood up, ready to make my way to the Fondazione to get started. "But all of this talk has made me anxious to start prepping the dresses . . . when can we leave?"

"You don't want a quiet day to recover from you trip?"

I picked up Christina's book of poetry, slipped the postcard inside, and folded my arms around it.

"Somehow, I knew you'd feel that way." In one smooth motion, she drained the last of her coffee, shoved back her chair, and rose to her feet. "Since I have commitments most days at the factory, I arranged for transportation to take you back and forth to the Fondazione; that way, you can create a schedule that works for your own convenience. In fact, I'm already late for a morning meeting with a potential client, so I have to run."

"Is Nico going to pick me up?"

"Not exactly, he's very busy with all of the renovation projects." She motioned for me to trail her out the kitchen door that led into the courtyard. As we emerged into the enclosed space, I noticed it had the same neglected air of the palazzo, with bare flowerbeds and dry fountains. Then she pointed at an old black bicycle propped up against a tree. "It's not fancy, but it will ferry you around the city."

"No." I held up my hands. "I haven't ridden one of those in years and wasn't ever comfortable on two wheels when I *had* to pedal one as a student. You remember my terrible sense of balance." Never having mastered the bicycle well as a child, I avoided it as much as possible.

"We all have to conquer our fears." With an air of determination, Rufina retrieved the bicycle, walked it over to me, and patted the straw basket fastened to the handlebars. "Trust me, it's sturdier than it looks, and the Fondazione is only a few blocks away. You could probably walk, but the bike is faster, *and* there's a place to hold your sewing tools."

"There has to be another option," I stressed on a pleading note.

Rufina shrugged. "If you want to wait until after I meet with my client, which might be close to lunchtime, then I can probably manage to drop you off before I head out to the factory . . . but I can't guarantee it." She took the book from me and placed it in the basket, then tapped the bike seat.

Paul would have told me to do it and face my fears—no matter how small.

Ten minutes later, I had placed my deceased husband's Murano glass compass in my bag for luck and was shakily steering the two-wheeled menace along the Piazza dei Signori, grateful that it was a fairly quiet area without too many pedestrians. Luckily, the autumn weather had turned sunny and warm, so I didn't have to deal with rainy, slick streets. But as I tried to navigate around the corner, the cobblestones caused the wheels to vibrate in an alarming way, and I almost ran into a stop sign. Tightening my grip, I somehow kept the bicycle upright, though my shoulder bag swung wildly to the side, nearly hitting a young woman who was strolling by with a little girl in hand. "Scusi!" I tossed off as I kept moving, and I heard a mild curse in response.

Clamping my arm down over my purse, I heard a car engine rev impatiently, but I didn't dare turn around. Then it sped past me with a squeal of tires and a sharp honk of the horn. At that point, I contemplated just walking the bike the rest of the way when I spotted a street plaque on the side of a building: Via Salerno. Quickly, I turned right onto the narrow avenue and was relieved to find it empty of people and cars. Heading to the end of the street, I finally braked in front of the Fondazione.

With a trembling hand, I brushed back my hair. *Surely it will get easier with practice.*

"Buongiorno, signora," Nico greeted me as he strolled out of the open front door; he was wearing the paint-splattered apron again. "Rufina called to say you'd be coming and I should look out for you—"

"Before I crashed into the building?"

He laughed as he steadied the handlebars so I could climb off the bike. Once I did so, I took in a deep breath, grabbed the poetry book, and followed him inside the immense foyer. As he propped the bike against one of the marble pillars, I noticed a scaffolding had been positioned next to the staircase.

"That's my next project while I help you with the exhibit," he said, sweeping a hand upwards to follow the arc of the stairs. "Some of the wood spindles are loose, so I have to check them one by one."

I followed his gesture and realized there were at least a hundred of them. "It's certainly time-consuming work."

"But better than painting." He hooked his thumbs in the front of the apron. "I've been doing that for so many weeks, and I can't rid myself of the chalky smell; it seems to permeate my clothes, my hair, even my skin. I will be glad to never see a can of paint again." He gave an exaggerated shudder. "It's much more preferable to help you set up those antique dresses."

"Just wait until you have to stuff mannequin arms," I quipped. "Everybody hates that part."

"I don't think it will be too bad." He looked down at me, a faint glow of amusement in his eyes that, in spite of myself, managed to lighten my mood after the wild bicycle ride.

"I'm surprised your brother agreed to Rufina's request to include the costume artifacts as part of the reopening since he didn't seem too enthused about the dress exhibit."

"She was very persuasive that it will bring people back to the Fondazione, especially women who are starved for fashion." Nico looked over his shoulder at the entrance. "It's been two years since the stabbing outside, but people still cross themselves when they pass by because they think the building is evil."

I shuddered. "Rufina told me all about the murder . . . and that your cousin was the victim."

"Tonio." His features shuttered. "He was almost like a second brother to me. We spent all our time together as boys, fishing and hiking along the river, but all of that ended when the Fascists took over. It was very sad . . ."

"I'm sorry about your loss." Placing a hand on his arm, I added, "It must've been a great shock, especially when the war was drawing to an end."

His mouth tightened. "It made no sense, even though rumors circulated around Verona that he stole something from the partisans and they had him assassinated, or that he was secretly involved with Fascisti who were thieving from locals and *they* killed him. But I never quite believed it. He wasn't a criminal or a traitor. He was a good man who loved all of us more than life itself, and if he took something that did not belong to him, it was because he had a good reason. No matter what, he didn't deserve to die like that."

"If he did, it must have been quite valuable—" I broke off as I saw Nico's eyes shift to a spot behind me. I sensed someone approaching and inhaled a woodsy aftershave with the scent of pine and musk. Instantly, I dropped my arm.

"Time to go back to work, mio fratello," Alessandro pronounced in a brusque tone as he handed a paint can to Nico. "You missed a few corners in the main gallery."

"Sì." Nico grabbed the handle and stalked off, muttering something unintelligible under his breath.

When he had exited, Alessandro stepped in front of me, glancing down with a slight frown. "Signora, I'm allowing my brother to assist you, but I want to make it very clear that I prefer you not discuss other matters with him besides the exhibit. We don't talk about the recent past in Italy. Nothing good can come from it."

"We were just making idle conversation when he mentioned his cousin Tonio," I began, taking in his casual look, with khaki work pants and a black T-shirt, stretched tight over his muscular chest. "It was harmless—"

"On the contrary, bringing up the unsolved murder can cause a great deal of ill will because people might start talking about the tragedy again and stay away from our inaugural exhibits. I cannot allow that to happen when it took me months to persuade the Verona leaders to even consider the possibility of repairing and reopening the museum, so I'm asking you not to meddle in things you don't understand."

"I meant no harm."

"Yes, I believe you. And yet the world is filled with people who have good intentions but end up causing trouble," he responded with a slight warning in his tone. "Wading into the unfamiliar waters of a foreign country, which has so recently endured a bitter war, can stir up nothing but ugly things lurking in the depths."

"You mean connected to Tonio's murder?" I pressed.

"Partly." He gave an exasperated sigh. "But also because it's dangerous to ask too many questions about *anything* that happened during the war. So let's just leave it at that." His gaze remained fixed on me for a few seconds, and it seemed as if he was going to explain further, but then changed his mind and headed for the stairs.

As I watched him ascend to the upper floor, passing the painting of the *Man with No Arms*, I clutched the Christina Rossetti book to my chest like a talisman, as I studied the portrait's main figure; it had a blank face, almost like the mannequin, but with truncated legs and missing arms. A disturbing piece of artwork in every way. It had no past, present, or future. Just nothingness.

I looked away.

Such a far cry from the lyrical beauty of Christina's verse.

But that was the reality I had come to in Verona to set up a simple exhibit, a place where even the art reflected a mute image of pain and suffering. How could it be anything else? In that moment, I realized that my job had just taken on more complexity than I had anticipated because I couldn't do it without delving into some unspoken truths.

I clasped the book tighter.

What have I gotten myself into?

CHAPTER 4

CHRISTINA

"Oh, my heart's heart, and you who are to me
More than myself myself, God be with
you . . ."

(*Monna Innominata*, Sonnet V)

Albany Street, London, England
21 May 1865

It had been a whirlwind of a week, planning, packing, and preparing myself for the long journey ahead.

But now, as I sat in my room with Dante Gabriel, I could take a pause and enjoy my last evening in London with my brother.

Everything was *almost* ready.

The whole process had taken up every bit of my energy, from dawn until dusk, which was probably a fortunate thing because I did not have time to keep rereading Papa's extraordinary letter. I had even taken a leave from my work at the Sisters of Mercy Convent to complete these travel tasks, which I probably found more time-consuming than usual because my mind kept drifting back to Papa's revelations. I still found it difficult to believe that he had a long-cherished love before he married Mama, and that he had conceived a son with his lover.

Peppina.

The woman whom he had met as a student in Naples and come to love with a passion that lasted through his life. Signor Pecora had discreetly omitted mentioning her name in his brief conversation with me, but I assumed she was the "other circumstances" that had been part of ending the circle of their friendship. Even in Papa's last days on earth, his thoughts had gone back to *her*. And his recollections of leaving her behind in Naples still conveyed the pain and regret he carried inside for the rest of his life. For a few moments, the image of my suitor, Charles, rose up in my mind, with his thin hair and bespectacled, scholarly air. *Will he be the last person I think about before I take my final breaths?*

Just then, I heard Dante Gabriel clear his throat from his perch, half lounging on my bed as he leaned down and scanned the items in my trunk. "Very neatly packed, with everything in its place. I could never do that, which is why I rarely travel. It takes too much planning, too much effort. Besides, what is the point of transferring all of our possessions from one place to another, when all we really need to carry with us is a sketchbook and a stick of charcoal." He peered closer at the trunk's contents. With a little click of his tongue, he reached for the basket pendant that had once belonged to Peppina and lifted it up by its chain. "Where did this come from? Your charming Charlie must have come into some money if he bought it for you, but perhaps he learned about investments and stocks when he took a break from translating biblical psalms. His brother is a mathematician, after all, so some of his skill with numbers may have rubbed off on your future husband."

"Do not be ridiculous," I admonished as I snatched the pendant from him. Dante Gabriel had been in and out of the house for days, seemingly diffident about our departure but, inside, no doubt anxious at being left alone at his Chelsea home in London; he hated it when he was left to his own devices. And that never boded well for his alcohol consumption. I had pleaded with him many times to come with us, but he would not change his mind. "One, I have not agreed to marry Mr. Cayley and, two, he did not give the pendant to me."

"It looks quite old, and expensive," he commented, picking up his charcoal stick.

"I doubt it." Slipping it into my velvet jewelry case, I snapped the lid shut and placed it atop the blue poplin walking dress. "It was a gift, and the person who bequeathed it to me was very . . . dear and far from wealthy; it holds sentimental value only."

That part was true.

He leaned back on one elbow, sharpening the point of his sketching tool as I bustled around the room. "Ah, that explains it: no doubt a trinket from one of your friends with the Society of Busybodies. I am sure they will miss you no end when you are away since there will be no one to help serve the lunches or scrub the floor." He twisted the charcoal stick around, carefully and expertly cutting the wood with a small knife until a few centimeters were exposed at the tip.

"I find my work at the Sisters of Mercy *very* rewarding," I corrected him. "And the other women who volunteer there are devoted to their good works for a higher cause, just like Maria and I are."

He laughed as he flipped open a sketching pad. "The convent suits our older sister, but it is not for you, Christina."

No, I would hate to be shut away in a nun's cell with only my thoughts for company.

"Your silence speaks volumes," he quipped. "As does the rainbow of colors in the dresses you are taking with you—quite a departure from your usual sedate, plain clothing."

"Aunt Charlotte had them made for me because she felt I needed brighter fabrics to match the warm, sunny Italian climate, although they are not exactly what I would have chosen for myself."

His mouth quirked upwards on one side. "I doubt you protested too vigorously."

He knew me too well.

I slid onto a chair in front of my vanity dresser and began to arrange the toiletries that I would take with me: jasmine cologne, a little tin of rice powder, and Crème Celeste. Certainly, they contained nothing that a proper lady would not use, but Mama and Maria would have none of it. I, on the other hand, reveled in the rich floral scents and the soft feel of cream against my skin, even if my olive complexion was not the pale English ideal for a woman. Still, I had my own look that proudly harkened back to Papa's Mediterranean ancestry along the southern shores of Italy.

When I was finished, I turned and leaned my head against my hand on the back of the chair.

"Stay still, that is just the angle I want." Dante Gabriel sat up and began to draw with quick, broad strokes, moving his shoulder and arm back and forth. Before I could protest, he added, "The afternoon light is slanted perfectly along your cheek, and I will lose it if you move. *Please.*"

Reluctantly, I complied. There were still a dozen little things I had to do before we departed the next day, but sketching always calmed my brother as he drew our family as various religious figures—Mama as St. Anne, William as the Angel Gabriel, and me as the Virgin Mary. Over the years, I had noted how his watercolors of "stunners" or the woman he loved pushed him into the darker regions of obsession, but re-creating our likenesses restored his spirits again. So I remained in place, watching how he kept the charcoal stick between his thumb and forefinger, palm facing down, so as to not smear his work. Head bent, hair falling over his face, he barely looked at me as his strokes gradually became smaller and smaller, feathering in the finer details. Once he was finished, he studied the sketch for a few minutes, then started to blend the edges with his fingers.

"You are going to die of boredom traveling with Mama and William for a month," he commented as he continued working on the shading. "She will be indisposed every other day, and he will drag you from museum to museum, educating you on the *artistry* of Renaissance painters—the lines, textures, and colors. All very technical. But he will never understand the passionate need to pour one's soul onto a canvas. It cannot be explained, only felt . . . he will drive you to distraction."

"So true, but I tolerate his 'academic' approach to life because, at heart, he is a dear and well-meaning brother. You know that only too well. It seems a small price to pay in order to see Milan and Verona, places I have only dreamed about. And Papa's old friend, Signor Pecora, has promised to connect with us once we arrive, so we shall no doubt see parts of the cities unknown to most English tourists." I had mentioned his visit at the convent to Dante Gabriel but omitted his reminiscences that had led me to the discovery of Papa's secret love for Peppina. It was not just Papa's instructions that led me to withhold that knowledge from my brother; if Dante Gabriel knew our father had loved a woman whom he essentially abandoned, and that she had subsequently taken her own life, it would no doubt inflame my brother's still raw emotions about Lizzie. "Will you not reconsider and go with us?"

"No." He brushed the side of his hand over the sketch.

"But think of the beautiful work you could create there," I pressed. "I cannot imagine that Italy, with its many . . . attractions, would not inspire you."

He raised his head, and a deep frown line appeared between his brows. "I can *paint* any woman I choose, but it is not *her*. Why go to Italy when I already know every face I behold will be a pale imitation of Lizzie, lacking all power to kindle my creativity? Without that, it is just placing color on a canvas, flat and dull. I have had other models, but none of them ignite my imagination with that Promethean spark that lights up my world. And anything less is hardly worth the aggravation of travel. No, I will stay in London and focus instead on my poetry—'an image in Life's retinue / That had Love's wings . . .'" His voice grew thick with emotion and he shifted his eyes away. "Maybe memorializing her in verse will be my saving grace."

"But I thought that you had decided not to compose verse ever again after you buried your poems with Lizzie—" I broke off quickly, catching myself before I caused my poor brother further anguish by reminding him of his last gesture of redemption toward his dead wife. On the day of her funeral, Dante Gabriel had been overcome with remorse and placed his small manuscript book in her coffin, nestled beneath her long red hair. William had tried to dissuade him, but Dante Gabriel had been too grief-stricken to listen to any appeals. So his unpublished poetry was lost forever.

He gripped the charcoal stick so tightly his knuckles stood out. "I am trying to write them from memory, particularly the sonnets from my 'House of Life' sequence about my years with her. Our first meeting. Our growing love. Our lost daughter. I do not regret burying the poems with Lizzie, but I now realize that was not the best way to honor her."

"You were heartbroken," I said gently.

"I was a fool." He held up the sketch and blew off any stray bits of charcoal, then considered it silently for a few moments. "I blame Papa . . . he filled our minds with his obsession about Dante and how we must aspire to the great poet's romantic notions about grand gestures in the face of the unattainable. Yet another reason not to visit Italy since it is the country that gave rise to Papa's hopeless delusions. It was an impossible effort to reach those same creative heights he expected of me."

"Still, it made you a brilliant artist—"

"But not a *great* one."

I could not argue with him on this point. In spite of his magnificent talent as a painter/poet, he had never quite fulfilled his own ambitious goals of fame and fortune. He formed the Pre-Raphaelite Brotherhood with no clear goals or principles, then he dropped out of art school before he had truly mastered the techniques of oil painting and wrote poetry only when it suited him. In truth, he lacked the discipline to touch greatness, but there was still time.

"I think you are too hard on Papa—and yourself." Rising to my feet, I arched my back as I took in a long, deep breath and acknowledged that, after sitting for my portrait so many times, it now took longer to stretch my muscles since I was in my thirties. Joints stiffened much more easily, another signal of the passing of time.

"On the contrary, I am being honest. He bankrupted us financially with his bizarre ideas about secret conspiracies hidden in Dante's *La Divina Commedia*, and, sadly, I have not succeeded in restoring our fortunes. But do not lose faith in me. I may have failed Lizzie, but I shall find a way to take care of my family." He handed me the sketch. "It is my gift to you, little sister. I may not be able to accompany you in person, but you and William and Mama will be in my thoughts while you are in Italy."

Glancing down, I saw the outline of my figure, chin resting on my folded hands as I stared off in the distance with dreamy eyes, a woman longing for a world as yet unseen and unexperienced. Yearning for something just out of her touch and fearing that it would never be attainable.

He saw too much.

"I shall be with you in spirit." Dante Gabriel grasped my hand and squeezed it briefly.

"Do not indulge yourself too much with your friends while we are gone," I teased.

"I could not do so even if I wanted to because they are all old married men now who are living in the country and spending all their time learning to handle wheelbarrows and shovels." He gave a mock shudder.

I smiled. "And yet the change of scenery might do you good . . . perhaps a holiday with William and Jane Morris at Red House?"

"Maybe."

They were particular friends of his, but their recent move to create a rural idyll outside of London held few charms for my brother. He preferred the chaos and crowds of the city. Before I could press him further, he made a quick exit in that odd, slouching manner he had of walking, hands shoved in his pockets with an attitude of defiance and *insouciance.* I knew my words would have little effect on his behavior because Dante Gabriel always went his own way, increasingly eccentric and volatile, but he had been fixed on that course for too long to change his behavior at this point.

A man in search of redemption.

Shaking my head to clear the thoughts of my brother out of my mind, I tried to focus once more on the task at hand: finish the last little odds and ends of my packing. I slipped the toiletries into small silk bags, tucked them inside the trunk's padded brocade pockets, and checked that Papa's box was nestled under my dresses . . . then my glance fell on the jewelry case. Before I could stop myself, I retrieved it and clicked the mother-of-pearl release button. As the lid flipped open, I slowly pulled out the gold chain and dangled the pendant in front of me. The little basket spun around, showing the delicate filagree at all angles, from the flat base to the braided handle. So pretty. Squinting, I studied the round, moss-green stone set in the center, trying to detect its value. Had Dante Gabriel been right in his impression that it was expensive? But it had no glimmer, no glow. Surely, a precious gem would have some type of sparkle. But this stone looked almost opaque . . . like old glass.

Papa said in his letter that Peppina thought it would bring only a modest amount of money for the rivoluzione, so it could not be that costly.

No, it would simply remain a cherished gift from my father in death because he found it too deeply personal to share with Mama or me or anyone else in life. Like Dante Gabriel's manuscript, it had remained sealed off from the rest of the world because neither Papa nor my brother could allow that part of their lives to see the light of day.

Until now.

Slipping the chain over my head, I gazed down at the pendant as it came to rest against my bodice, almost as if it were meant to lie there. I would wear it in Italy to honor Papa and remind myself that something once lost could be found and should always be treasured. Perchance, it would bring me luck in my travels.

★　★　★

Days later, as I gazed out a rain-streaked window in our Paris hotel, I remembered my hope for a pleasant trip with a wry grimace. Our journey had begun with a thunderstorm when we boarded a boat to Calais, and the rain had not let up at all—long dreary days, though somewhat revived for William when we visited the Salon to view Manet's *Olympia*. I had not been impressed with the artist's idealized view of prostitution because I knew its grim realities only too well from my interactions with some of the abused young women who showed up at the Sisters of Mercy. But William was happy to view the avant-garde painting and then visit with Parisian art critics who dissected every aspect of the work. Most of the time, I remained in the hotel, restlessly drifting around its elegant rooms as I tried to escape Mama's incessant complaints about the dampness inflaming her arthritic joints. I did not dislike Paris, but I was fixated on our destination in Italy.

And I could not wait to depart.

We finally set out under cloudy skies for Lucerne and, a day later, boarded a horse-drawn diligence to cross the Alps at the St. Gotthard pass. At that point, miraculously, the rain stopped. As we made the ascent, it felt like we had been transformed into eagles, soaring high toward the peak, and then swooping low in descent along the mountainside garden of pink Alpine roses and blue forget-me-nots, as if I could ever fail to remember the road we traveled or the awe I felt at seeing the landscape. It had been burned into my mind. Even Mama temporarily abandoned fretting about her aches and pains on that thrilling stage of our journey.

We arrived at Bellinzona, the capital of Tincio, and I took in the lovely Italian faces and musical Italian speech, varying little from that of the various émigrés who had visited Papa over the years at our London house, but somehow feeling different. Italy was now real, not just a place my father and his friends talked about, but one I was about to truly experience. *The land that speaks to my heart.* The gloom of Paris had been worth it because it was a stepping stone that brought me here.

After spending the night, we traveled to Milan by carriage to stay at the Palazzo Antica, a hotel where William had stayed several times. When we pulled up, I was delighted to see a Baroque-style building on the corner of a quiet street; it had two tower-like ends, joined by a one-story, flat-roofed entrance. With its pale yellow façade and lace-curtained windows, it had a soft, delicate appearance in the midafternoon sun.

"Are you pleased?" William asked as he helped me out of the carriage.

"I could not have chosen better." The balmy late-day air settled around me like a comforting blanket of warmth. It had been cold in the Swiss mountains, and I welcomed the more moderate temperatures of this Mediterranean city. It thawed the chill that had clung to me since Paris.

William smiled and reached for Mama's hand to assist her, and as she emerged from the carriage, she exclaimed, "Why this hotel looks like one of Dante Gabriel's paintings—lit with a golden glow. I so wish he had decided to accompany us."

I saw William's features tighten, and I hastened to add, "Thanks to William, we have perfect accommodations. And do not worry, Mama, we can record our daily activities to share with Dante Gabriel when we return home; it will be almost as if he were with us." After she gave a brief nod and moved toward the hotel's entrance, I heard William heave an audible sigh of irritation. Of course, Mama would have preferred Dante Gabriel's presence. For the hundredth time, I acknowledged that it could not be easy for William to always be effortlessly upstaged by his older brother, even when he was absent. It had to be especially galling on this trip when William had arranged every minute detail of the journey and took responsibility for overseeing that everything worked smoothly, but Mama could think only of Dante Gabriel, even as we strolled through the quietly elegant hotel lobby with its small glass dome and pale green marble floors, pointing out how our older brother would be enthralled by the frescos. I quickly interjected once again how astonishing it was that William could find such a charming place that fit our meager budget.

She offered him a small smile of gratitude but added no words of appreciation.

I would speak to her privately about the matter later.

Once I had settled into my room, I threw open the tall French doors and strolled onto the small balcony, a little space that contained a wrought-iron table and two chairs, surrounded by potted bamboo trees and a flowering vine-covered arch, creating almost a grotto-like feel in the middle of the city. Moving forward, I inhaled the scent of jasmine flowers, letting the fragrance engulf me with its sweet aroma. *It was perfect.* And I was finally alone. After two long days of travel in the close quarters of our carriage with my family, I welcomed the respite of being lost in my own thoughts in solitude. A few snatches of conversations floated up from passersby on the street below during the hour of the passeggiata, the evening walk, and I paused to listen to how the Milanese spoke my father's native language with the words lengthened and pronounced precisely.

Una bella notte.
A beautiful night.

Each word seemed overly enunciated, more musical than Papa's loose, easy way of speaking Italian after decades of living in England, and it was much easier for me to translate.

As I eavesdropped, I closed my eyes and absorbed the sounds as if they were melodies once lost and now found, sweeping me along with their familiar call. I could not move or think

or speak. Remaining motionless on the balcony, I felt something stir inside, an ancestral connection to this unfamiliar land.
For so long, I had written poetry about what it felt like to be
"shut out," the feeling that I could never take part in the vibrant
voices around me:

> The door was shut. I looked between
> Its iron bars; and saw it lie,
> My garden, mine, beneath the sky . . .

And even though I now stood apart on my balcony, I could
hear the song that reached up and touched my being, claiming
me as a daughter of the soil with an unstoppable power to set me
free from the restraints of my life. The door had creaked opened
now and I was eager to see what lay beyond.

★   ★   ★

The next morning, I came back to reality as the unwilling tour-
ist on William's tightly packed schedule. He ushered Mama and
me around the city from one museum to the next, never stopping very long except to record a particular artist in his daily
journal. We visited the Pinacoteca Ambrosiana to see the *Adora-
tion of the Magi* by Titian, the Museo d'Arte Antica to view a collection of sculpture and decorative arts from the Middle Ages,
and the church of Santa Maria della Grazie to take in DaVinci's
The Last Supper painted on the wall of its former dining room.
I thought them all quite beautiful, but in truth I far preferred
nature's riches to art treasures, yet did not want to disappoint my
brother, who was most anxious to see that Mama and I had a full
tour of Milan's famous works.

After a light lunch al fresco at a small trattoria on the Via
Senato, I pointed out that a crowd of pedestrians were making
their way toward a beautiful park across the piazza.

"Shall we join them?" I posed, curious about the canvas-covered monument at the entrance. "It looks like they are unveiling a statue."

William checked his silver pocket watch and shook his head. "We are slated to see the Duomo before teatime, and it must be taken in without haste, section by section. In fact, my planned tour of the magnificent interior will take several hours to complete since I researched every aspect thoroughly before we left London. Trust me, you will be awestruck at the cathedral's Flamboyant Gothic style; it is the only one in Italy with flame-like spires and pointed arch windows. The dukes of Milan chose the architecture to impress French and German royalty, and spared no expense, from the pink Candoglia marble exterior to the golden statue of the *Madonna of the Nativity* at the top." His voice rose in excitement. "Not surprisingly, it took almost five hundred years to build such a remarkable structure—just imagine."

I almost groaned audibly, realizing William's tour would make it *feel* like five centuries. "I truly anticipate seeing it, but I would also enjoy a bit of spontaneity—"

"We cannot alter our schedule." His face turned mulish.

"But should we not also partake in the unexpected events that present themselves to us?" I countered, noticing the crowd had grown.

William signaled to the waiter that he wanted to pay the bill. "We can always read about it in the newspaper tomorrow."

"I do not want to only read about events; I want to enjoy them in person," I bristled. "What is the point of coming here and seeing only museums?"

He looked taken aback. "Christina, you are becoming overwrought—"

"I can assure you, I am not—"

Mama held up her hand to silence us. "Please do not argue, my dear children. I agree with William that we should set aside enough time to appreciate his beloved Duomo this afternoon, but I also think Christina's suggestion is reasonable; there is nothing wrong with taking a short detour now and again . . . and I too would like to see the statue's unveiling since it is drawing such a crowd." With a smooth smile pasted on her face, she rose and opened her lace parasol in a smooth, practiced motion. "Shall we?"

I refrained from responding, but inwardly a glow of delight lit inside of me since I knew William would never disagree with Mama. I had triumphed, albeit in a small way, but it was something. As I stood and shook out my blue poplin walking dress, I held out my arm for my mother to lean on. "Grazie, Mama," I whispered as we strolled off while William finished up with the waiter, still grumbling under his breath.

"William is well-meaning, my dear, and he takes such good care of us," she reminded me with a brief glance over her shoulder at him. "But I wish he would allow himself to be a little more free-spirited."

"Like Dante Gabriel?"

Her eyes caught mine with a flash of amusement. "Maybe not *that* impetuous."

"Two brothers could not be less alike," I observed as I matched my steps to Mama's slower ones. In her early sixties, she was showing her age on various fronts, from stiff joints to memory lapses, but she had been remarkably energetic on our journey thus far. Her Polidori side of the family were known for their longevity, except for her brother, John, who had been the famous poet Lord Byron's physician and died too young from the stress of depression and gambling debts.

As if reading my mind, Mama added, "I fear Dante Gabriel is too much like my own brother, too high-strung for his own good. The artistic temperament has its own curse to bear." Her grip tightened on my arm as she stumbled slightly on the loose stones outside the garden's gated entrance. "And women must shoulder the weight of their inconstant behavior."

Was she referring to Papa? Did she know about Peppina and their son who died in infancy?

I let the moment pass and then noted a plaque on the gate's stone pillar: Giardini Pubblici—Public Gardens. The crowd had increased around the statue, but I could still make out the expansive, well-maintained grounds in the distance, with small hills and neat rows of chestnut trees. It looked like St. James's Park in London, a small, neatly elegant outdoor space among the clustered buildings of the city, its chirping birds and aromatic flowers competing with the world of man.

"I may need to sit for a few minutes to catch my breath from the heat," Mama said, her chest heaving a little unsteadily. "But please stay here or you will not be able to see the ceremony. Not to worry, for I will be fine on my own until William arrives."

I hesitated, but Mama waved me on as she took several halting steps toward a wooden bench under a large sycamore tree. Once she had seated herself, I began to focus my attention on the statue again, when I heard someone call out to me in a slightly familiar voice: "Signorina Rossetti!" I turned to behold Giovanni Pecora and, instantly, I offered him a wide and welcoming smile.

"Come stai?" he exclaimed, quickly edging around the throng on his walking stick with a taller, younger man in tow.

"Molto bene," I responded warmly, reaching out my hand to him. Then I pointed out Mama, promising to introduce her after the ceremony. "My brother, William, should be here shortly as well."

"How fortunate that we ran into each other here, of all places." He gestured toward the statue, drawing me away from the bystanders whose murmuring grew louder. "It is such an important day for Italia because this monument is to be dedicated to our first prime minister of our United Kingdom of Italy, Camillo Benso, Count of Cavour. A soldier, a politician, and a man who believed in freedom of both thought and action. Sadly, he died after only three months in office; no doubt, the strain of being such a tireless patriot took a toll on him. But he achieved much in his life . . . it is bittersweet that your father could not be here today because it was his fervent dream to see the Risorgimento."

"At least we can share the day with his comrades in arms." My eyes misted over, thinking about all the years Papa had spoken of the unification of his native country; it would have caused his heart to burst with pride.

"You are Gabriele Rossetti's daughter?" The younger man came forward, a touch of incredulity in his query. "He was a hero to those of us in my generation, a poet and a revolutionary. His brave, selfless acts in the early days of the revolution inspired me to fight in our recent war of independence with Conte di Cavour. It is my great honor to meet you." He bowed his head briefly and, as he lifted it again, I caught my breath at his compelling light blue eyes, firm features, and the confident set of his shoulders. Clean-shaven, the corners of his mouth tipped slightly upwards as he stared down at me with a pale, serious face framed by brown hair glinting in the sun. My heart fluttered wildly in my chest and, for an instant, he appeared to be the only person in the world who seemed alive and real; everyone else faded away into mere shadows.

Because the birthday of my life
Is come . . .

"I must apologize for my son's rash behavior in speaking out before I have had the chance to properly introduce him to you," Signor Pecora's amused voice interjected, breaking the spell of the moment. "May I present my son, Angelo?"

"Piacere di conoscerti." He shook my hand, holding it a fraction longer than normal. "My father told me that you are a poet like your father and have achieved some fame in England. Your family must be very proud of your accomplishments. I personally have little skill with words, yet admire those who can stir hearts and minds with their beautiful verse."

I gave a short laugh. "Truly, my work is not quite so . . . exalted. But my family is very generous in their support of my literary inclinations, especially my brother, Dante Gabriel. He did the illustrations for my upcoming book of poetry, and they are remarkable in the way they give shape and form to my creative vision . . ." I trailed off, becoming aware that I had scant understanding of what I was saying under Angelo's admiring gaze. "I also have an older sister who is quite scholarly."

"How lucky you are to have siblings," he replied. "And I should like to see your book when it is published."

Signor Pecora slipped an arm around his son and exhaled deeply. "My wife and I had hoped to give my son a brother or sister before she passed away, but it did not happen. She is greatly missed."

Immediately, I conveyed my condolences to both of them. "To lose a loved one is truly a wound that takes a long time to heal." *Like Dante Gabriel—if he ever could be made whole again.*

At that moment, a dignified gentleman stepped onto the platform in front of the statue and announced the ceremony was about to begin. He donned a pair of round spectacles and then slipped a piece of paper out of his jacket pocket; as he carefully unfolded it, the crowd gradually quieted. A quartet of young men in crisp, open-collar white shirts and dark pants lined up on one side of the platform, their musical instruments in hand.

"That is the mayor of Milano," Angelo whispered in my ear. "A good man, but he can be known to be quite long-winded

on these types of occasions, so you might want to prepare
yourself—"

Signor Pecora leveled a severe glance at his son.

I stifled a laugh, trying not to notice the scent of Angelo's
cologne with its faintly citrus spice odor. *Earthly and sensual.*

The mayor cleared his throat loudly, "Buongiorno, signore
e signori."

He continued with an acknowledgment of the beautiful day
that had brought us all together and invoked the patron saints of
Milan before he signaled for the musicians to play an introduc-
tory piece, announced as "Inno di Mameli."

The title sparked a vague memory, but I could not pinpoint it.

As the band struck the first chord, the audience began to
sing the stirring lyrics, and I grew more puzzled as to where I
had heard it.

> *Fratelli d'Italia,*
> *L'Italia s'e desta;*
> *Dell'elmo di Scipio*
> *S'e cinta la testa.*

> *Brothers of Italy,*
> *Italy has awakened;*
> *Scipio's helmet*
> *She has put on her head.*

As they sang out, the images of fighting for the cause of
liberty ignited a memory in my mind. *Of course.* It was the Italian national anthem, and I knew where I had caught snatches
of it: Papa's study. A few years before he passed away, one of his
old friends, who had recently returned from Italy, appeared at
our house and said he had something to share with him, for his
ears only. After they shut themselves behind closed doors, Papa's

friend started to sing something in a low voice, but I paid little attention. Later, however, Papa was always humming the tune under his breath.

Now I understood why.

I glanced over to check on Mama and saw her eyes filling with tears as they caught mine in a moment of recognition at what the song meant.

How Papa would have loved hearing it today.

"You know our anthem?" Angelo inquired, as he looked down at me.

I nodded.

"We sang it every day as we protected our fortress in my hometown, Verona, and it bonded us as Fratelli d'Italia—Brothers of Italy. Our souls were stirred to never surrender, and that is how we won our War of Independence." His chest swelled in pride. "I am happy that I will be able to tell my future children that I played a part in the Risorgimento, if only a small one."

"But every role is significant," I assured him, moved by his devotion to his cause, though it made my own scribbling and volunteer work with the Sisters of Mercy seem somewhat trivial. "I so wish women could contribute in such a powerful way, but sadly, we are relegated to only insignificant tasks."

Angelo blinked in surprise. "That is not true, Signorina Rossetti. As a poet, you must realize the importance of the words which you compose. Like our anthem, they can transport people into worlds that they can only dream about, and that gives them hope. The women of Milan published special issues of the *Corriere delle Dame* during the struggle for unification, reshaping a fashion periodical into a political force by filling it with patriotic songs and poems." His voice rose as the crowd's version of the anthem grew more impassioned. "I shall obtain a copy for you, if you would like to see one."

"Indeed, I would." *Fashion and politics.* I never quite realized they could be entwined. "It may inspire me to new directions in my own poetry."

He smiled broadly, then picked up the singing at the chorus, "Siam pronti all morte, / L'Italia chiamo—We are ready to die, / Italy called."

Once the anthem ended, everyone clapped and cheered, and I found myself caught up in the excitement that rose up in a wave of pride. Then the mayor proceeded to give the highlights of Camillo Benso's career, stressing the many sacrifices he made for his country on the road to unification. As he paused at various points in the count's life, people clapped again and, eventually, he stopped speaking and reached for the blue silk curtain that covered the statue, acknowledging the artist, Antonio Tantardini. With a flourish he yanked it down as a lone trumpet rang out.

I held my breath in anticipation.

The audience instantly turned silent as they took in the bronze sculpture of the imposing statesman, chiseled with his arms stretched forward, as if to embrace the crowd, holding an open book in his right hand. Slightly disappointed, I found it not unlike many of the statues of important men that graced the London squares . . . until I noted Tantardini had included a half-clothed female figure seated boldly at the base in the act of inscribing Cavour's name on the front plaque.

"You see, the spirit of freedom is embodied in a woman," Angelo murmured to me alone. "And *she* is the one who is writing history."

I stared at her for a long moment, taking in her daring and confidence, and finding it more inspiring than the Cavour figure for all of his striking dignity.

"Actually, the Milanese gossips say the sculptor included la bella donna because she was his lover," Signor Pecora added with a cynical twist to his lips. "I would not be surprised."

"Oh, Papa, if that were true, he used her as a model to convey his idealism." Angelo gestured toward me and added, "You embarrass Signorina Rossetti with such talk."

"On the contrary, you forget that I have a brother who is an artist, Dante Gabriel, so I understand how female beauty can embody a man's greatest aspirations and, sometimes, his greatest disappointments, the highs and lows of life." I scanned the statue again, thinking of the many afternoons I had spent in Dante Gabriel's studio, watching him paint one of his "stunners" as Guinevere or Beatrice. Of course, Lizzie became the very embodiment of his fantasies. "To see the female form so dominate the sculpture is rather refreshing, and is it truly any different than a sonnet written about an unattainable love? Isn't creating such beauty a statement in itself?"

Angelo beamed in approval, but Signor Pecora did not.

"At any rate, it is a great day for Italy to honor such a hero," I hastened to add, not wanting my father's old friend to think I was too outspoken. He had been so kind in his donation to the Sisters of Mercy and his generous offer to show us around Milan; I could overlook some of the old-fashioned views of his generation.

Signor Pecora gave a grudging nod.

As some of the audience members surged forward to shake hands with the mayor, I glanced over at my mother and spied William approaching her with a glass of water as she fanned herself vigorously. "If you would like to stay here, I must see to my Mama since she is not used to the heat—"

"Oh no, I should like to meet her," Signor Pecora interjected quickly. "I find myself growing a bit overheated as well.

We Italians tend to spend midday indoors, especially during the summer months, which are unusually hot this year. I am ready to leave."

He held out his elbow and I linked my arm through his, slightly disappointed that it was not Angelo escorting me away from the crowd, but he had been drawn to the side by a friend who hailed him with an enthusiastic greeting. They slapped each other on the back and began an animated conversation, gesturing with their hands and raising their voices to be heard above the din of the crowd. When the band started up with another tune, Angelo and his friend quickly moved toward a quieter spot of the piazza where a young woman waved them over, and they disappeared under a colonnade. As I craned my head to try to find them again, I felt Signor Pecora's gentle nudge bring me back from my daydreams.

"You must excuse my son for abandoning us," he said in a rueful tone. "He is a very popular young man, especially with the young ladies."

Oh.

"Did you have a pleasant trip here, signorina?"

"Indeed, yes." I forced myself not to look over my shoulder as we strolled toward Mama and William. "I found traveling through the St. Gotthard pass in the Alps to be such a thrilling adventure, and the Italian scenery is lovely, just as my father always told us."

He tilted his head upward briefly. "I believe he is looking down upon us today."

"I felt that as well."

Slowing my pace, I took a few moments to compose my thoughts. "I wanted to tell you, Signor, that after we met in London, I decided to hunt around for my father's box which you said he brought with him from Italy. I suddenly felt curious to see it again because, when he gave it to me right before he died, I simply stored it in the back of my armoire. I never gave it much thought after that. But when I examined it more carefully a week ago, I found . . . a secret compartment, of all things."

Signor Pecora halted.

Quickly, I related the general contents of Papa's letter, along with the hidden Dante book and pendant.

"I am astonished." His raised his thick, gray brows. "Gabriele was not the type of person who withheld the truth from anyone. He was honest and straightforward in his dealings with every person who came into his orbit. As am I. When I met you in London and discussed my friendship with Gabriele and Fabiano, however, I hesitated to include Peppina out of sensitivity to your family. Did he not tell any of you that he once loved a young woman named Peppina?"

"No." I had nothing else to add. In truth, it was still very difficult for me accept that my beloved father had neglected to inform us about this significant part of his life in Italy when he told us repeatedly about everything else. How could he have kept all of it locked inside his heart for so long?

Oh, Papa, and why did you feel it necessary to reveal it only to me and so long after your death?

Signor Pecora's face took on a pained expression. "I am sorry that my appearance caused you to learn about your father's deception in such a sudden way, but, since he left you the letter, it seems that he was trying to unburden his soul before his passing into heaven. I can only add that we all loved Gabriele and, while he cared for Peppina with the passion of his youth, he would not have married your mother without a mature man's depth of feeling. Do you think your mother knows about her?"

"I cannot say for certain." I shrugged, noting that William was motioning us toward them. "Papa wrote in the letter that he never admitted to the relationship openly, but he thought Mama may have guessed. Then again, he penned those lines a few days before he died, so he may have made a deathbed confession to her in a last-minute attempt to clear his conscience. I have no way of knowing for sure unless I share the contents of Papa's last communication, and I am afraid to do so. What if she did not have any knowledge of Peppina? Learning about it now, ten years after Papa's passing, would do nothing but tarnish his image in her eyes."

Glancing down, Signor Pecora ground his cane into the gravel path, crushing the small stones beneath the tip. "I wish I could advise you on what would be best since I am partly responsible for the dilemma in which you now find yourself, but only you can decide on which course to take. I can assure you that I had only the best of intentions when I contacted you in London, yet I somewhat regret it now."

"Oh no, I do not blame you at all, because you helped to bring the truth to light," I said firmly. "Hearing your stories about Papa brought him back to life again, and I look forward to hearing more of them. For the rest, please keep it just between us; I told my family that you had met Aunt Charlotte and that you and I became acquainted in London, but nothing else. We are traveling to Verona next, and I shall find a way to honor Papa's request to return the Dante volume . . . and spare Mama's feelings."

Nodding, he smiled as we moved forward again. "You have your father's courage and determination, Signorina Rossetti. I will assist you in any way possible and happily welcome you and your family to my city of Verona."

"Grazie, signor."

As we approached Mama and William, I made the introductions and they greeted Signor Pecora warmly in Italian. I glanced around the piazza to see if Angelo had reappeared, but he was nowhere to be seen. A little twinge of disappointment tugged at me.

"But you speak our language beautifully, Signora Rossetti," Signor Pecora was saying to my mother as he bowed and kissed her hand.

"I am half Italian." Mama smiled up at him. "My mother was English, but my father, Gaetano Polidori, emigrated from Tuscany, and he made certain that my siblings were fluent in his native tongue. I believe you already made the acquaintance of my sister, Charlotte, when you recently stayed in London."

"Sì—a chance encounter. In fact, she was the one who mentioned your daughter's work at the Sisters of Mercy and that you were traveling here, so it was most fortunate that I met her; otherwise, I would never have had the opportunity to meet other members of my old friend's family on such an auspicious day," he replied, straightening again. "Sadly, Gabriele and I lost touch after he left Malta, as is often the case when people are separated by such a great distance, and I rarely traveled to England."

"He would have welcomed you to our home," William said as they shook hands.

"So your sister said . . . it was *my* loss." Signor Pecora shifted his glance to my mother again. "And one that I am pleased to rectify."

"As are we." Mama inclined her head.

As we chatted for a little longer, the crowd finally began to scatter and the band members packed away their instruments, no doubt ready to take refuge indoors from the blazing sun. If anything, it had grown hotter as the afternoon progressed, and I too began to long for the coolness of my room at the Palazzo Antica.

William pulled out his pocket watch again. "Signor, we are about to take a tour of the Duomo and would be delighted if you would care to accompany us. I have been planning this visit for months, carefully studying the history of the church, its architecture, and the artistry of the stained-glass windows. I wanted to begin with the Aribert and Visconti coffins, then view the statues near the main altar while taking in all of the exquisite windows along the way."

"Ah, my favorite is the twenty-fifth window above the altar of Santa Prassede, one of the oldest in the Duomo, on the northern side. It feels like being covered in a blanket of light when you stand beneath the precious glass," Signor Pecora reflected. "You may not know that this particular window is attributed to the artist Niccolo da Varallo and was sponsored by the College of Apothecaries in homage to San Giovanni Damasceno—their patron."

William's face kindled in excitement. "I did not, sir, but would be most appreciative if you would care to join us and share your expertise. It is a dream come true to have such an accomplished scholar take us through each part of the Duomo, though, of course, I do not wish to impose on your time."

Please, let him be busy.

"Not at all; my afternoon is completely free." He reached down to help Mama rise, but she seemed a little unsteady, rocking back on her heels. "But perhaps your mother is a bit fatigued?"

"Yes, indeed." I stepped forward quickly to take Mama's arm. "It might be best, William, if I escort her back to the hotel so she can have a cup of tea and a little breather.

He frowned. "But you will miss my tour."

"I think Mama's health needs my attention more right now, and I can always take a brief viewing of the interior tomorrow on my own."

The look of horror on my brother's face almost caused me to laugh aloud.

Before he could protest, Mama declared that she would prefer to return to her room and for William to carry on without us.

"But you do not know the way back to the Palazzo Antica," he persisted, obviously not ready to acquiesce yet.

"I shall escort them," Angelo declared as he appeared at my side once more. "I know a short, backstreet route there, if you are feeling well enough to walk, Signora Rossetti."

Mama agreed readily, and before William could further protest, we quickly moved off, with my mother taking Angelo's arm. I took my place on the other side of him and noted approvingly how he measured his steps to match Mama's. We exited the piazza and strolled toward a narrow, winding street.

"Thank you so much, signor, for assisting us. My mother is not used to such exertions, especially on such a warm day, and I fear it has taxed her strength." However, even as I heard myself say the words, I became aware that Mama seemed to pick up her pace smartly the farther away from William we found ourselves. *Brava, Mama.*

"It is my pleasure, Signorina Rossetti. I must apologize, though, that I temporarily abandoned you after the statue was unveiled."

"Oh, I completely understand. Your friends wanted to spend time with you."

"Sì, but I mainly wanted to buy you a copy of this week's *Il Corriere delle Dame.*" He handed me a thin pamphlet with an illustration of a fashionably dressed woman and the headline: "Risorgimento, Forever!" "This is the journal that I was telling you about; it is written and published by women who believe their words have the power to alter history—like you."

I smiled in pure delight.

As I took it from him, our fingers brushed against each other, and I glanced up at his unusual eyes; now they gleamed like a morning sky of promise and hope. And it seemed like the dawn of something new and fresh and real in my life. Could this feeling be what Dante Gabriel had felt when he first saw Lizzie?

Mama coughed lightly, and I broke off my gaze, tucking the pamphlet into my bag.

The moment passed, but something had happened between Angelo and me, small and tentative, but undeniably true.

The rest of our short walk passed in a blur of winding, crooked streets, earth-toned buildings, and cloudless skies, with passersby hurrying around us when Mama stopped to take in a store window or gaze at a garden gate. En route, I barely even registered what Angelo was saying, except that he had read my father's poetry and political tracts and even quoted some of his favorite lines, which he had memorized. I was charmed, to say the least.

By the time we arrived at the Palazzo Antica, I did not want our conversation to ever end, but Mama was visibly flagging at that point. "Signor Angelo, I would ask you to stay for tea, but I think my mother needs to rest quietly for a little while." I paused. "I hope we shall see you and your father again while we are in Milan—"

"Most certainly," he interjected. "Papa has some banking business to conduct that should be finished up rather quickly; after that, we are free."

Yes.

My heart quickened. "We are booked to take a short cruise on Lake Como tomorrow evening, so perhaps you both would like to accompany us . . ." I trailed off, not certain if I were being too bold.

"It would be our pleasure." The corners of his mouth tipped upwards, then he kissed my hand and strolled off, whistling the Italian anthem.

As I watched him disappear around a corner, I heard Mama cough again, louder and more deliberately this time. Turning, I found her eyes piercing the distance between us with a probing query.

"What?"

"Nothing."

Gritting my teeth in annoyance, I refused to justify my invitation to Angelo, and an awkward silence descended on us until the hotel manager appeared. While fussing over Mama, he ushered us both inside the cool, airy lobby. Then he signaled for a young man to help Mama up the stairs and informed me I had two letters awaiting me at the front desk.

"Perhaps *Mr. Cayley* has penned a note to you," Mama said, stressing his name, before she headed toward the stairs with her escort.

A twinge of guilt instantly nagged at me as I realized that I had completely forgotten about my suitor.

Out of sight, out of mind . . . perhaps because he has never been in my heart.

Hesitantly, I picked up the letters and was relieved to see Dante Gabriel's familiar sloppy handwriting. As I opened it, I wandered into a small alcove off the side of the lobby; it held a lone balloon chair, upholstered in a richly colored red brocade, and a delicate tea table. Seating myself, I began to read the note:

25 May 1865

En route to Bexleyheath
Dearest Sister,

I am writing this letter on the train to Red House to see William and Jane Morris, which will show you how glum I am because I hate the countryside. But I have been rattling around my studio for two days, and I cannot stand it any longer, and visiting Maria does not help. Her religiosity has become insufferable. To wit, the evening prayer over dinner last night lasted almost a quarter of an hour, and my food had turned quite cold before I could taste one forkful of mutton.

Even worse, I have taken a chill and feel quite unwell, making it difficult to distract myself by painting or teaching. All of London seems even more dreary when you are away: gray skies and endless drizzle that cause my mind to drift into dark avenues, even to thinking someone was shadowing me. I am hoping that the Morrises will raise my spirits with their cozy home, but I fear it will only remind me of what I have lost.

Pardon my peevishness. I hope to be more cheerful when I write again.

Your dejected brother,
Dante Gabriel

P.S. Do not let William drag you to every museum and church in Milan.

I grimaced and refolded the letter.
Peevish, indeed.

Still, I would write to him that evening and try to improve his mood by describing the sights we had seen and the people we had met. But not Angelo. I would keep my thoughts about him to myself, including my invitation that he and his father join us on the Lake Como cruise.

And I will wear the same blue poplin walking dress that I had on today when I met him.

Then I glanced at the other note and noticed it was not from Dante Gabriel. In fact, there was no return address. Puzzled, I opened it and scanned the single line:

Tuo padre mi ha tradito.
Your father betrayed me.

"Trust me, I have not earn'd your dear rebuke,
I love, as you would have me, God the
most . . ."

(Monna Innominata, Sonnet VI)

★

28 January 1843
Milan Italy

Per abbigliamenti da passeggio o da visite non abbiamo da additare altri abiti, fuorche quelli di raso all reine, ovvero di damasco, guarniti di velluto, di nastri o di passamani . . .

For walking or visiting attire, we have no other clothes to choose, except those of royal satin, or damask, garnished with velvet, ribbons, or trimmings . . .

Il Corriere delle Dame
(di Mode, Letteratura e Teatri)
Ladies' Courier
(of Fashion, Literature, and Theater)

CHAPTER 5

MARIANNE

> "'Love me, for I love you' and answer me,
> 'Love me, for I love you' so shall we stand
> As happy equals . . ."
>
> (*Monna Innominata*, Sonnet VII)

Verona, Italy
October 1947

Alessandro and I saw little of each other during the first week of my work on the exhibition; he kept to his duties at the Fondazione while I remained in what I now called the "alabaster room," crafting the initial stages to display the dresses. Occasionally, he hovered by the door when Nico was helping me, and I sensed his presence before I actually saw him. It was as if the air turned unnaturally quiet. Then he would appear in the doorway, and I'd know he was listening to make certain I wasn't making any further inquiries about the murder. Apparently satisfied, he would then vanish as quickly as he turned up. It all seemed a bit strange, but I did my best to ignore him.

Yet something about Alessandro always lingered, even when he wasn't there.

Today I worked alone on the blue poplin walking dress, which was stretched out on one of the tables, checking the seams to make certain none of them had split and gauging whether the material could take the stress of the underpinnings needed to create the proper period silhouette, including padding, petticoats, and arm stuffing. Without those accessories, the garment would look flat and lifeless, and that would spoil the presentation—a travesty for a costume curator, especially one who'd become obsessed with making Christina Rossetti come alive through her clothing.

Certainly, her dresses were typical of proper Victorian women, but after I'd begun reading her poetry, I saw the complexity of her inner world, exploring forbidden subjects for her time. So, who was she—truly? I found myself thinking about the lush images in her verse, often about love and passion, and wondering if she had composed them about the man she met at Lake Como. Was he the object of her deepest desires? I was also surprised by the sensuality of Christina's poems, enticing and even erotic at times. One longer piece, *Goblin Market*, was a disturbing tale of two sisters, one of whom becomes bewitched by eating the fruit of goblin men, and the other who saves her by squeezing the goblin fruit on her skin for the sister to taste and break the spell:

> *Squeez'd from goblin fruits for you,*
> *Goblin pulp and goblin dew.*
> *Eat me, drink me, love me . . .*
> *For your sake I have braved the glen*
> *And had to do with goblin merchant men.*

Those were hardly the lines one would expect a Victorian lady to pen. They had a tinge of thinly veiled sexuality, raising more questions in my mind about Christina's secrets that she may have hidden behind the lines of poetry. What had occurred while she was in Italy? Something amorous? So life-altering that it caused her to leave these lovely garments behind, along with mementos of her visit?

I reached into the pocket of my apron and slipped out the Lago di Como postcard that I had found sewn inside the dress, then set it next to the bodice, imagining Christina in the frock as she strolled along the shores of the lake on a pretty summer day. Poplin was a perfect material choice for a walking dress, being a plain weave—light and versatile—with a smooth, lovely sheen that doesn't wrinkle. She could've worn it all day without the fabric losing its freshness. Even after all these years of being folded in the trunk, the garment's puffed sleeves and double skirt with its fringe trim had a crisp and fresh appearance. I looked down at my white shirt and wool pants under the apron, machine made and utilitarian, as befitting this era, and I frowned. Christina's feminine, hand-stitched pieces spoke to me in a way modern clothing never could.

Every antique dress has a unique story to tell . . .

"Marianne, look what I found," Nico exclaimed as he strode into the room, carrying a decrepit mannequin, an early twentieth-century style with a wooden torso positioned atop a metal stand. No arms, no legs. It was typical of the kind tailors used at that time, and it was shaped in the style of a man's chest.

Oh no.

I forced myself to smile so as to not dampen his enthusiasm as he explained how he had found three of them, stashed in an old horse barn outside of the city, and bartered with the farm owner to sell him the mannequins at an inexpensive price. He had agreed, needing the space to store his horse feed.

As I approached the form, I wrinkled my nose because it reeked of straw and dung.

"The wood looks solid, so I won't have to do any repairs; the other two are outside and in pretty much the same shape." Nico spun the mannequin around, so I could see it from every angle. "I know it smells bad, but I can do something to remove the odor."

"Yes, that's the first thing that needs to be done." I tapped my chin, stalling for time as I tried to imagine how in the world I could remake this thing into a suitable mannequin for a Victorian dress. "If you could take this one back outside with the others, spray them down with a heavy dose of white vinegar and let them air out, that should take care of the barn stench; then I can plan how to transform them into a semblance of a female form. It's going to be . . . tricky."

His expression took on a shade of disappointment.

"But it's a good foundation, and we can build on it," I added hastily. "All we need is some rubbery padding to fill out the torso and hold the underpinnings, then maybe create soft arms out of nylon to support the sleeves . . . it should work just fine." Trying to keep my tone light and encouraging, I still struggled to imagine how we'd duplicate the hourglass figure of the nineteenth century on this tailor's dummy, but we would find a way. I'd once made a mannequin out of straw and burlap for an exhibit at a small gallery outside of Boston due to wartime scarcity of materials at home, so I could manage this too. Creativity and commitment. Those qualities could make any clothing exhibit successful, and I felt both of them stir inside of me again since I'd come to Verona, dampening that constant sense of self-doubt that I'd had since Paul's death.

But he had supported me, even when my own parents doubted my career choice. This was my vocation.

You have to believe in yourself and the importance of your work, Paul would always say to me when I had moments of uncertainty. But then I had him to remind me of that when I faltered. Now all I had to rely on was myself, and as I took another dubious look at the mannequin, I realized I would have to dig deep into all of my skills and experience.

"What is that awful stink?" Rufina said as she took a few steps into the room and then stopped with a grimace. "It reeks like a dirty animal."

I exchanged glances with Nico.

"You might say that." I watched in amusement at the wide berth she gave the noxious mannequin. "Nico found three of them in a horse barn, but hopefully we should be able to clean them up so their pungent odor doesn't rub off on the dresses."

Her brows rose in skepticism.

Tilting my head back and forth, I eyed the torso from several angles. "All I can say is they're better than not having a form at all. If we had to place the dresses on hanger mounts to exhibit them, we would lose the whole sense of the woman underneath the garment, even if we attached quilt batting or mattress padding. We couldn't fill out a life-sized shape needed to re-create Christina's 'body.' At least the torso gives us a foundation." I hated exhibits when dresses were placed on hangers. They were very popular when I was in design college because they had a modernist appeal, but with historical apparel, I preferred to develop a sense of how the clothing was actually worn at the time, and that meant a padded form beneath the clothing. Granted, it still left much to the viewer's imagination, but it was easier to visualize a woman's figure with a three-dimensional display.

"I see your point," Rufina conceded, drawing back from the torso as she produced a handkerchief from her pink leather bag and held it up to her face. Today she wore a smartly fitted gray skirt and jacket, with high-heeled shoes of brushed suede. Her red curls were swept up in a French roll and her lipstick matched her bag. *So typically chic.* It was the kind of attire I knew she reserved for high-level business meetings. As if she could read my mind, she added, "I have an appointment with vendors from Milan today who might finally commit to stock our Lake Como factory's finest silks again, *if* I can persuade them that the quality is as good as, if not better than, what we produced before the war. I'm going to give them these samples and invite them to the exhibit to sweeten the pot; that way, they'll have time to make their decision before they travel here to Verona—but not too much time." Rufina winked as she unwrapped a small silk bundle and handed several swatches to me.

"I know you'll be able to work your magic on them." I held up the top piece of luxurious burgundy-colored silk and ran my fingers along the natural weave, soft and gossamer light. The rest of the pieces were just as beautiful. "How can they not be impressed with the fine weave? It's perfection."

She managed a small tentative smile. "I hope our final product has the quality it once did."

"All of that and more, from what I can tell." I passed the pieces back to her, careful not to have them touch the mannequin. The silks produced nearby were second to none because, as I had learned from Rufina, the mulberry trees around Lake Como, which are the main source of silkworms, were planted centuries ago and created a perfect environment for the insects to produce the long, thin fibers that were harvested and woven into lustrous fabric. Of course, everything came to a halt during the war, but now, if there was a chance the business could be revived, Rufina would be an integral part of it. "I think the Milan stores will be delighted to sell the Rovelli silks again."

"Certo," Nico echoed.

She carefully rewrapped the swatches and set them on the table where the poplin dress lay. "It's sort of fitting that Christina bought a silk postcard of Lago di Como."

Picking up the souvenir, I could feel the texture wasn't quite as refined as Rufina's silk, and the material had thinned a bit over the decades of storage in the trunk, but the painted scene of the sailboats on the lake stood out quite vividly with the billowy white clouds and turquoise-colored water. "Still, it's puzzling why she stitched up the postcard inside the dress's pocket. Even if the trunk was somehow mistakenly left behind, which is hard to believe, I can't imagine why she hid the postcard, especially one with such a romantic inscription: *I met him here and first heard the nightingale sing.* If it had been mine, I would have kept it close as a cherished memory." Like I did with Paul's compass; it was never far out of sight.

"Speaking of that, I might have someone who can shed a bit of light on our elusive poet," she proposed. "Remember when I told you a few days ago that I left a message for Dr. Rupert Harrison, a literature professor at the University of Padua? Well, he called back this morning and I related a few details of our little discovery. He was very excited to speak with you. I figured you might need a little break from working on the exhibit, so I made an appointment for you to meet with him this afternoon." She gave me the time. "I know it's a bit last minute . . ."

"Today?" I blinked, rapidly calculating how I could make time for the trip. "But I've got to mend the poplin's hem, reinforce some of its lace trim, and clean the bodice by the end of the week. I just don't know if I can leave the project for that long." Then my inner voice said, *Do it.* How could I decline a meeting with the man who might provide answers to the questions that had been haunting me since I began working on the exhibit? "On second thought, I can probably complete those repairs on schedule if I put in extra hours over the next couple of days. Of course I'll meet Dr. Harrison."

"It's only an hour's drive from here, so maybe Nico could take you?" Rufina ended on a question as she turned to him. "That would be the quickest way to make it there and back."

Nico grinned. "Sì, it would be my pleasure to take you there, Marianne—"

A throat-clearing sound in the doorway interrupted him.

Alessandro was leaning against the jamb with his arms folded. "Nico will be too occupied with his painting duties to go jaunting around the countryside," he said, strolling into the room. Then he sniffed the air around the mannequin and frowned. "I assume *that* is the source of the stench?"

"I'm afraid so, and there are two more of them in the court-yard just as foul smelling, but I have already told Nico how to eliminate the odor," I explained quickly. "They should be fine after a white vinegar cleanse."

"Just so they don't taint any of the other exhibits," Alessandro continued.

"Of course." Biting my lip nervously, I didn't want to do anything that would jeopardize the Fondazione's priceless art-work, but I desperately needed these mannequins for my dresses. "And I don't require Nico to drive me to Verona when he's so busy. I'll take the train."

"That will be twice as long since it stops in San Bonifacio and Vicenza along the way since there is no direct service yet." Alessandro surveyed the dingy tailor's dummy for a few more moments, then closed his eyes briefly as he rubbed his forehead with a weary sigh. "Nico, this mannequin needs to be moved out of here immediately and cleaned, then you can resume your painting. *I* will drive Signora Baxter to Padua since I need to pick up a sketch that a patron of the university decided to loan to the Fondazione."

Nico's shoulders sagged, but Rufina clapped happily, exclaiming, "Perfetto!"

Yes—perfect. I would be confined in a car for hours trying to make idle conversation with a man who made me uncomfortable. "Truly, I don't mind taking the train—"

"I will pick you up at Rufina's palazzo around—" He broke off and glanced at Rufina, who raised three fingers. "Two o'clock. That should give you enough time to finish up here and be ready."

Do I really want to know about Christina Rossetti's secrets enough to agree to his offer?

Am I that obsessed?

"I'll be waiting outside," I responded.

★ ★ ★

I had to push all thoughts of my trip to Padua out of my mind so I could concentrate on mending the poplin's hem by hand; it required painstaking work with a very thin needle, starting at the seam and working invisible thread across the torn section with tiny, even stitches—the old-fashioned way, except I had a lamp off to the side that illuminated the fabric with a bright, unforgiving light in case I made a mistake. Thankfully, I had learned the technique in design college, anticipating that antique dresses would always have some type of damage along the hem, especially those from the nineteenth century, when the bottom of dresses often swept along the streets. After about an hour, I sat back and surveyed my handiwork, viewing the hem from the front and back with a critical eye. Only the first stitch could be seen from the inside seam and it was an almost microscopic knot to hold the rest of the stiches; nothing showed on the outer part of the skirt.

Satisfied, I took a few moments to simply absorb the full length of the dress, imagining how beautifully it would drape on the refurbished mannequin, like a dream from the past that had gradually turned into reality. And I had to admit that this sky-blue poplin was my favorite of the three dresses, maybe because it was the first one I had lifted out of the trunk. When I'd slid it out of the tissue paper, the fabric seemed to exhale in a whisper of relief to see the light of day again. Certainly, nothing about it was atypical of an 1860s Victorian frock: fitted top with lace, two layered sleeves, waistband, and flared floor-length skirt. And yet . . . its very existence after being hidden away for so long gave it an air of mystery.

The Verona church bells rang in the distance with a single chime.

Time to wrap it up.

I had to bike back to the Villa di Luce and ready myself for what would no doubt be an awkward car ride with Alessandro. Why couldn't he have just let Nico drive me? But I already knew the answer: he didn't trust me not to ply his brother with questions about the murder along the way, and of course I would. It would be too tempting . . . all I could hope for was that speaking with Dr. Harrison would make it worth the trip.

Reluctantly, I switched off the light, covered the poplin dress with a thin cotton sheet to protect it from any dust particles, and left the room.

Exactly an hour later, I stood outside the entrance of the villa, waiting for Alessandro. I had taken a brief shower, freshened my hair and lipstick, and wore a belted, buff-colored dress—with my Schiaparelli scarf—and a matching cardigan sweater. Nothing too fancy. I didn't want him to think I was making an effort to look attractive for him, but I also knew that Italian women took a more formal attitude to the type of clothing they wore in public than Americans. In my bag, I carried Gabriele Rossetti's letter and the Lago di Como postcard to share with the professor.

I gazed up and took in the clear, cloudless skies; it had turned out to be a crisp autumn day with a bit of a chill in the air, just right for a drive through the countryside. *If only I could relax enough to appreciate it.*

At precisely two o'clock, he pulled up to the curb in an old-style convertible touring car: a sleek, silver, two-seat Alfa Romeo. With Alessandro looking very handsome and relaxed behind the wheel, I had to take a minute to adjust to this new incarnation of my boss. I thought I even detected an air of good humor about him as he slid out of the driver's side to open the door for me with a slight smile.

Is it possible we might become friends by the time we arrive in Padua?

While I settled inside, I noted that, in spite of the car's elegant make and model, it was somewhat worse for wear: the leather seats were split in sections and the dashboard was missing some glass covers over the dials. But it had a pleasant musky smell of cedarwood and nutmeg—masculine and outdoorsy. As Alessandro climbed back into the car, we were almost shoulder to shoulder in the tight confines of the interior, and I leaned a little to the right to keep our arms from touching each other.

He shifted the car into gear and then pressed down on the gas pedal, causing us to spring forward in fits and starts as the engine sputtered a few times, but it kept running as we made our way to the end of the street near the Adige River. We turned left and paralleled the twisting, curving waterway out of the city, gradually leaving behind the crowded Verona streets for quieter country lanes.

After about fifteen minutes of silence while I gazed at the rolling hills and sycamore trees, I couldn't stand it any longer and finally spoke up, "I was surprised you volunteered to drive me to Padua since you're so busy."

He raised a brow. "You think I don't like you?"

"I'm not sure."

"Certainly, I appreciate that you came to Verona to help with the Foundazione's reopening, but it's not quite that simple. Every step we take forward in this country means we could tread on something that takes us backwards, so there's no room for carelessness. As a stranger, you don't know who or what you're walking over; there are minefields everywhere." Alessandro steered past a vineyard with its rows of newly planted vines stretching far back from the road and gestured toward the fields with a tilt of his head. "In fact, there were unexploded ones over there at one of the wine estates that survived. It belongs to the Sartori family, who took a year after the war ended to clear the groves of the mines and start to bring the vines back. Painstaking labor and endless bank loans. They could've walked away, but they chose to stay, put what happened behind them, and restore their ancestral lands. Coraggioso—brave. The bombs might have littered the fields, and the earth under those vines soaked with the blood of violence, yet we Italians prefer to focus on the new life and new growth." He threw a brief glance at me. "When I saw you the first time, looking at the painting of the *Man with No Arms*, I could tell you were the type of woman who had to look beneath the surface, crack open the door, and poke around in things that don't concern you."

"I *am* a costume curator, and my job is to delve into the history of artifacts." I raised my chin combatively. "How am I supposed to do my work if I can't research the past?"

"For the dresses—only," he said firmly.

"But I can't do that unless I know something about the woman who wore them and why she left them here, hidden in a trunk," I pressed. "*And* how they connect to the Fondazione."

His fingers tightened on the steering wheel. "If you would restrict yourself *only* to researching Signorina Rossetti's cloth-ing, that would be fine, but you've already pushed beyond that in asking Nico about the death of his cousin. He doesn't need to be reminded of Tonio's murder, nor do I."

"Maybe your brother needs to talk about it, and I certainly wouldn't share anything he told me in confidence—"

"That crime was never solved, so did it ever occur to you that the killer might still reside in Verona, which could put both Nico and you at risk? I don't want anything to happen to my brother . . . or you, for that matter." He took in a deep breath. "After all, you *are* a guest in my country."

Sitting back, I let his words sink in and stole a look at him. His face had taken on a worried expression. Was Alessandro's previous warning for *my* sake? I had taken it as his labeling me as a meddlesome "outsider" who was bristling against his rules, which I would have to admit was true to some extent. "I apolo-gize if I made a few missteps in my first week. I honestly want nothing more than to make the exhibit a successful part of the Fondazione's reopening."

The wind picked up, swirling the fallen leaves around us in a cascade of paper-thin, copper-tinted foliage. Alessandro reached behind my seat and then handed me a soft plaid blanket which I spread across my lap.

A thoughtful gesture.

Perhaps we truly had a chance at being friends, after all.

Smoothing down the blanket's fringe, I commented, "I wasn't expecting you to show up in a convertible."

"It doesn't belong to me—not really," Alessandro responded with a faint smile. "My father bought it years ago, a special edition Gran Turismo that was made in 1930 as a road-going version of the Alfa Romeo race car. Papa always dreamed of being a sports car driver, but he studied engineering and built bridges and railroad tracks instead. Yet he so loved taking it out on the narrow lanes outside of Verona, and even taught me to drive in it." He pointed at the tattered dashboard. "It was damaged badly in the bombings, even though I had hidden it in a friend's barn near Bergamo, so I decided to rebuild it to honor my father. For some reason, I couldn't just let it be taken away for scrap metal when it was his great joy."

"Rufina said he died of influenza—along with your mother?"

Alessandro nodded. "It happened before the war during the same outbreak that took Rufina's parents. It was a sudden, brief epidemic, but many Veronese families lost older members. I suppose it's why I'm so protective of Nico; he is my only relative left."

"I understand. Being an only child, I would've loved having a brother or sister." *And felt less lonely.* "Perhaps that's why I'm so close with Rufina; she is like my sister, and I wish I could've grown up with her like you and Nico did."

"Actually, during our early years, I saw her only infrequently since she's closer to Nico's age, and I left here early to study art history in Florence, then lived in Rome." He stared straight ahead, eyes unblinking. "I wanted to experience la dolce vita, the beautiful life that I thought I could find only in such a large, sophisticated city as an aspiring artist. Vibrant and exciting. And I had my family's money to do whatever I wanted."

"That sounds typical of every young man—"

"I was naïve like so many of my friends, focused only on creating and exhibiting art that I thought would change the world." His voice took on a note of bitterness. "We drank and drove fast cars and enjoyed beautiful women; I even had a brief marriage, but my wife, Isabella, left and later divorced me when the party ended and the black shirts took over our country, destroying everything that our families once stood for. Maybe if my friends and I had paid more attention to what was happening, we might have been able to help stop their rise to power, but we didn't and that was our sin. I returned to Verona only when my parents were dying, and by that time northern Italy had become a hotbed of Fascism. There was little I could do, except resist joining them, manage our estate along with the Foundazione—and take care of Nico. Being fifteen years older, I tried to become his surrogate father, as best I could, and protect as much artwork from falling into the hands of the Nazis—a paltry contribution, but I was considered too old for active service in my late thirties."

"Every act of defiance is important . . . and Nico?"

"I would not permit him to fight with the army since he was too young. But he was involved with the local partisans, which was dangerous enough."

We approached a curve in the road, and Alessandro slowed down for an elderly man in a baggy gray jacket who stood on the edge of the crosswalk with a small dog on a short leash. We stopped and he waved, then made his way haltingly across the lane toward a bus stop, tipping his cap, which held a military insignia on the brim. Once he reached the other side, Alessandro sped up again. "The world saw Italy as undivided about the war, but that was far from the truth; most of us had little inclination to fight battles of conquest, especially when it took centuries for Italy to achieve its own Risorgimento. So when we saw our chance to fight the Fascisti, we did, but it cost so many lives, including my friends and family members, that most of the rural areas are made up now of only children and tired, old veterans who've seen too much death and destruction. We can never replace all the young men we lost or cure the ones severely wounded; I'm only thankful that Nico survived the madness with his life and limbs intact—many did not."

A sudden thought occurred to me. "*You're* the one who painted *The Man with No Arms*, aren't you?"

"Sì," he said shortly. "But I have no desire to produce art any longer."

"Yet you couldn't part with that piece. It must mean you have not totally given up on your dream—"

"That flight of fancy ended with the war."

A cloud passed across the sun, casting a shadow over the road ahead, then drifted on.

"I'm sorry for what you and everyone else has suffered," I said, scanning the hilly terrain, scarred by deep grooves. "I heard about some of it from Rufina in her letters, but we were removed from the worst of it in America—"

"Yet you, too, suffered when your husband was killed." He cast his eyes in my direction, not the usual furtive glance of emotional awkwardness at hearing about my widowhood; this was simply matter-of-fact. "Rufina told me that he died fighting in Germany."

"Yes." I tucked the blanket around my legs. "Paul was a photographer—talented and free-spirited. We were married almost eight years when he enlisted and was killed near Berlin. I know I should feel proud of his service, and I am, but I also resent that he was taken from me at such a young age." *We hadn't even had time to plan for children.*

"So it appears as if we have something in common: we both had people we cared about taken away from us during the war," he observed quietly. "Sometimes being a survivor seems almost worse, but if we don't honor their memory by living our lives, then they died for nothing."

"I suppose that's true . . ." I thought of Paul's Murano glass compass and how I always kept it close at hand; it was in my bag today with the postcard. "But it's not easy, is it?"

"No."

I liked his direct assertion, with none of the tepid, senti-mental reassurances people usually added afterwards, murmur-ing how Paul would've wanted me to find purpose and meaning again. In all honesty, I didn't know what my husband thought about my future without him, so how could anyone else pre-tend to understand? Paul and I had never spoken of it before he left for Germany, even though there was a silent understanding that he might not return, and I would have to continue alone. Maybe it was impossible to plan for such an occurrence, and it could only be dealt with by improvising each day without any goals or expectations. Just moment by moment . . .

"We're almost there." Alessandro's words broke into my thoughts, and I snapped out of my reverie, realizing we were approaching the outskirts of Padua; its elegant medieval and Renaissance buildings looked to be mostly intact, with a few dam-aged walls or missing roofs here and there. He pointed at a single ruin, as if reading my thoughts. "Most of the air raid damage was north of here in the Arcella district—near the railway—but this part of Padua saw heavy bombing for months. In the aftermath, it was almost miraculous that most of the precious art and archi-tecture in the old town center emerged relatively unscathed, espe-cially the Giotto frescoes in the Scrovegni Chapel."

As if on cue, the traffic slowed and the streets grew more crowded. When we approached a large piazza, the open-air market was teeming with early afternoon shoppers, filling their baskets with fresh produce and loaves of crusty bread, as they browsed each vendor. My mouth watered slightly, and I real-ized that I'd had nothing to eat since an early breakfast, but we couldn't take time to stop now since it had to be close to my appointment. "Professor Harrison said he'd meet me at the Palazzo Bo at the university, just inside the courtyard. Do you know it?"

"Sì—Cortile Antico. It is the historical core of the university and one of the oldest parts of the main campus, from the thirteenth century." Alessandro made a right turn that took us down a narrow road with fewer pedestrians, but with a rut-filled, uneven surface. As the car thumped along, he added, "I've been there many times for art exhibits, and I'm still awed by the Great Hall, decorated from floor to ceiling with the coats of arms of important students and faculty. The great Galileo once taught from a podium in that hall."

"How extraordinary." My eyes widened as we approached a busy square dominated by a block-long majestic palazzo of blanched stone.

He slowed down and then halted in front of an arched entrance embellished with double pillars on either side and an elaborate coat of arms above. "The courtyard is just through that gate. I have to drive to the other side of campus to pick up the painting, but I'll meet you back here at the Pedrocchi Caffe in an hour." He pointed at a classically columned building across the street, overflowing with young students bundled in their jackets and sweaters at the outside tables.

"That should give me enough time." I reached for the door handle, brushing aside any help from him to alight from the car. "See you then."

As Alessandro waved and drove off, I remained there for an instant, not quite sure what had happened between us, except that I felt something stir inside of me that I hadn't felt in a long time. A tiny tendril of a new emotional connection, tentative and unfamiliar, but stretching outward nonetheless.

Not wanting to examine those feelings any further, I turned and strolled through the open iron gate as Alessandro's words echoed through my mind: *Nico is my only relative . . .*

It explained some of his wary attitude toward me. Would I not be equally protective if he were my only brother?

"Are you Mrs. Baxter?" A tall, slightly stooped older man with a shock of white hair asked in a British-accented tone. "I'm Rupert Harrison."

"Marianne." Smiling, I extended my hand. "Sorry I almost walked right past you."

He shoved his reading glasses atop his head and clasped my fingers warmly. "No need to apologize. This university can be a bit overwhelming with its complex web of buildings and court-yards; it took me years to learn how to navigate its labyrinth of old and new, now made even more confusing with the postwar renovations."

"You're most kind, and I so appreciate your meeting with me on somewhat short notice." Actually, the open-air, square courtyard looked more like a monastic cloister with its terraced columns and medieval tower.

"It's my pleasure—truly. As a literature professor, I was intrigued when your friend Rufina called to say you had uncov-ered something new about one of my favorite poets. My spe-cialty is nineteenth-century English literature, and I've studied Christina Rossetti's work for much of my career. Even more fortuitously, I'm working on a new collection of essays on the Romantic and Victorian poets who spent time in Italy, so I was intrigued to learn if what you have found might have some impact on my research. Is it a lost manuscript?"

"Not exactly . . . more like three lost *dresses*."

"Oh." He seemed taken aback. Obviously, Rufina had omit-ted to explain fully the nature of our discovery.

"But there was also a letter written by her father," I added hastily, producing the document from my bag and handing it to him. As he pulled down his reading glasses, I explained the details of the hidden trunk and what we had found inside. "I'm setting up the exhibit of Christina's clothing for the Fondazione in Verona and could use any information that you might be able to pass on about her. It will help me re-create a sense of who she was as a poet *and* a woman. But I also have to confess that I've become somewhat obsessed with knowing exactly what happened to her while she was in northern Italy."

"That might be difficult because she recorded very little about her time here, only a few notes to friends. She was quite a secretive person in many ways, especially in her correspondence, much of which she burned toward the end of her life," he said, scanning Gabriele Rossetti's words, blinking rapidly as he absorbed the content. "You actually found this letter in Christina's trunk?"

"Yes, it was tucked inside a sleeve of one of the dresses."

Eventually, he looked up and stared at me with a gleam in his eyes. "It seems Gabriele had a few secrets of his own, as well."

Just then a door swung open, and a few dozen students streamed out of a classroom, their voices raised in eager discussion; they swarmed around us, and Professor Harrison took my arm to draw me aside. "All of the afternoon classes are ending, so let's go to my office where it's quieter."

"Yes, *please.*"

He led me across the square toward a small archway that connected to another courtyard, this one with various sized and shaped stone monuments. At the far end, he gestured for me to step into a red-carpeted hallway, then we headed in the direction of what appeared to be a more modern wing. As we passed a door left ajar, I stopped for a few moments, peering into an immense hall that seemed bathed in light reflected from the frescoed ceiling and burnished coats of arms on the walls. The room stood empty, except for the velvet-upholstered chairs that encircled the podium in neat rows.

"That's the Aula Magna, the Great Hall. It was initially the dining room for the School of Law, but now it's reserved for official ceremonies. I once heard the Italian poet Carlo Gadda give a reading here when I first came to teach; it was riveting."

"How did you land a job at this incredible university?" I asked as we continued on.

"I'm half Italian on my mother's side and half ardent scholar on my father's side; he was a lecturer in the literature department at the University of London, so I had the advantage of being bilingual and having constant exposure from a young age to all of the great English authors and poets—an unusual combination."

"Did you stay during the war?"

He gave a brief nod. "I couldn't leave my students since many of them were involved with the Italian resistance; there is a network of tunnels under the campus that they used to carry out their sabotage efforts, and I helped any way I could; being an old man, I could come and go without the Germans paying attention to me—the invisibility of advanced age." With a ghost of a smile, he reached into his pocket for a set of keys and let us into a tiny office that seemed to be built of books stacked in every conceivable space, even on top of the desk. "But, if anything, my longevity has made me more determined than ever to play my part in history, just like when I applied for a position here and wore down the faculty search committee with sheer persistence."

I laughed. "That's nearly the same way I was accepted to design school in Boston: I kept sending appeal after appeal to the selection committee and campaigned relentlessly for a year to achieve a place in their textile program, and they finally agreed." After removing some books from a chair, I sat down. "Maybe it's that same drive that's pushing me to find out more of Christina's story, because I just can't seem to get her out of my thoughts. Partly, it's an occupational hazard. When I touch antique fabrics in order to get a sense of the feel, sound, and smell of the person who wore the garments, it's a very intimate act in many ways. But it's also because her poetry seems to suggest that she was not a typical Victorian woman."

Rupert slid into a chair behind his desk and shoved aside a small pile of books so he could lay out Gabriele's letter. After he donned a pair of gloves, he carefully smoothed down the crinkled edges. "As I said, Christina was unusually private, even for her time. But perhaps that's because the Rossetti family was so famous, from her father who became a well-known Dante scholar with a large circle of friends in London, to her two brothers who were founding members of the Pre-Raphaelite Brotherhood, a collection of young artists with Dante Gabriel as their leader. Christina was on the edge of all of this celebrity, frequently sitting as a model for the artists, contributing poems to their journals, and even finding herself engaged to one of them as a young woman. But she never could fully participate in that Bohemian life because she was also a *lady* who had to devote herself to worthy causes, like her sister, Maria, who eventually became an Anglican nun. In spite of her unconventional family, Christina, like most Victorian women, had few 'respectable' options, aside from marriage."

I let his words sink in with a depressing thud of understanding. "It must've been a difficult path for her to walk, seeing the freedom that her brothers enjoyed to express their art, and yet not being able to fully enjoy that same kind of liberty herself. So sad. But at least she had her poetry for solace."

"She did achieve great renown for her verse, especially the work that featured illustrations by Dante Gabriel. She was even considered as a possible candidate for England's poet laureate later in life, but she was too ill at that point to accept." He reached behind him for a book and flipped it open to a page with a black and white drawing of a young woman cutting a lock of her hair as an offering to the ratlike gremlins that surrounded her. "This engraving is from one of her most popular pieces, *Goblin Market*."

"I've read the poem . . . It's sort of sinister." I swallowed hard, noting how one of the goblins grinned slyly as he held out a tray of fruit with a ripe pomegranate—enticing and tantalizing.

Brother and sister seemed to have shared the same bizarre vision of temptation.

Rupert snapped the book shut. "I agree, but Christina's poetry is often read superficially, ignoring the undercurrents that hint at unspoken, dark yearnings—"

"The Fata Morgana," I cut in, pointing at the scrawled phrase on Gabriele's letter. "She didn't just write the phrase on her father's letter; she wrote an entire poem about a 'blue-eyed phantom' that she chases but, somehow, he always eludes her grasp—a ghostly mirage like a male version of the magical creature, Morgan le Fay. He enchants Christina, yet she can never catch him, and it makes her weep. It's really quite intriguing. But aside from that poem, I haven't read much more than a short selection of her work, and I'm certainly not a scholar, but don't you think that her constant theme of lost love means something beyond the poetry itself?"

"Possibly. However, it was not all that unusual for a Victorian female writer to code her feelings within certain images and metaphors, especially if she was unmarried. It was an accepted way to express love and sexuality in nineteenth-century English society, which habitually repressed women."

I glanced down at the *Goblin Market* illustration again, focusing on the woman's alluring expression, with her full, round cheek and luscious lips, parted to taste forbidden fruit. "But she traveled to Italy and maybe . . . something changed?"

Rupert leaned back in his chair and rubbed his chin meditatively. "From what I remember in my research, she was in her mid-thirties when she traveled to northern Italy, around May, in 1865, with her mother and brother, William, but nothing in his letters from that summer mentions anything other than a rather touristy trip through Milan, Verona, and Brescia. Unremarkable."

"And yet, if she also carried out her father's last wish to return the Dante book to its rightful home in Italy, she could've had some kind of . . . adventure, unknown to her brother." I produced the Lago di Como postcard and set it in front of the professor. "I found this souvenir sewn inside the pocket of one of her dresses."

"How fascinating . . . and that is definitely her handwriting." Rupert slipped down the reading glasses again and studied the postcard silently for a few minutes. "In one of her notes to her friend Anne Gilchrist, Christina describes taking a cruise around Lake Como and hearing the nightingale, but she included nothing about meeting anyone significant there or anywhere else. And her family was very close, so it's likely William was with her at every stage of the trip, but he may have omitted parts of it in his letters to friends. Who can be certain? Then again, she may have hidden certain things from William, including her deeper emotions around a new acquaintance or her mission to return the Dante book. But considering her father's consuming preoccupation with Dante's poetry, I don't believe the rest of the Rossetti family would have been surprised at the latter."

I leaned in. "What do you mean?"

"Gabriele Rossetti wasn't simply a Dante scholar, even though he started out that way in his younger days as a lecturer at King's College in London. Gradually, he became completely consumed with the idea that Dante's poetry contained hidden symbols and messages from the Illuminati—a secret society—that the poet placed in his verse to hide them from the Catholic Church. Gabriele grew so immersed in his theories that the college let him go from his teaching position. Still, he continued poring over every line of Dante's work, day and night, trying to find the 'key' to the concealed messages. Of course, he never did, and the growing compulsion became almost a mania. His health suffered and he became unemployable, which had a financial impact on the Rossetti family, who had few resources during the best of times."

"How awful, especially for Gabriele's wife and children."

"They certainly suffered," he agreed, tapping his fingers on the postcard as he peered at me over the little half glasses. "But what I find interesting is that Gabriele had been dead for a decade before Christina traveled to Italy and carried out his wishes. Why did she wait so long?"

"Perhaps she couldn't afford to travel until then?"

"Maybe." His voice sounded skeptical as he handed me two books with worn leather covers. "At any rate, I wanted to give you this biography on Christina and a collection of her brother Dante Gabriel's most famous paintings, including some of her, like *Ecce Ancilla Domini*. They might help you grasp a fuller sense of her life. I will say, though, after Christina returned from Italy, she broke off a budding relationship with her suitor Charles Cayley, and wrote a series of very sensual sonnets called the *Monna Innominata*—the hidden woman. It might be relevant or signify nothing at all."

A mere coincidence that she turned away a potential husband and penned sonnets about a hidden woman—only after meeting a man in Italy?

Not likely.

"I wish I had something more definitive for you, but as a scholar, I can't jump to conclusions based on a hunch and an old letter . . . perhaps you can dig up something further in your restoration work that I haven't found."

Picking up the postcard, I placed it and Gabriele's letter inside the pages of the biography and gently set the books on my lap as if they were precious cargo. "I'll try my best and call you if I find anything else in the other two dresses; I haven't begun to prepare them yet, so they too might provide some unexpected insights."

Rupert rose on slightly unsteady feet. "I have a class in ten minutes, but I'm happy to meet with you again, should you have something else to share."

"And in the meantime, I'll send you word when Christina's dress exhibit will open in Verona," I added, gathering up my things, slightly disappointed that I hadn't found any startling information that shed light on the unknown parts of Christina's life. "It would be wonderful to have you attend."

"I'll be there," he vowed.

As I started for the door, I paused. "One other question: did anything noteworthy happen in Verona around the time that Christina visited northern Italy that might have been linked to her return of the Dante book or anything else?"

"Not that I recall." He placed his hands on the desk, propping himself up while he considered the question. "Oh, wait . . . didn't Gabriele's letter say he left Christina a pendant, along with the poetry volume?"

"I believe so. It belonged to his lost love, Peppina,"

"It might not be pertinent, but there is a local legend about the Menigatti family jewels—a priceless emerald Renaissance suite with a brooch, earrings, and pendant that was stolen from their Verona palazzo during the early nineteenth century, the building that is now the Fondazione. Unfortunately, the fate of the brooch and earrings are unknown, but there was a rumor that an English lady had brought the pendant back to Italy, though nothing seemed to come of it, but I believe that was right around the time Christina traveled here. Of course, many English women journeyed to this area." He shrugged. "Oddly . . . another rumor about the same jewelry arose right at the end of the war, when some of my student dissidents said they'd heard about a famous emerald pendant that one of their members had found and was going to sell for food and ammunition. But he was killed and I never heard anything else about the pendant."

My breath caught in my throat. "Was his name Tonio? The young man who was stabbed outside the Fondazione?"

"I don't remember his name, but I believe that's where it happened . . . such a senseless tragedy."

"It had to be him. Do you think the two events are somehow . . . connected?" Even as I said it tentatively, I knew firmly that they *had* to be tied together as if by a silken bond that stretched through time. "If so, the question is where did the pendant and earrings finally end up? Christina may have inherited part of the set from her father, but there's no mention of the earrings in Gabriele's letter. And how did Tonio come to find the pendant? It might be helpful if we knew what the jewelry actually looked like."

"I . . . I think I've seen it here in Padua." He straightened slowly. "Not the actual set but a Renaissance portrait of one of the Menigatti ancestors wearing all three pieces, which was loaned to one of the university's museums before the war. As I recall, the gold settings appeared fairly simple, but the emeralds were stunning—not sparkling, but with a deep, forest green glow. There was something else that caught my interest in the painting, but for the life of me, I don't remember that either . . ."

A tiny thrill passed through me, followed by frustration at the absent-minded professor. "Where is the portrait now?"

"Unfortunately, it was probably destroyed or stolen, along with so much of Italian artwork." His voice trailed off, but then he snapped his fingers. "But . . . since it was part of a university exhibit, it may have been photographed for the archives. Let me look into it, and I'll call you."

I managed a small smile, clinging to the hope that a photo of the suite might have survived. "Thank you, Professor, for all of your help. Although Christina is a bit of an enigma, at least I have a sense of who she was and can build on that with the books you've given me."

"Buona fortuna."

Good luck.

I'm going to need it.

As I exited the office, I retraced my steps down the hallway and through the courtyards to the entrance and took stock of everything I had learned from Rupert. Christina was about my age when she had arrived in northern Italy, and something had happened to her that changed her life forever: she remained single but wrote passionate sonnets—perhaps to this unknown lover? A Victorian woman who lived in the shadows of her own secrets.

I know more about her outward existence but little about her inner being . . .

"Marianne!" Alessandro shouted from the other side of the street, where he sat at a little table, sandwiched between two groups of students, chatting away in loud, spirited conversations. The silver Alfa Romeo sat parked out front. As I crossed the lane, dodging the cars, I kept a tight grip on the books Rupert had given to me. They were my lifeline to understanding Christina's world. *The woman. The poet. The legacy.*

When I approached Alessandro, he was talking with a couple of the students, looking quite animated. He turned to me, easing into a smile, and I felt breathless for an instant at his radiant vitality, so different from the tense, over-burdened man who stalked the hallways at the Fondazione.

"I ordered you a zabaglione—a creamy custard made with marsala wine, and a coffee."

"Grazie mille." My stomach growled at the sight of the delicious-looking dessert as I took the small chair next to him and set my books on the table. "This seems to be a popular place."

He nodded. "The Caffe Pedrocchi has been a student haunt since the mid-nineteenth century; it was even the site of an uprising plot at one time," he commented, sipping his coffee. "You can see the bullet hole upstairs where one of the revolutionaries was shot in the Sala Bianca."

"I think I'll pass." Picking up a spoon, I tasted the zabaglione and closed my eyes briefly at the heavenly blend of sugar and sweet wine.

"Was your meeting with the literature professor helpful?"

"Yes and no." In spite of my desire to devour my dessert, I forced myself to put down the spoon and take a long drink of the strong, acidic coffee, so I could consider my response to him. *Should I tell him* everything? "Rupert is an incredible scholar and filled me in on a lot details about the Rossetti family that I probably wouldn't have been able to learn about myself; however, he didn't have much insight on Christina's travels in northern Italy, other than the places she visited. Apparently, she was quite a private and guarded person her entire life, writing poetry that seemed very sensual, but somehow also vaguely ambiguous; penning letters about everyday details of her life, but nothing too intimate; enjoying close family relations, but keeping her friends at arm's length. It's hard to say who she was really . . . and that makes preparing the exhibit of her dresses that much harder."

"Maybe she's all of those things, a contrast between the public and private woman, inscrutable to the end."

I looked up at him in surprise, as if he'd switched on a light in a dim room. *Of course.* "And finding that Lake Como postcard in one of the dress pockets would bear out your suggestion: that she hid things from her personal life. I haven't had the chance to thoroughly examine the other two dresses, but I'll wager there are other items tucked away in a bodice or sewn into a hem which could be very . . . revealing."

He set down his cup in the saucer and asked casually, "Did the professor say anything else?"

My thoughts were already spinning ahead to the garments that awaited me in Verona, but I came back abruptly to the present at his seemingly innocent query. "Just that he would try to research the Dante book and pendant which Christina's father mentioned in his letter to her. He thought the former could be located through a library search of antique volumes, and the pendant might have something to do with some local Renaissance jewels that went missing years ago." Finished, I set the spoon down and sighed in contentment; then I picked up the coffee cup to drain the last of the rich, pungent liquid. "He said he would call me when he had more information."

"And the professor didn't know anything else about the pendant?" Alessandro pressed further.

Tell him the truth: Rupert caused me to speculate that the pendant might be linked to Tonio's murder. Then again, I had no proof.

I shifted my glance to a little group of students at the next table. "Not really."

After a few minutes, he signaled the waiter and paid the bill. "It's growing late, so we need to head back to Verona. I want to secure the sketch that I picked up and make certain that Nico cleaned up those foul-smelling mannequins; our exhibit date is approaching fast and we can't have that stench permeating the Fondazione."

"Of course, I'm ready to leave." I rose, retrieving my books, and headed for the car with Alessandro following closely behind. *He knows I'm not telling him the whole truth.*

After he helped me into the car, he took his place behind the wheel and we inched into the late-day traffic. I noted Alessandro had placed the framed drawing, wrapped in plain brown paper, in a small, narrow space behind the driver's seat. "Who is the artist?"

"You'll have to wait and see . . . I'm not displaying it until the formal opening of the Fondazione." He smoothly steered the car through the web of busy streets, and we reached the edge of Padua's historic district in a short time—then onto the open road toward Verona. I inhaled the crisp, fresh air with its autumnal scents to distract myself from what I had just done, and the countryside seemed to pass in a blur on our return trip as we talked about superficialities like the weather and the upcoming fall festival season. I said nothing more about Christina Rossetti's pendant. If I touched on it, even briefly, I probably would have admitted that there had been more to my conversation with Professor Harrison.

Still, I felt uncomfortable about my deception. I wasn't normally a person who lied, even by omission. Paul and I had never held back anything from each other, and my relationships with family and friends were built on total candor. But in this instance, telling the truth might mean revealing a vital piece of information that could jeopardize my exhibit, and I couldn't bring myself to just give it up yet.

By the time we pulled up in front of Rufina's villa, my discomfort had turned into full-fledged guilt, and I quickly started to climb out of the Alfa Romeo, but Alessandro grabbed my arm.

"I'm glad we had this opportunity today to learn a little more about each other," he said, lifting my hand to his mouth briefly in a soft kiss. "It will make our work days more pleasant, knowing that we have been so frank and sincere about our past lives and our future dreams. We're now amici."

"Friends," I echoed as I grasped the books and alighted from the car. Without looking back, I let myself into the villa and heard Alessandro drive away before I closed the door behind me. Closing my eyes, I exhaled deeply. Then I called out to Rufina, but there was no answer; she was probably still in Milan at her meetings, at which I was relieved because she knew me too well and would immediately guess that something was wrong.

I needed time to think.

Ambling into the kitchen, I set the books on the table while I put the moka pot onto the stove. I needed another strong cup of coffee to contemplate what I should do next: confess to Alessandro or keep up the pretense until the professor had something concrete? While I waited for the water to boil, I absently flipped through the pages of the book with Dante Gabriel's various portraits, most of them watercolors, of a hauntingly beautiful, sylph-like female model with flowing red hair who was unknown to me. Then I spotted the charcoal sketch of a mature woman with more of a Mediterranean look: olive skin and a smooth, dark-tressed chignon. She leaned her head on folded hands, looking off into the distance with a wistful gaze. It had to be her. Then I saw an inscription next to his signature in the bottom corner of the portrait: *Christina—May, 1865.*

Her brother's drawing had been created around the time she had visited Italy.

I stared at her features in delicate repose, charming and poised, yet somewhat exotic. But did her tranquil expression cloak passionate emotions for a particular man that she expressed only in her poetry? *Had anyone really seen into her innermost self?*

I understood that kind of concealment all too well because I, too, now had secrets.

CHAPTER 6

CHRISTINA

"'I, if I perish, perish' Esther spake
And bride of life or death she made her fair
In all the luster of her perfumed hair . . ."
(*Monna Innominata*, Sonnet VIII)

Milan, Italy
28 May 1865

I barely slept that night after reading the note about my father. By the time I finally drifted off into a fitful slumber, it was well into the small hours of the early morning, and I managed only a short nap, during which I experienced a bizarre nightmare in which I was trapped in a windowless room with Dante Gabriel while he attempted to paint a portrait of his lost wife, but her face kept changing into a skeletal image of a dead woman. He grew more and more agitated, flinging his brushes across the room as he cried out in anguish. Gasping, I struggled to awaken as I saw him slam the painting against the wall again and again . . . and with a start, I became fully conscious, realizing the sound was a firm tap on my door.

Sitting up quickly, I took a couple of calming breaths until I felt my heartbeat settle into a steady rhythm again.

Dear God, what caused such a hideous dream?

Then my eye fell on the note, which I had left on the nightstand:

Tuo padre mi ha tradito.
Your father betrayed me.

"Christina? Are you all right?" William called out from outside my door, followed by another loud knock.

"Yes . . . yes, I'm coming," I exclaimed, gradually becoming aware that the sunlight was streaming into my bedchamber. It was almost midday. Quickly, I rose and donned my wrapper, feeling a little shaky as I moved toward the door. Swinging it open, I saw my brother stationed there, fully dressed, with a shadow of concern in his eyes, and I stammered, "I . . . I was up very late writing poetry last night and decided to sleep in this morning. Not to worry, I am quite well."

"I am so relieved." He visibly relaxed. "Mama has been asking for you all morning. Apparently, her neuralgia has flared from all of the walking yesterday, and she is now confined to her room in need of your company to soothe her nerves over an early tea." A touch of asperity threaded through his voice; I suspected our mother's constant ailments were trying his patience at this point of the trip, especially because he had so carefully and thoughtfully planned our itinerary. "That is, if you do not mind missing our return tour of the Biblioteca Ambrosiana to see Pietro Bembo and Lucretia Borgia's love letters; it's rumored there is also a lock of her hair kept with them."

"Oh no, not in the least," I assured him quickly, though I was somewhat intrigued to read their correspondence. "Mama's needs must be attended to first. Actually, she has done quite well, considering the intense heat and unfamiliar surroundings. You know how she likes her routine at home in London; this entire trip has been a challenge to her settled ways."

"I suppose so." He sighed audibly and adjusted his suit jacket. "Perhaps after a day of rest, she will be able to accompany us on the Lake Como viaggio this evening, since the cruise lasts only a few hours—to Bellagio and back. But if she prefers to remain at the hotel, I think you and I should still go, especially because Signor Pecora sent a note after breakfast that he and his son, Angelo, would like to join us."

"Indeed, it would be unforgivably rude to decline," I murmured, striving to hide the budding happiness that grew inside me at the prospect of this evening's excursion. "But I will try everything I can to raise Mama's spirits enough to accompany us tonight."

"That is all you can do." Shaking his head, William turned and strode down the hallway, grumbling to himself the whole way. Then he stomped down the stairs with hard, heavy steps. Biting my lip to keep from smiling, I closed the door and allowed myself a few minutes to fantasize about skimming along the waters of Lake Como with the beauty of nature all around us, in the pleasant company of Angelo . . . and his father. I could not conjure up anything more magical.

And I would not dwell on that note about Papa; that could wait for later.

But first things first; I had to cajole Mama into a better mood.

After a hasty toilette, I sought out my mother and found her reclining on a chaise lounge in her room, staring out the window at a large chestnut tree, while an untouched tea service sat nearby on a silver tray. As I drew closer and greeted her, she rolled her head to the side and extended a hand to me. "Oh, Christina, where have you been? I have felt out of sorts all morning with only William for company, and he had his head buried in some book about Caravaggio the whole time. I do not think he heard a word I said."

Probably not.

"You know how absorbed he can be when it comes to studying Italian art," I pointed out, taking a seat next to her as I clasped her fingers in a reassuring grip. "I think it is because he has such a mundane job that barely engages his creativity at all. There is so much more to William than just being a clerk in the Excise Office, keeping track of custom duties and taxes. He has the sensitive nature of an artist."

She released my hand, then held a tiny vial of smelling salts up to her face. "Sad to say, though, he does not possess the talent of one who could make a living at it, so choosing the civil service was a good choice for him and us."

"I think he is aware of that, Mama." I held my tongue from adding anything further, knowing that William *had* to make the decision at sixteen to take employment at an occupation that he found dull and boring because our family teetered on the edge of poverty. Papa had become too ill and reclusive by that point to support us financially, so William had made the sacrifice to work in an office all day, allowing Dante Gabriel and me to spend our time in creative pursuits. "But we need to encourage him to feel that his efforts on our behalf are fully appreciated."

"Oh, I try, my dear." A touch of concern shadowed her eyes. "Do you think he doubts it?"

"Of course not, Mama, but reminding him now and again might not go amiss." I picked up the pink flowered china teapot.

"Do you feel well enough to have a cup of tea with a slice of the chocolate torte?" Aunt Charlotte used to make this particular Italian pastry when I was a child, and I still loved the rich, sweet taste.

She sat up and gave her assent for me to pour the tea. "Just a small piece of the torta, though."

As I filled her cup and placed a little wedge of the torte next to it in the saucer, I mentioned in passing that I had received a short note from Dante Gabriel. "He was on his way to visit William and Jane Morris at Red House, so they will keep him company while we are here. You know he does not do well when he is alone."

"No, he is like my poor, dear brother John in that way, driven by inner demons that the rest of us cannot quite comprehend, and we need to help him keep them at bay." She nibbled on a piece of the torte, then took a sip of tea. "Their brilliance shines brightly, but when the shadows come, the darkness can eclipse their whole world and nothing seems to matter."

I knew she was thinking of that midsummer morning when she found his lifeless body in his room; his death was pronounced later to be of "natural causes," but everyone believed he had deliberately taken an overdose of a fatal drug. *Dead at twenty-six.* Though Mama and I had never spoken about it, I think she feared Dante Gabriel might do the same if he were left to his own devices too long.

Like poor Lizzie.

But we would never let that happen to my brother.

"You forget that, while Dante Gabriel might have Uncle John's obsessive tendencies, he also has your common sense," I reminded her.

"I pray that to be true. And I wish I had understood better how to help John, but I was a girl barely out my teens when his life took such a dreadful turn. If I had to do it over again, I would have attended more carefully to his melancholia." She crossed herself. "All of that happened over forty years ago, and I have no idea why I brought it up today."

"Maybe being in the country of our ancestors makes us think about the past, how our families are connected to this land and what they have passed down to us, both the good and the bad. I have thought about that inheritance since the day we crossed the border into Italy and how it has shaped our characters: the creative streak runs deep in both the Polidoris and Rossettis."

A tiny smile ruffled her mouth. "Certainly, your father believed that poetry was the highest art, and it could bring out the divine side of humanity. He was never happier than when expressing himself as an improvisatore, composing poems on the spot, swaying the emotions of crowds who would listen to him. It was quite a talent and very much part of his youth in Naples, which proved useful when he emigrated to London as a mature man and took a post as a professor of Italian. His pupils were captivated by him. I wish you could have seen him as he was then: full of fire and intensity, always believing that his beloved native land would eventually unify under one flag."

"It would have delighted him to his very soul," I added, noting happily that Mama was reviving, particularly when she spoke about Papa. "And I do have cherished memories, as a child, of Papa coming home from a day of teaching and lying down on the hearth rug as he read to us by firelight, never allowing William and Dante Gabriel access to books which Maria and I did not also have. We were all educated equally, and I am so grateful to Papa and you for that gift."

"I wanted nothing more than to marry a literary man and fill my house with children and laughter and love, and I did have that at first." Her smile faded a bit. "I just did not fully realize that one cannot support a family on poetry alone, and the very qualities that I loved in your father also made life a never-ending battle to barely manage our bills; it is also unfortunate that his health suffered so severely under the strain of his teaching and scholarship, especially after he became so immersed in his Dante learnings. It changed him."

I had seen it too, through the eyes of my girlhood. My boisterous, outgoing Papa became increasingly furtive and reclusive, often not wanting to leave his study as he expanded his reading into treatises on freemasonry and alchemy, and other kinds of unusual texts, which he believed had influenced Dante's *Divine Comedy*. Papa grew thin and nervous, often unable to eat more than broth and bread—until his final collapse. Yet, as he shut the rest of us out, I knew he loved us, even if I had only his letter to me as proof. "Do you regret marrying Papa?"

"Of course not, my dear." She set her teacup aside as her eyes grew tear-filled and misty, like clouds on a watery dawn. "I followed my heart and loved him to the day he died, and I had four wonderful children: you and Dante Gabriel—my 'storms'—and William and Maria—my 'calms.' All so different but so precious to me. We have had our struggles, but what family has not? I only regret that I did not plan better for you and Maria to make advantageous matches—"

"But that hardly matters since she intends to take her vows as a nun," I cut in quickly.

"And you have Mr. Cayley awaiting you in London. He may not be the most dashing man, but he is steady and reliable and will make a good husband."

I glanced down at my lap at my ringless fingers. "You make him sound like your lapdog, Mama."

"Oh no, I simply meant that he could provide stability for you, making this stage of your life more comfortable."

"I do not want a dull and vapid existence, no matter how secure . . . I want what you and Papa had together. No marriage is perfect, but your love sustained you through those later years with their many difficulties."

She exhaled in a deep sigh. "But I thought you were fond of Mr. Cayley."

"I *do* care for him." Struggling to explain my doubts, I attempted to harness the sudden surge of emotion. *I want the heights of passion, even if it means braving the depths of pain. Otherwise, what is the point?* "I am not sure if my regard for Mr. Cayley is the same kind of love that I have dreamt about and, if it is not, I would prefer to occupy myself with good causes than be wedded to a man who inspires little beyond . . . respect. At some point, I fear that kind of relationship would drift into mutual displeasure at best, and tedium at the worst."

Mama caught my hand. "Sometimes women are offered only so many choices, and if those offers pass by, they may not return again."

Of course, she echoed what I had already realized: I was no longer young, and Mr. Cayley might be my last chance at matrimony. After already having called off one betrothal at nineteen when my fiancé, James Collinson, decided to leave the Anglican Church and the Pre-Raphaelite Brotherhood, I waited almost fifteen years for another suitor to appear. So Mama was right in that regard. In spite of my modest success as a poet, I had neither the social position nor the money to stave off the ambiguous existence of being a middle-aged woman without a husband. At least Maria would be the bride of Christ; I would be the family spinster.

In truth, I probably would not hesitate to accept Mr. Cayley's offer of matrimony when we returned home . . . were it not for meeting Angelo. Even after our brief first encounter yesterday,

I felt a wave of intense emotion that I had never experienced before—certainly not with Mr. Cayley—and I wanted to give it free rein. Let it take me into unchartered territories. Only then would I know for certain if it led to a destination where my heart could be like that "singing bird" about which I had only written.

The freedom to love and be loved.

"I have not formally entered into any engagement with Mr. Cayley, but I can assure you that I would not dismiss lightly an offer from him."

She released my hand. "I am very glad to hear that, because most men would expect a considerable dowry, which, unfortunately, you do not possess as the impoverished daughter of an Italian immigrant—"

"That might not matter so much outside of England," I interjected. "Papa is considered quite a hero here in Italy and is much admired, so a prospective suitor could consider that connection more important than an advantageous financial settlement."

"My dear, I think that is improbable," Mama said gently as she poured herself another cup of tea. "And I do hope you are not entertaining foolish hopes that would lead you to behave in a manner that would be unseemly, because when we return to London, you do not want to have to conceal anything from Mr. Cayley."

I seated myself again and jerked the chair forward with a sense of indignation. "I would never act in an improper manner, but if my affections become engaged elsewhere, I *will* follow my heart and, by all means, tell him the truth. In such matters, a lie can do nothing but fester like an old wound that will not heal."

"Yes, deceptions can poison a relationship, no matter how well intentioned. I have often thought that if Dante Gabriel had told us right from the beginning that he loved Lizzie and wanted to make her his wife, it might have saved them from so much distress. But he kept those aspects of his life hidden from everyone, and delayed their union for too long." She gestured toward me with the teapot, and I shook my head. "I partly blame myself for what happened because we had all heard rumors about their association, and I should have simply asked him to be candid about his intentions toward her."

"We all pretended not to know and, after Lizzie's death, it created such a bitter divide in the family," I reflected, remembering how Dante Gabriel had lashed out at all of us after Lizzie's funeral, blaming Mama in particular for not welcoming her into the family because his deceased wife was only a shopkeeper's daughter. "I am glad Papa was not alive to see that discord because it would have hurt him very deeply to see us split apart from each other."

"But we have reconciled again and vowed to harbor no more half-truths."

Occupying myself with slicing another piece of the torta for Mama, I kept my glance down, so she could not see my expression. I had not told her about Papa's letter to me, conveying his last request and desire for secrecy as I carried it out. If I did, I would have to reveal that his thoughts had drifted back to Peppina, and their dead son, during his final days. And I refused to be the one who tarnished Papa's image for her. He said that she might have guessed, but how could I know for certain without telling her the whole story?

No, I would hold my tongue about Peppina—for now.

However, as I handed Mama another thin slice of the torte, I inquired whether Papa had ever mentioned Signor Pecora.

"I really do not recall," she responded with a helpless shrug. "Your father had so many friends from Italy about whom he talked incessantly—poets, artists, and musicians—that I can barely register their names. Many of them were fellow patriots from his days as a student in Naples, so he probably did mention him."

"But unlike most of them, Signor Pecora never came to visit us in London," I pointed out.

"Sadly, no. I would have enjoyed meeting him."

Watching Mama revive somewhat as she finished her tea and torta, I was happy to see her cheeks take on a pleasant color and her eyes a bit of a sparkle again. "Then you will be delighted to know that he and his son have proposed to accompany us on our Lake Como cruise this evening, so you will have the opportunity to further your acquaintance with him. He has promised to share some of his adventures with Papa from their student days in Naples."

She waved her handkerchief dismissively. "I am hardly up for that kind of exhausting journey, but you and William must go and enjoy yourselves. I am perfectly content to remain here and read, as long as you promise to pass on any particularly riveting stories about your father. I imagine Signor Pecora must have quite a few, considering how radical Gabriele was during those days. I will want to hear it all."

"I promise."

"And one other thing: you must also vow not to forget that you are almost engaged to a worthy man in England, and nothing can interfere with that."

I did not respond.

★ ★ ★

By late afternoon, I could barely contain my excitement as William and I rode the train toward the town of Como at the southernmost tip of the immense lake. The landscape took on a soft pastel quality as if the sky had spread out a blanket of dreamy tranquility over the entire area, beckoning us into this area of inland seaside towns. Sweetly compelling.

But I felt anything but serene as we approached our destination.

All I could think about was that I would see Angelo again. Hear his voice as he spoke about poetry and politics. Smell the faint fragrance of his cologne. It felt as if his presence had already imprinted onto all of my senses, and every part of my being waited to be brought to life again when I saw him.

"Christina, you are very quiet," William pointed out from the seat across from me. "Are you feeling fatigued after spending the day with Mama?"

"No, quite the opposite. I am eagerly anticipating our sail around Lake Como," I responded as I idly fingered the sleeve of my walking dress. I would not allow my long afternoon of placating Mama to spoil this evening. It was too precious. Nor would I let that vicious note about Papa diminish my high spirits, though I had decided to share it with Signor Pecora to see what he thought.

Nothing would distract me from embracing the joy of this night.

It seems as if I have been waiting my whole life for it.

"You look quite flushed, almost like a young girl on Christmas day," William pointed out with a curious stare. "And you are wearing that same fashionable dress you wore yesterday, not your usual sober black garb."

I looked down at the layers of poplin in the skirt, each one decorated with fringe and lace. "It was a gift from Aunt Charlotte, along with two other frocks I brought with me. When she presented them to me, she said that, while London suited my usual 'drab and dreary' wardrobe, it would not do to walk around as if I were in mourning when in Italy."

He gave a short chuckle. "Our aunt is never one to mince words, but in this instance, I agree with her; it is refreshing to see you in the vivid attire you used to wear—and even a pretty necklace. Aunt Charlotte was most generous to provide you with jewelry, as well."

"It was gifted to me from a dear . . . person." My hand covered Peppina's pendant. "Not too vain for a woman of my years?"

"How is it vanity to embrace beauty?" William raised a brow. "Your poetry is a celebration of how rich, colorful images move our innermost feelings, so why should you not adorn yourself in a similar way?"

I smiled. "Thank you, William. You are such a dear brother. No matter how dramatically self-absorbed I become, you always bring me back to practical sensibility."

"The calm to your storm?"

The train jolted a bit as it steered around a sharp curve that led toward the station ahead, and I braced myself against the side. "Truly, I try to be more composed, like Maria, but as I grow older, it seems to become even more difficult."

William turned his face toward the window and stared at the landscape as the hills gradually shifted into mountains. "Oddly, I find it grows easier to be mellow with age. Once I took the job at the Excise Office, I gave up any hope of achieving the creative ambitions I longed for, painting the kind of 'stunners' who parade through Dante Gabriel's studio, having young artists hang on my every word, and exhibiting my work to adoring audiences. Much as I wanted that kind of existence, I have come to accept that it was not to be my lot in life." His tone remained even and complacent. "I admit I sometimes feel envious that all of those gifts were bestowed on my brother and he has squandered them at times, but my love for him is greater than any feelings of resentment. He was born to be an artist, much as you were born to be a poet . . . and I was born to be a paper shuffler. A man who plans and organizes. Still, I sometimes wish it could have been different for me, and that I would have been granted a measure of his talent with paint or your genius for words. It would be . . . nice."

My heart squeezed in pain at William's nostalgic tone.

"But we cannot change our nature, can we?" He fastened his glance back on me.

"Yet the creative life demands that you dwell in the depths of darkness or the heights of joy; it can be utterly exhausting to give expression to those feelings again and again," I said quietly. "And the demons that drive us can become our masters if we do not control them."

"The goblins you wrote about?"

I nodded. "They appear when you least expect them, but when you try too hard, they remain beyond reach." Like most poets, I spent many nights trying to summon just the right word, the perfect metaphor, only to find the struggle pointless and give up, convinced that I would never write again. Then the morning would come and the words would flow again. "It can be an agonizing process."

A half smile crossed his face. "But so worth it when you consider the final product."

"Indeed."

The train began to slow down, and I spied the station ahead—a small, bare building with few windows. Even though I wished with all my heart that I could give my brother what he wanted, it was not mine to bestow on him. I could only love him for the many kindnesses he provided every day. "William, if I have not said it recently, I so appreciate everything that you have done to make this trip an unforgettable experience for Mama and me. I will never forget it."

"It has been my pleasure, even though you missed my long and detailed historical tour of the Duomo," a thread of humor touched his voice. "I shall make certain that I provide you with lengthy notes, so you can read them at your leisure."

I laughed. "And then quiz me on them, much like Aunt Charlotte did when she was our governess."

"Exactly."

As the train halted, we both rose, in harmony once again. We acknowledged and admired each other's strengths and weaknesses, and there was something comforting in having such a shared history with one's sibling. Nothing came between us for very long because the calms and the storms balanced each other, and we knew it.

We followed the smattering of fellow travelers down the aisle toward the exit door, William leading the way. As I descended the steps, I reached out for him to help me, but when I felt a grasp, I realized it was not my brother. It was Angelo. He stood there in a dove gray suit, smiling up at me as the sunlight glinted down on his face.

"Buongiorno, Signorina Rossetti."

I knew in that moment with absolute certainty that I had not been wrong; our meeting yesterday had been fated.

. . . *the birthday of my life*
Is come, my love is come to me.

Dante Gabriel had quoted those lines sarcastically in our dining room in London, but now they were real and true.

"Ah, Mr. and Miss Rossetti, I trust you both had a relaxing trip here," Signor Pecora chimed in as he appeared at his son's side, drawing my attention back to the present.

"We did, indeed," my brother responded. "And I am so pleased that you were able to obtain tickets for the cruise at this late date and make time to join us. Unfortunately, our Mama is a bit indisposed, so you will have only the company of Christina and myself on the sailboat, but I hope we will make up for her absence with our eagerness to see sights along Lago di Como."

"I trust she will recover quickly." Signor Pecora inclined his head. "And I do not think you will be disappointed in our magnificent lake, especially at sunset when the little towns clustered along the shoreline take on a golden glow. It is enchanting." He gestured toward a waiting carriage. "Please allow us to escort you to the dock."

Before I could take Angelo's arm, William drew him to the side with his usual erudite observation: "I understand Como is the third largest lake in Italy and one of the deepest, initially settled by the ancient Romans and shaped almost like an upside-down 'Y' with the towns of Lecco and Como at its lowest arms. It is quite extraordinary when you look at it on a map, almost as if a divine hand carved it into the earth with the letter in mind."

I bit my tongue, remembering our recent conversation on the train ride and his many sacrifices for our family.

But, dear God, William. Please do not scare him off with your pedantry.

Angelo responded politely with a short history of the area, explaining that Lecco had more stark scenery and small coves, but the town of Como was more developed, with elegant villas and lush gardens.

As we climbed inside the ornate gilded carriage adorned with the Pecora family crest, William sat next to Angelo and plied him with questions about exactly when the ancient Romans had settled the area and whether we would see any ruins. Instead of growing annoyed, as I was wont to do with my brother's incessant curiosity about historical details, Angelo seemed more than happy to provide extensive answers to every question.

My esteem for him rose even higher.

"I see your brother is fascinated with antiquity. My son also loves to talk about the past, so they shall no doubt get on well," Signor Pecora commented in a low voice from his place next to me. "But what about you, Miss Rossetti? Are you also interested in such things?"

I paused as the carriage moved forward slowly along a narrow, cobblestone street. "Of course, I am intrigued by history, but as a poetess, I prefer absorbing the beauties of nature and writing about how they appeal to all of the senses." Gazing out at the elegant villas and terraced gardens, my focus instinctively moved to the distance above and beyond. "I have never seen a sky this shade of blue, with the translucency of porcelain. Truly, it takes my breath away and I can hardly wait to capture it in verse."

He smiled. "You have the soul of a poet—like your father. When he, Fabiano, and I were boys, growing up in Vasto, we would roam the rocky shoreline, cutting open the bellies of local calamarello—cuttlefish—to seek out their ink for Gabriele's drawings; then he would sit in the window of his family's house that overlooked the Adriatic and sketch the images of ships far off at sea while improvising poems about the sailors' lives. There was nothing not transformed by his imagination."

"He loved composing poems on the spot; it was one of his great talents."

"Gabriele always believed he was descended through the Della Guardias on his father's side, noted for being great men of letters and their stubborn nature—"

"Hence, our family motto: *Frangas No Flectas*—Break Not Bend." I had heard Papa mention that philosophy many, many times over the years and found it both admirable and distressing. It made him strong and focused in how he wanted to achieve success, but willful and dogged in how he achieved it, never able to bring himself to compromise, not even for the financial security of his own family.

"He brought that same poetic fervor and unwavering fixity to our lives as student revolutionaries later in Napoli, living by his wits as a poet-orator, writing patriotic odes about freedom and justice, and dedicating himself to the Carbonari as the voice of the people. He was inspirational and never gave in to political pressure to tone down his poetry; instead, he chose exile in London where he could win over others to our great Italian cause." His eyes softened, smoothing out the lines of age that radiated around them. "But those are the ideals of young men, and I am sure Gabriele had to temper his views once he had a wife and children to support. That is what growing old is all about: responsibility and moderation. I had to embrace them myself, though such restraint does not come naturally to me, either."

For a moment, I hesitated to reveal that Papa never found such a middle way, not wanting to disrespect him: "My father worked hard to provide for us, though his absorption with Dante and, later, ill health made it difficult for him to teach."

Signor Pecora crossed his legs, flicking a tiny speck of dust off his immaculate pants. "I am sorry to hear that, but I know he did his best."

Taking a brief glance at William and Angelo, who were still absorbed in their conversation, I leaned in closer to Signor Pecora, "I have to admit that Papa took his scholarship to an extreme level, and it resulted in his being let go from his post at the University of London, which made him overly suspicious that he was being treated unfairly, perhaps even targeted. In reality, not everyone in the academic world appreciated the tenor of his studies. Even my grandfather Gaetano would not print some of my father's treatises because he felt they were a little . . . outlandish."

"Gabriele could see things that others could not, so perhaps he made others uncomfortable."

"Or he may have seen conspiracies where none existed," I responded. "The Dante book that I told you about, which was hidden in his box, had all sorts of Papa's annotations about secret symbols in the verse, as if the great poet had placed them there for only my father to locate centuries later. I cannot imagine that to be even remotely possible. Papa had to be experiencing some type of delusion at that point. But at any rate, he knew enough to realize the error of his ways in keeping a stolen book all of those years when he asked me to restore the volume to the Biblioteca Capitolare. We are leaving for Verona tomorrow, and if you are at back at your residence, I would appreciate your help in returning it."

"Yes, we depart for home tomorrow as well." He gave a brief nod. "I said I would assist you in any way possible, and I meant it sincerely. It will be my pleasure to contact the director of the biblioteca since I know him personally; no doubt he will be pleased to have the book returned to their antique collection. Actually, the Capitolare is the oldest library in Europe, with an amazing collection of manuscripts that date back to Roman times, so you will no doubt find it quite fascinating. Dante Alighieri himself was a scholar there for six years."

"I look forward to it." I lowered my voice to a whisper as our carriage lumbered past a Romanesque Duomo, more typically Italian than the cathedral in Milan. "But there is one other matter I wanted to discuss with you. When I arrived at our hotel yesterday afternoon, someone had sent me a note, saying Papa had 'betrayed' him, but it was unsigned. Do you know what it might mean? I found it worrisome, to say the least."

"Dannazione," he hissed between gritted teeth. "Pardon me, Signorina Rossetti, I did not mean to use such language in front of a lady, but that is an inexcusable act, especially because it is a complete lie. Your father was never disloyal to anyone. But I must admit that not everyone in this part of Italy supported the Risorgimento, because they had sided with the Austrian invaders to make a profit; they associate your father with the unification and their own loss of favor. Although he left our country long ago, his very name was one of the sparks that kindled the fire of patriotism to help us achieve our freedom. Please do not think that vicious note reflects the feelings of the majority of my countrymen, rather only a disgruntled traitor to our cause and nothing more."

I exhaled in relief.

"The last few years have been difficult, but I hope the hard feelings on both sides will lessen as time passes." His glance fell upon his son. "Even Angelo still speaks of vengeance against those who fought against us, but I remind him that, as a Catholic, he should embrace forgiveness."

"By all means." I took in Angelo's face, animated as he conversed with William, and it was hard for me to believe that he could hold vengeance in his heart, but there was something in his eyes which I had seen yesterday, a fleeting glint of raw pain that suddenly appeared when he saw his friends, perhaps because they also reminded him of the ones he had lost in the fight. "He must miss those in the brotherhood who gave their lives for the sake of liberty."

"Angelo mourns them in his heart, though he says little about it." Signor Pecora transferred his gaze to me. "Friends come and go in our lives, but when they are taken before their time, it is a tragedy."

"Speaking of absent friends, in my father's letter he said Fabiano was quite distraught when he told Papa that Peppina committed suicide." I took in a deep breath and exhaled slowly, trying not to imagine that conversation. "Do you think Fabiano might have turned up here for the celebrations, and when he found out my family and I were here, wrote the note because he still held a grudge against Papa?"

Signor Pecora drew back, seemingly startled. "I suppose it is possible. Certainly, Fabiano and I had both observed their relationship dissolving, and he seemed to feel the tragedy of it more than I since he held Peppina in high esteem. But after she threw herself into the sea, your father departed for England and Fabiano disappeared before I could speak to either of them about it . . . they never even said goodbye."

As his words sank in, I reflected on the many times Papa could be so caught up in his world of politics and poetry that he scarcely noticed us. Benign neglect. "I am sure Papa cherished your friendship. And if Fabiano were here and wanted to meet with me, I would be happy to share the contents of Papa's letter with him so he could see for himself that she was on his mind during his final days." I touched the pendant. "I wear this in memory of Papa and her."

"She would be honored." He inclined his head. "I shall make inquiries about Fabiano, and if he contacts me, I will convey your generous offer. However, if he wrote the letter, I will make it very clear that he cannot cause you further upset with such comments." He patted my hand. "At any rate, do not concern yourself about it because I will not allow anything to spoil your cruise on Lake Como."

"Spoil what, Papa?" Angelo inquired, his brows raised in puzzlement.

"I was simply assuring Signorina Rossetti that we shall make this a memorable evening for both William and her."

Angelo broke into a wide smile. "Sì."

And it was.

From the moment we arrived at the dock at Lake Como, I was enthralled at being at the southernmost tip of the immense body of still, blue waters that stretched north as far as the eye could see. Narrow in width, the lake seemed to twist and turn in a snakelike fashion, with little towns clustered on either shore, mountains rising up behind them, which were covered in thick trees.

Even Dante Gabriel could not have painted a more vivid scene.

"So, what do you think of our lake, Miss Rossetti?" Angelo asked as he escorted me to a small, anchored sailboat which was rocking gently as the waves lapped against the dock. William and Signor Pecora had already boarded and were strolling toward the bow, while two young Italian sailors stood on deck, waving a greeting at us. I kept a tight grip on the rail on the steep gangway but, even with my walking dress hem's shorter length in front, I tripped slightly, and Angelo steadied me with a hand against my back. Feeling his palm through the material of my dress, it was like a warm radiance extended from his fingers into every part of my body.

"It looks almost too pretty, if such a thing is possible," I said, noting the sun had started to sink toward the horizon, casting slanted rays of light that shimmered across the lake's surface. "Nature truly puts us to shame when we try to re-create such colors and sights and sounds."

"Even with your poetry? I think you could capture its essence well." He guided me up the last part of the gangway and onto the deck toward the seats at the stern. "It appears you have fallen in love—"

"What?" I caught my breath.

"With Italy," he finished as we sat on the opposite side of an older couple who were holding hands. Gray-haired and somewhat weathered in years, they still had an air of devotion and tenderness around them. *A loving affection that was evident to all.* And I had to remind myself that our family would be in northern Italy only a short while, and nothing permanent could come of any liaison with the son of my father's old friend.

Still . . .

Angelo turned to me. "Yet many other English poets have tried and succeeded to capture the magnificence of our country in verse, even the great Lord Byron, who wrote, "Italia! oh Italia! thou who hast / The fatal gift of beauty."

"I could never dream of approaching the greatness of his poetry," I said with some asperity. "He was able to take on the world as his backdrop, but I am afraid my verse shows the smallness of a woman's existence and the themes are more . . . domestic."

"But I have to take issue with you on that point, signorina, because I read the entire volume of your poetry which my father gave to me last night, *Goblin Market and Other Poems*; he bought the book when he was in London, and I thought it was uniquely creative. The lyrics have a deceptive simplicity, and the sonnets a classical polish: 'Remember me when I am gone away, / Gone far away into the silent land; / When you can no more hold me by the hand, / Nor I half turn to go yet turning stay.' It is pure Petrarchan elegance . . . such lines of love and redemption are more than 'domestic themes.'"

For a few moments, I could not decide what delighted me more: the fact that he had read all of my poems in that volume in one night or that he had memorized some of the lines. "You do me too much honor, signor."

"I am only telling the truth, and surely literary critics have praised your work similarly."

I gave a short laugh. "I am afraid their reviews have been only somewhat enthusiastic when reviewing my poetry; certainly, they do not see me on the same level as my male counterparts."

"That is nonsense," he said firmly. "Did you read the copy of the *Corriere delle Dame* that I gave you?" When I nodded, he continued, "I told you how it has become an important journal of patriotic spirit during our recent struggle for unification, but I did not mention that its founder, Carolina Lattanzi, began it in 1804, as a pamphlet to promote women's emancipation in Italy. She was a pioneer in her belief that women are the equal of men. And, yes, she included articles about fashion and theater, but her real focus was on how literature and poetry written by women is as good as, if not better than, that written by men. It is what I also believe."

Astonishment flooded through me. Not even Dante Gabriel, who illustrated my work and worked on my behalf with publishers, truly saw me as his equal. "I can only say that it is utterly refreshing to hear a man voice such sentiments. I did read the *Corriere*, and I found it intriguing that some of the female writers expressed such firm political ideas. Even though I contributed lyrics to my brothers' literary magazine, *The Germ*, years ago before it folded, I have never seen a journal like the *Corriere* in England."

"Since you speak and write in Italian, perhaps you might contribute one of your own poems to the *Corriere*; I can assure you, it would be most well received by readers, and not only by women. Men, such as myself, would be moved by your work, as well."

"Because I am Gabriele Rossetti's daughter?"

"No, because you are *Christina* Rossetti—the famous poet."

My spirits soared as if they had grown wings.

Just then, I felt a breeze pick up, and the two young Italian sailors who had greeted us cheered and began to hoist the sails. A slightly older man wearing a captain's hat appeared and announced we had enough wind to set off; he then signaled for William and

Signor Pecora to make their way back from the bow, exclaiming, "Siamo pronti a partire."

We are ready to depart.

They hurried along the side of the boat and took seats next to us. William's eyes were lit with the fire of a new adventure, and he silently mouthed to me, "Are you not glad we came?"

"I am overjoyed."

One of the sailors untied the lines to the dock, and the captain turned the wheel slightly so the sails caught the wind and puffed out like white bellows, causing the boat to pull away from the dock. Scarcely minutes later, we were skimming along the lake's stillness with the only sound the quiet rushing of the water as the boat sliced through the surface. I closed my eyes for a few moments and inhaled the subtle, perfume-like scent that seemed to cling to the lake, so unlike the murky, salt marsh odor of the lake near Grandfather Gaetano's country house. In contrast, Lake Como smelled like flowers, sweet and blooming in the night air.

"The scenery must look very different from your home in London," Angelo observed.

"That is an understatement; no two places could be more dissimilar." I reached down and trailed my fingers in the water; it was surprisingly cool after the heat of the midsummer day. "I have lived in London my entire life, with the typical fog and gloom, but I spent the summers at Grandpapa's country house in Holmer Green in Buckinghamshire, which was quite lovely with its hedgerows and little creeks. Yet it pales in comparison to this."

"Speaking of London, if I may be so bold as to inquire whether there is a special someone who awaits you there?"

"No," I responded quickly.

In the dusky light, I could not see William, but I *felt* his startled reaction.

"Certainly I have had suitors, but I am not engaged at the moment." And it was true. Mr. Cayley had not offered a formal proposal of marriage.

"Then you are free."

"Yes, I am free."

The boat keeled a bit to the right as the wind blew stronger, and Angelo inched closer, his fingers almost touching mine. Then I heard the high-pitched trill of a bird off in the distance, which grew into a loud, throaty whistle until it stopped abruptly.

"A nightingale," Angelo said, as the evening drew in and stars began to appear in the sky. "They come out only at night with their haunting melodies to remind us that, even in the dark, there is the light of song. Though some do not see it that way, I consider it a good omen to hear one."

I met him here and first heard the nightingale sing . . .

The next hour passed in a daze as Angelo told me anecdotes about the historic towns along Lake Como's shores that housed vineyards and olive groves, and described the splendid villas of aristocrats from all parts of Europe. The couple across from us joined in the conversation, but William and Signor Pecora remained fixed on a more mundane discussion of churches built here during the Middle Ages. *Oh, William, you are missing everything.* As the wind shifted slightly, the captain announced that we would make port at Bellagio for a short while, and I spied a smattering of partially lit buildings on a little inlet.

After we tied up at the dock, the sailors set out the gangway again, and we all trooped off the boat onto a cobblestone street that curved along the shore with slanted alleyways that rose up behind the main avenue. Signor Pecora steered us toward an open-air café with a few tables under an ivy-covered pergola that provided cover. As he ordered refreshments from the owner,

I noticed that Angelo was heading toward a shop that was open nearby, and after hesitating for a few minutes, I followed him.

By the time I arrived, he was already exiting with something in hand. "I wanted you to have this to remember our trip."

He held out a silk postcard with two sailboats painted on it, along with the words Lago di Como.

As I took it from him, I held it close while we lingered in the night air, without moving or speaking for a short while. No words were needed. Then, as we turned to rejoin the group, a shadow darted out of an alleyway—quick and sudden. It turned out to be a man, shrouded in a cape, who grabbed for my pendant, yanking hard on its chain. But when it did not break, he tried again even harder; then Angelo appeared and my attacker pushed me away with a violent shove before he ran off.

My legs buckled, but Angelo caught me in his arms, shouting for help as he managed to keep me on my feet.

He had saved me.

CHAPTER 7

MARIANNE

"Thinking of you, and all that was, and all
That might have been and now can never be,
I feel your honour'd excellence . . ."

(*Monna Innominata*, Sonnet IX)

Verona, Italy
October 1947

I had finally finished installing the blue poplin walking dress on
the mannequin.

As I stood in the alabaster room of the Fondazione, admiring the form, now filled out with padding and petticoats to create just the right Victorian figure, I moved one nylon-stuffed arm so it was in a bent position. Perfect. It had taken some time and extensive cleaning for the old wooden mannequin to be suitable for such a garment but, somehow, Nico and I had done it. The dress looked as if Christina Rossetti were actually wearing it, right here and now. We had decided not to try and re-create her head, even though I knew what she looked like from the portraits and sketches her brother had done of her. But adding a head to a mannequin was problematic since then I would have to fashion some type of hair to adorn it, and realistic wigs were scarce.

No, a headless form was best for this exhibit.

And it seemed appropriate since, even after reading Christina's biography, there was still so much about her I didn't know.

What happened to her in Italy?

Did she fall in love?

Who was the man she met there and why did she leave him to return to England to a reclusive life?

"The dress looks fabulous," Rufina commented as she strolled into the room, her flat heels clicking on the marble floor. More casually dressed today, in a red sweater and black checked pants, she slipped on a pair of cotton gloves. Halting in front of the poplin, she stared at it for several minutes, her fingers tracing the white lace along the neckline. "How did you make the crinoline for the skirt? It billows out perfectly."

"You won't believe this, but Nico found some fishing net, which we arranged into three tiers bound with strips from some old corsets that belonged to his grandmother; then I placed a light layer of cotton around it, almost like a makeshift petticoat, to protect the skirt fabric and let it fall to a natural drape." I lifted the hem and cotton so she could see the stiff fishing net underneath.

"How inventive, and almost too realistic," she said, admiring my handiwork, then took a quick look at herself in the large oval mirror that Nico had positioned in the room, next to a padded bench. "It appears as if Christina just stepped out of time, and you can almost see her shadow inside the fabric, not quite living and not quite dead."

I shivered slightly. "Please, don't go on like that. It's eerie enough to be working with her garments, knowing that *she* wore them, especially when I still have so many unanswered questions about her life. You know how I've told you it is with costume exhibits when you grow too close to the subject; it can be spooky. I have to keep reminding myself that I'm working with an artifact, like a piece of pottery or old coin, and not become *too* emotionally involved with the piece."

Rufina cast a sidelong glance of skepticism in my direction.

"All right, perhaps I've already tiptoed past that line, but I don't want to make it any worse." I removed my apron, setting it on the empty table where the poplin had lain. The other two tables still had the remaining dresses spread out, and I hadn't even begun preparing them. "I already feel her presence too often."

"It's part of the job." Rufina shrugged and turned toward me. "Speaking of our ghostly Victorian poet, did Rupert Harrison call you with any more information about her?"

"No, but I'm hoping that I'll hear something today; it's been almost a week since I saw him, and I'm getting a little anxious to fill in some of the blanks about her life. I still don't have a solid theme for how the exhibit connects to Italy, aside from that 'Daughter of a Native Son' idea, which doesn't exactly thrill me now that I've had time to think about it. And without something captivating to attract locals, I'm not sure a lot of Veronese will be interested in simply viewing a nineteenth-century English poet's dresses." I pursed my mouth, knowing that, while *I* was obsessed with historical costumes, most people didn't share that interest and needed a reason to attend an exhibit, one that would fire their imagination.

But what?

"You'll find a way to draw them to the exhibit—I'm sure of it." She squeezed my shoulder in reassurance. "By the way, did you ever tell Alessandro *everything* the professor mentioned to you?"

I winced. Of course I had related the whole conversation to Rufina and *most* of it to Alessandro, omitting only my speculation about Christina's connection to the emerald pendant involved with Tonio's murder. "Actually, I was waiting until I heard from Rupert with something definite that would link her with the jewel. Otherwise, there doesn't seem to be any reason to share it with him and jeopardize our budding . . . friendship."

"Amicizia? Is that what you would call it?" Her scarlet-tinted lips spread into a wide, knowing smile. "I think it's edging closer to something more significant."

The artful way she emphasized the last word made me laugh. "We've started sharing coffee and cake together here at the Fondazione, that's all. I would call it more of a cordial exchange of information."

But was it really? Rufina could always read people so well, especially when it came to love. She had known that I was attracted to Paul before I fully realized it, urging me to get to know him, a photographer who couldn't offer me a traditional type of marriage but, rather, an interesting one where we could both pursue our arts. And I had taken a chance on building a life with him and never regretted it. But with Alessandro, it seemed more complicated. He was wounded; I was guarded and still grieving. Not to mention, we came from two very different worlds. I wasn't sure that, even if our feelings for each other grew stronger, it would be enough to bridge the divide between us.

And I wasn't foolish enough to think his brief "drop-ins" were prompted only by his newly acquired interest in my restoration work; he wanted to make certain I limited my research to Christina Rossetti's life and not Tonio's murder. I sensed he knew I was withholding something, but he never asked. Instead, our conversations always inched toward my visit with Professor

Harrison; then I'd grow vague and he'd drop it—until the next time.

"You've turned pensive, which means you're questioning yourself again." She faced me, arms folded across her sweater. "You have to fight that sense you always have of being an outsider. How many times do I have to remind you that life is not meant to be lived with timidity? I know it's tempting, but we can't have survived all of the horrors of the war and then be afraid to embrace a new life. That would be almost a greater tragedy."

She's right, of course.

"But a new relationship can't be built around a lie, no matter how small," she pressed.

I reached up and removed my headband, then smoothed down my short bob. "During our car trip to Padua, Alessandro shared some heartfelt, personal details, and I did as well. It seemed like we were bonding; then, when he questioned me about my talk with the professor, I didn't want to do anything to tip us backwards, so I took the coward's way out, deciding silence was best until I had *concrete* information to share. When I do, I'll have to tell him the whole story, though I'm not sure how he will react." I set the headband next to my apron. "I don't know how to handle Alessandro; he's disturbing and intense, so different from Paul. I feel like I'm in over my head."

"That's because you and Paul were young and untested when you married, and he had a quiet nature—sort of introverted. It gave him the perfect eye for taking pictures because he never tried to imprint his own emotions on his subjects, yet it also didn't make for . . . fireworks in your everyday life together—"

"I was never bored with him," I felt compelled to add.

"I'm not saying that," she said, obviously picking her words slowly and carefully. "I just meant he was your first love when everything was sweet and new and shiny, whereas Alessandro is a mature man with passionate beliefs and a rocky past, and you're a woman with some experience behind her. Accepting his nature might not be easy, but you're not the same woman you once were either. A second go-around on love is always going to pose problems, but I think it's worth it. Isn't that what you wanted when you came here? A fresh start?"

"I came here because you twisted my arm," I corrected her playfully. "And . . . I would've lost my mind if I'd stayed another day in Boston with nothing but my memories to keep me warm at night."

"You won't have that problem if you share Alessandro's bed."

I cast a warning look in her direction, but I felt a flush run through my body at the thought of his arms around me, our lips touching and hearts beating as one. *Don't allow yourself to dream. It will lead to nothing but a world of hurt again.*

"All right, but don't say I didn't warn you." Rufina waved her hand. "So which dress are you going to work on next? The muslin day dress?"

"No, I decided to take on the green silk frock." I moved toward the table where it lay. Like most Victorian evening dresses, the neckline dropped off the shoulder, dipping slightly in the center, with short sleeves and, of course, the usual wide skirt. The fabric was adorned with tiny black leaves, matched with an almost Gothic-style black velvet trim along the hem. Very, very elegant. "It looks like it's maybe been worn once or twice, so it should be easy to fit on the mannequin because I don't have to repair any part of it. None of the seams have been stretched; there are no stains, no tears." I paused, scanning it up and down. "It took me ten days to finish the poplin, but I'll need only half that time to prepare this piece; that leaves me plenty of time to work on the last dress."

Rufina moved to stand by my side. "From everything you told me about Christina, this one seems really fancy for her . . . and a little out of character, since you said she preferred more subdued attire."

"She and her sister, Maria, were not known for their stylish tastes, but I have a theory about that. Her two aunts were quite fashionable, so they may have had the dresses made for her specially for the trip since it was, after all, the first time she had traveled out of her own country, and to Italy, where people like vivid colors. Hence the bright blue poplin, the emerald green silk evening dress, and the sunny yellow figured muslin day dress. A total change from the usual dark colors she wore, which makes it all the more intriguing why she left them behind."

"I don't know that you'll ever solve that mystery, but I'm sure you won't give up trying," Rufina said drily, as she touched several delicately shaped black velvet roses sewn along the edge of the bodice. "This part of the evening dress is quite pretty, but it seems to be a separate piece of fabric from the rest of the outfit."

I nodded. "That's a 'bertha'—it's a folded band of material, sometimes pleated or adorned with embroidery, which was fitted around the low-cut neckline to add a degree of modesty; they could also be decorated with pearls or other jewels as a show of wealth. Victorian women loved the bertha because it was quite versatile and could be removed and worn with other evening dresses. Generally, they were made of white lace because that complemented every dress, but this one seems to have been made specifically for this garment because the black velvet roses and trim on it match that of the skirt."

"A rather expensive outfit for an impoverished poet, so your theory might be correct: a more affluent relative had it made for her, and clearly one with an eye for fashion." She stepped back, chewing on her lower lip. "There is something, though, that is a little crumpled about the center velvet rose. Can you see it?"

I leaned down. "No, it looks like the rest, except larger."

Rufina touched one of the fabric petals with her gloved hand. "In the center, it looks like the velvet pile is slightly crushed, as if something lay on top of it."

Reaching for my magnifying glass, I scanned it close up. "Your vision is better than mine because I can't see any difference—" Then I stopped midsentence, noticing how the innermost velvet petals were indented in the shape of a . . . pendant. I straightened and lowered the glass.

"What is it?" Rufina queried

"I think Christina must have worn a pendant with this dress," I said slowly and carefully. "That would've been where it rested if it had been on a long chain, right in the center of the black rose."

Rufina swung her glance in my direction as she realized the import of what I had just said. "Could it be one her father gave her?"

Hesitating, I took another peep at it through the glass. "Since we don't know what Peppina's pendant looked like, I can't say for sure. Most Victorian women would have worn some type of necklace with an evening dress, generally something simple on a long chain so as to not break up the line between the neck and shoulders, so that's a definite possibility. But for the rest . . ." I gave a helpless shrug. "If the professor can find an image of the Menigatti jewels, we might have a better idea as to the pendant's shape and size, then see if it matches this indentation."

"Let's hope you hear from him today, because the suspense is killing me, and I can't afford to be preoccupied now that I have vendors committed to featuring our silks," she tossed off with an air of nonchalance.

"Oh my God, you didn't tell me. That's wonderful news!" I exclaimed, hugging her tightly. "After your meeting in Milan, you didn't say anything, so I thought it might not have worked out."

Her face brightened into a beam of elation. "I heard only this morning. Two major managers called me and said they were very impressed with the quality of the silk and were willing to place rather large orders; that means I can move beyond creating fabrics just for locals, maybe even expand into European markets again, running an office in Paris like we did before the war. It's a dream come true." She laughed. "I never thought I could ever feel . . . well, optimistic, again. But your coming to Verona has brought me good luck for the first time in years."

"I don't think my arrival had anything to do with it," I responded, still holding onto her arm. "You have worked day and night to make this happen, and I couldn't be more pleased. And it shows that dark times do end eventually."

"Sì," Rufina agreed readily. "On that note, I have a hundred things to do this week, so I'll let you get back to restoring the evening dress." She started to turn away, when she took one last glance at the garment. "Why did she choose rose nere—a black velvet rose? Isn't that the color of mourning and death?"

"Not always. In the Victorian 'language of flowers' it is also interpreted as a new beginning, sometimes even a representation of rebirth, which might be what it meant to Christina."

"Maybe, but I still find it a little bleak. I would have gone with a red rose, symbolizing love and passion." She winked at me before she took a few saucy steps toward the door. "Then again, *you* could wear the black rose since this is your fresh start."

"I'm perfectly content with things as they are now—"

"Was there any doubt of that?" Alessandro said as he walked into the room with two small cups of espresso perched on a silver tray, followed by Nico, who clutched a bag which I knew contained two cornettos—the best part of my late morning break, which I shared with Alessandro.

Rufina looked over her shoulder and mouthed silently before she exited, *Tell him the truth.*

I gave an imperceptible shake of my head, then greeted both brothers warmly, "Can you stay, Nico?"

He rolled his eyes. "I have to finish repairs on some of the oak floors upstairs, then replace two missing window panes and fill in a section of crown molding."

"Time is wasting while you're complaining to Signora Baxter," Alessandro commented, setting the tray on the empty table, where the poplin dress had recently lain. "I don't need to remind you we are only two weeks away from our opening date, and we must make certain that everything is perfect for our inaugural exhibits. I'm depending on you, Nico. You and I both need to keep working hard to stay on schedule, and I will join you shortly to help with the floor repairs, but first, if you could bring in the items in the hallway."

"Sì—scusa." He acquiesced, setting down the bag and then leaving, only to return a minute later with the other two mannequins, each one with the wooden torsos beautifully cleaned and polished to a high sheen. With a flourish, he placed them in front of me; when he let go, they remained steady on their refurbished pedestals.

I clapped my hands excitedly, marveling at his handiwork. "They look absolutely beautiful, Nico. Grazie mille."

"Prego."

He started to say something else in Italian, but Alessandro cleared this throat with deliberate intent. "I also need you to buy more paint."

The younger man stalked out of the room without another word.

As I sat on the bench, I commented, "I don't mean to overstep, but aren't you being a little hard on your brother? He's worked ten-hour days to make the Fondazione ready for its reopening, and I certainly couldn't have completed the first dress display without him. His assistance has been invaluable."

Alessandro handed me one of the small cups filled with deep brown liquid. "Not to worry, Nico knows I appreciate his efforts to make this event successful, but he can be a little irresponsible if I don't keep him on track, like my paint request just now. Nico never carries money, so every time I send him on an errand, he's back in ten minutes to pick up cash that he forgot." Alessandro handed me a crescent-shaped sweet and took a seat next to me, reaching for his own coffee and cornetto. "But I will try and not be too harsh with him."

I nibbled on the pastry, its flaky layers melting in my mouth. "It's not that I don't understand the drive to make an exhibit perfect, knowing only too well how it becomes a total obsession. I once spent three days trying to mend a tiny tear in a pair of antique gloves, pricking my fingers so many times that they swelled up enormously, to the point that I couldn't even hold the needle and an assistant had to finish it for me. I told Paul that I had an allergic reaction to a fabric cleaning fluid." I laughed shortly as I took a sip of my espresso. "But I have to say, the gloves looked impeccable by the time I installed them with a turn-of-the-century wedding dress—a beautiful soft pink tulle."

"So, you share my passion for excellence?" he said, without surprise. "I wouldn't have known from the long hours you've spent in this room, bent over those dress tables, arranging and rearranging the material."

I took a brief glance at the mannequin featuring the poplin dress, every fold in place. "It's odd, but each exhibit always starts out for me as a job, but then it becomes a labor of love."

"Lavoro d'amore," Alessandro echoed, following my gaze and staring at the dress for a short while. "I've had many accidents with installations, as well; the worst was when I fell off of a ladder as I was trying to hang a piece of artwork at just the right angle, cutting my face on one of the rungs as I went down on top of the painting, cracking the frame." He pointed at the jagged scar along his jawline that I had noticed when I first met him, which did nothing to take away from his attractive face; it anything, it gave a sexy asymmetry to his almost too-handsome features.

"When I first met you, I thought it must have been a war wound."

He gave a short laugh. "Nothing so dramatic—just pure clumsiness brought on by extreme fatigue. I should've waited until morning when Nico was here and could hold the ladder for me, but I couldn't stop myself. It had to be just right before I could let it go. And the funny thing is, because of the damage to the frame, I couldn't even include the painting in the exhibit. Sometimes that kind of fixation backfires . . . literally in your face, even though I told everyone I had cut myself shaving." With a lingering twist to his mouth, he broke off another piece of the cornetto, chewed it slowly, and then took a drink of his espresso. "Injuries aside, did your husband support your preoccupation with work?"

"Sort of." I mulled over the question, not having thought about it in a long time. "He loved developing his pictures in the darkroom, but he knew how to set it aside, unlike me. What about your ex-wife? Did she adjust to your long workdays?"

"Never . . . not even during our early years together." His features darkened. "Though I was more carefree in my lifestyle as an artist, I was always distracted in the middle of creating a painting, and it was a constant source of conflict between us.

If the Fascisti had not taken over, ending all of our hopes and aspirations, I believe she still would have left me then, because I would block out everything and everyone when I was going to show my work, as did my friends. It was a world in which she didn't want to play a part. So there you have it: the age-old story of the sacrifices we make for the things we believe in, but I still believe it's worth it in the end."

"After the upheaval from the war, maybe it's all we have left." I recalled the many times I had been late for dinner or missed an event that Paul and I had planned; if only I could go back and reclaim that time with him, I'd gladly do it. "Then again, I thought my husband and I had a long life stretching out in front of us, with unlimited opportunities to create shared experiences together. But it turned out to be quite the opposite, and I regret those lost moments, though *he* never complained."

"Maybe we've gathered a bit of wisdom along the way," Alessandro observed, "and will find a way to balance work and life in the future."

Now it was my turn to laugh. "I doubt it."

"So do I." He drained the last of his espresso. "Have you decided how you want to set up this room for your exhibit?"

"Not completely, but I have some ideas." I scanned the alabaster room, with its eggshell walls, white marble floors, and pale, high ceilings decorated with pearly tinted crown molding. "The room is actually perfect for a costume installation because it's like a blank canvas for the dresses that will make their colors and textures stand out, but because there are only three of them, I need to build some kind of historical reference points to fill out the display area. Since the big draw of the exhibit is Christina Rossetti herself, I was thinking of including posters with selections of her poetry and reproductions of some Pre-Raphaelite art by her brother, Dante Gabriel, which Rufina has requested from a London gallery. They would all create a social context for the dresses. As for the theme . . ." I paused. "I originally thought to center the exhibit around her father, but somehow it just doesn't feel right, even though his letter was part of the artifacts in the trunk. As you know, my research on her has taken me in other directions, including the mysterious man she met on Lake Como, her love sonnets, and her later reclusive life in London. It all points to—"

"A *Romeo and Juliet* theme?" he posed. "Fitting for Verona."

"Certainly, star-crossed lovers, except I don't know what forces conspired to separate them forever."

"Has Professor Harrison turned up anything new?" he asked, seemingly occupied with brushing pastry crumbs off his gray pants.

I stiffened.

A seemingly casual question, but the mood subtly shifted.

"I'm hoping for a call today, but he did say at our meeting that it would take him some time to go through the Padua University archives since the campus was so damaged during the Allied bombings." I kept my eyes on my espresso cup, worried that Alessandro would see something in my face that aroused his suspicion. "The books he gave me were very helpful in understanding her life, her family, and her poetry; yet there's nothing about her time here in northern Italy, which is the part I most need to know about. He was going to research if there was any mention of her in local records, any event that occurred during her stay that could be linked to her and reveal this man's identity."

Tell Alessandro the rest of it. He'll never forgive such a deception.

"So, this 'unknown Romeo' is the crux of everything?"

"It seems that way." I set my cup aside, folded my hands in my lap, and took a deep breath. "Rupert did actually mention something else which . . . um . . . could be relevant, but he wasn't sure until he found an artifact that showed—"

"Marianne!" Nico shouted from downstairs. "Professor Harrison is on the telephone and wants to talk with you."

I hesitated.

Nico yelled up again, "Alessandro, there is a banker waiting to speak with you in your office—right now!" he added with loud urgency.

We both rose to our feet simultaneously, then I spoke. "It looks like we'll have to continue this conversation later."

"I hope so." He stood as well, not moving as our gazes locked. I felt his breath on my cheek, as he leaned his head down, almost brushing his mouth against mine.

"Alessandro!" Nico exclaimed again.

Exhaling in frustration, he straightened and stepped back. "I had better go before our banker decides to withdraw his loan to reopen the Fondazione." Still, he waited . . . then, finally, strode out of the room.

The moment passed . . .

Afterward, I vowed to tell him everything—clear the air, for his sake and mine, and face the consequences. I was totally committed to the exhibit, but I couldn't lie to him any longer now that we had formed a bond. But first, I needed to talk to the professor. Quickly, I descended the stairs to a small room connected to the lobby where Nico was stationed next to the phone. He held out the receiver to me, then left.

"Hello, Professor Harrison?" I asked eagerly.

"Marianne, I have to apologize for taking so long to contact you, but finding information on Christina Rossetti's days in Italy has proven quite difficult. I searched through our antiquarian library collections to see if there were any newspaper articles or scholarly papers about her visit but, sadly, I turned up nothing."

Damn.

"There was little else documented beyond the facts that I related to you: she traveled to Milan and Verona, along with a few other cities, then returned to London, broke off with her suitor, and became rather reclusive in her later years." He coughed lightly. "But . . . and this is quite interesting, I did learn from one of her brother William's letters that, at some point on their trip, they connected with one of her father's old friends from his revolutionary days, a man named Giovanni Pecora."

"Who was he?"

"No one of particular historical importance; however, he married into the Menigatti family—"

"The same ones that owned the famous jewelry?"

"Yes."

The connection to Christina?

"At least it was some piece of factual evidence about her . . . and I saved the best for last: I found the archived photo of the Menigatti ancestor's portrait wearing the entire jewelry set, and even though it's a black and white picture, it shows quite clearly what each of the emerald pieces looked like, especially the pendant."

I almost dropped the phone.

"I have to see it—today, if possible," I blurted out. "I can catch the train to Padua this afternoon, if you have time to meet me—"

"There's no need. I figured you'd be anxious to see the picture, so I decided to drive to Verona this morning and meet with you in person. In fact, I'm in the city now, and after I run a brief errand, I could meet you at the Piazza della Erbe, near the fountain, in about an hour. Maybe we could have lunch while we look the photo over?"

Excitement flowed through me as if I were being showered in glitter. *At last.* "I would *love* to have lunch. And I have had a development in my work that might connect to the pendant, but I'll save it for our conversation. I'm too charged up to talk about it right now."

"I'll see you shortly then. Oh, wait . . . and I finally remembered the unusual thing about the actual painting when I saw it years ago: the woman wearing the jewelry had icy blue eyes—very atypical even for a northern Italian." He hung up, but I didn't. I simply held the receiver tightly to my chest for a few moments, my mind racing as I recalled Christina's opening image in her poem, "Fata Morgana": *A blue-eyed phantom.*

Was the man that Christina met in Italy related to the Menigattis? Someone she cared about so deeply that she wrote a poem to him long afterwards as a "phantom" who still entranced her?

Okay, I was getting ahead of myself.

Before I could let my thoughts spin completely out of control, I replaced the receiver and forced myself to concentrate on the pendant again. If it appeared to be similar to the indentations on the black rose, I had a thread, albeit a tentative one, that tied Christina to the jewelry. *What then?* I didn't know, but I felt convinced it would lead to the identity of Christina's mystery lover and maybe even shed light on the murder that had happened at the end of the war.

Quickly, I dashed up the stairs and grabbed my small leather bag, slinging its strap over my shoulder while I took one last look at the evening dress. As I stared down at the black velvet rose, I tried to memorize the shape of the indention to share with Professor Harrison: the lower part was a small square, with the upper part in a separate curved section, almost like a handle. I reached for the magnifying glass again to get a closer look, just in case I had missed something, and I noticed the very center had the petals layered over each other completely. Picking up one of my long basting needles, I gently separated them and found what looked to be a tiny folded note.

How had I missed that?

I slipped on my cotton gloves and used a pair of tweezers to pluck out the wafer-thin paper and then set it on the table. My hands shaking in anticipation, I edged open each corner, to reveal . . . a little charcoal sketch of a woman wearing the silk evening dress, along with a pendant and what appeared to be matching earrings. Positioning the magnifying glass directly over it, I gasped. Even though it was a rough outline, without a lot of detail in the woman's face, it was unmistakably Christina Rossetti.

Holding my breath, I scanned the rest of the portrait and found the artist's name scrawled at the bottom: Angelo Pecora.

Drawing back, I lowered the glass. *Pecora.* But hadn't Dr. Harrison told me Christina's father's old friend's first name was Giovanni. So, was this his brother? . . . son? If it were the latter, that would make him probably around Christina's age. I peered at the image again, focusing on the charcoal strokes, each one with a sense of tender reverence. It *had* been sketched by a loving hand, clearly someone who cared about her, perhaps the son of Giovanni Pecora.

Was he *the one she sailed with on Lake Como? And the "blue-eyed phantom"?*

As I worked it out, it seemed the unknown fragments of her days in Italy were coming together to form a clearer picture, and I might be able to fill in some more of the gaps at lunch. *Her life and her love all those years ago.*

I refolded the sketch and wrapped it in a piece of cotton, then slipped it into my bag. As I peeled off my gloves and reached for my cardigan, I wished fervently that the professor would know what all of this meant, especially if the earrings and pendant in this drawing matched the photo of the Menigatti jewels.

Checking my watch, I realized that I had only thirty minutes before my meeting at the Piazza della Erbe. I hurried downstairs toward the entrance of the Fondazione, halting for a few seconds in front of the closed door of Alessandro's office, where I could hear him inside talking, presumably with the banker. Debating whether or not to interrupt and confess what I was about to do, I reached for the doorknob . . . but stopped myself. There just wasn't enough time. I'd tell him when I returned, fill him in on all of the details and pray he would understand.

Once outside, I buttoned up my cardigan; it had turned cool under a gunmetal-gray sky.

Then I climbed onto my bicycle and took off down the Via Salerno. Unlike when I'd first arrived in Verona, I'd now mastered the two-wheeler and could dart in and out of traffic just like everyone else. Making a few quick turns, I pedaled hard toward the piazza in the historic center of Verona and reached the square in a quarter of an hour. I'd actually made it early. I slid off the bicycle, keeping a hold on the handlebars as I waited next to the Fontana dei Madonna Verona, the ancient Roman fountain with its *Lady of Verona* statue, a queenlike figure who watched over the city's good fortune.

Perhaps she will bring me luck today as well.

In spite of the dreary day, the market vendors had already set up under their usual tents at the center of the piazza, and it was bustling with locals buying fruits, vegetables, and anything else for sale. I craned my head to see around the throng of people and, finally, spied Professor Harrison, who was a head taller than everyone else. Smiling, I waved at him and he nodded in recognition and headed toward me.

But as he cleared a group of young couples with their baskets, a car came careening toward them at high speed, causing everyone to scatter, except for the professor. Frantically, I yelled out his name, but he kept moving forward. Instead of pulling to one side, the car seemed to aim right for him, even accelerating right up to the instant it hit him, causing his body to roll over the hood and then slam onto the street. I cried out in shock. Several women screamed and men rushed to his aid, but the car never stopped; it sped away before I could catch a glimpse of the driver.

In a panic, I threw down the bicycle and shoved my way through the crowd until I reached Professor Harrison. I gasped at what I saw. He lay motionless, his arms and legs splayed out at odd angles, with blood trickling out of one side of his mouth. As I knelt down, I frantically felt his wrist for a pulse and located a faint one. *Thank God he was still alive.* But his breathing grew labored as he turned his head toward me and pressed something into my hand.

Then his eyes shuttered.

"Time flies, hope flags, life plies a wearied
wing;
Death following hard on life gains ground
apace;
Faith runs with each . . ."

(Monna Innominata, Sonnet X)

★

3 March 1844
Milan, Italy

Ogni popolo, ogni secolo, ogni nomo si e fatta
un'idea differente fella belleza.

Every people, every century, everyone has a
different idea of beauty.

Il Corriere delle Dame
(di Mode, Letteratura e Teatri)
Ladies' Courier
(of Fashion, Literature, and Theater)

CHAPTER 8

CHRISTINA

"Many in aftertimes will say of you
'He lov'd her' while of me what will they say?
Not that I lov'd you more than just in play . . ."
(*Monna Innominata*, Sonnet XI)

Verona, Italy
31 May 1865

"I know this may sound insensitive, but that 'incident' at Lake Como two days ago turned out rather well for us, now that we are installed in such charming surroundings," my mother commented from her comfortable position on a gold brocade settee in one of the lovely upstairs sitting rooms, painted all white. "Signor Pecora's palazzo here in Verona is truly magnificent— lovely furnishings, exquisite artwork, and a library unparalleled by anything that I have seen. Your father would be most pleased to see us here at his old friend's home."

"Mama, it was a bit more than an 'incident' since someone tried to steal my pendant and then knock me down," I reminded her drily from my chair across from her, touching the little basket-shaped trinket where it lay against my bodice. "I am lucky not to have sustained any injuries." My elbow had a slight bruise, but it caused little pain and was covered by the long sleeve of my muslin day dress.

"Oh yes, of course. I did not mean to say that I *wished* you to have been harmed—just that some good had come out of a bad experience." She leaned her head back against the pillow that a servant had placed there for her. "I found being dragged around from one hotel to another rather exhausting. I am content to spend a few days relaxing in the palazzo while you and William see the sights of Verona."

And have an army of servants to indulge your every whim.

In truth, I agreed with her, though for a different reason.

I could not deny it *was* a grand and majestic home in that understated way of old Italian wealth, but with a faintly Moorish look. Positioned at the end of a street lined with similarly palatial residences on the Adige River, the palazzo stood out with its unusual combination of a Gothic façade and pastel frescos painted across the exterior. Apparently, one of the Menigatti ancestors had visited Morocco and Tunisia and become enamored with the architecture and art, altering the palazzo's exterior to suit his tastes. I liked its exotic appeal.

But for me, the appeal of residing at the Menigatti palazzo lay in my proximity to Angelo. I saw him constantly.

The morning after we arrived, he made certain that all our needs were met, arranging a light breakfast for Mama and me in a charming dining room that overlooked the river and then showing William their extensive library; afterwards, my brother had disappeared among the trove of books, and I had not seen him since.

Today, after I settled Mama in her bedchamber for a nap, Angelo escorted me along the Via Salerno so I could post a letter, pointing out the various ancient basilicas and piazzas along the way, without the didacticism of my brother—just a sense of pride in his native city. And the Painted City enchanted me with its dreamy combination of frescoed buildings, ivy-covered entrances, and potted flowers everywhere.

"I see why Shakespeare set his famous play here," I commented as we strolled past a jewel-like church. "The city has a certain romantic quality about it."

"Ah, *Romeo and Juliet*. Everyone associates Verona with that play, but it was not based on a true story that took place here. Certainly, we have had feuding local families, but the story of the Capulets and Montagues is completely fictional—"

"But it is based on an old Italian tale, is it not?"

"Sì, a story by Masuccio Saleritano, but in that version, Marriotto—Romeo—is executed for murdering a nobleman, and Gianozza—Juliet—dies of a broken heart." He steered me under a stone archway with open bronze doors. "Supposedly, *that* tale came from actual events that occurred in Siena."

I laughed as we emerged into a courtyard. "So the whole tragic story is merely a fabrication? My brother, Dante Gabriel, will be so disappointed, because their tale has inspired some of his best work."

"There is nothing wrong with being inspired by legends, even if they are only partially true." He gestured toward the ufficio postale.

"Surely, you are not a cynic," I teased, reaching in my bag for my letter to Dante Gabriel at Red House.

His face turned serious. "I do not believe one should die for love . . . one should *live* for love."

"I so agree." My breath caught in my throat as I gazed up at him. "And write about it."

"*Your* poetry, of course."

Still smiling, I turned and strolled into the post office, feeling lighter and happier than I had in years. Walking along the streets of Verona with Angelo had erased the memory of two days ago when I had been attacked—almost. My mind sometimes flashed back on the shadowy man darting out of the alley, his hand yanking at my pendant. Then a sense of stark, raw fear would rise up inside of me, causing my heart to race. After a few deep breaths, I could calm down again, reminding myself that, after all, I had grown up in London, a city not unknown to crime, where my own father had been robbed at gunpoint as a young man. Still, nothing like that had even happened to *me*.

I gave myself a mental shake as I rejoined Angelo. As Mama had said, out of that near-miss came this opportunity to become more acquainted with a man who intrigued me more than any other whom I had met, and though our time together might be fleeting, I was determined to enjoy every moment in his company.

The splendour of the kindling day . . .

I would hold nothing back on experiencing the joy of being together.

And I did not.

We meandered around the historic center where I saw the Castelvecchio, a medieval fortress built of rough stone, and the open-air Roman arena, a perfectly preserved structure built of pink limestone. Then we stopped at a café along the Adige River, lunching on the local dish of risotto al tastasal and amorone wine. A heady mixture of history and savory delights. By late afternoon, I was growing a bit tired, but Angelo proposed one last stop: Juliet's tomb.

I could not resist.

Angelo guided me outside the city walls to a large, gated garden. He paid the entrance fee and we passed along a heavy overhanging grape vine to a little chapel where a stone sarcophagus lay, made of red marble; it had no lid and sat empty, except for a lone lit taper in a socket at the bottom. A deserted tomb of a fictional character, and yet there was something stirring about seeing this shrine to Shakespeare's heroine.

"It is quite moving, but I cannot say why," I whispered.

"Maybe because so many people, especially English poets, have come here to pay homage not so much to the playwright but to the *spirit* of his subject. Many literary men are rumored to have taken a tiny piece of the tomb to remind them of the enduring quality of love when they find their donna perfetta."

"Is there such a thing as a 'perfect woman'?"

"To *one* man's eyes, it is the perfection of recognizing one's soulmate." He turned to me as he stressed the last word.

It penetrated my heart, as if he had found the key to all of the emotions I had been holding inside for so long. It felt both intoxicating and frightening because I could no longer pretend that I would settle for less than what he offered. I wanted to delve into all of the emotions I had only previously dreamed about, and in keeping with the sentiment, I revealed to Angelo the story of Papa's first love, Peppina.

Our fingers entwined as we remained motionless for a long time in front of Juliet's tomb, simply watching the candle burn in the darkness.

The famous crypt may have been a representation of an imaginary couple, but what I felt for Angelo was real.

True love.

I had no idea how long we stayed there, but when we returned to the palazzo, it was too late for tea, and I decided to take supper alone in my room since Signor Pecora and Angelo had a prior engagement that evening. Still reveling in the bliss of my day, I did not want to listen to William explain some new artistic theory he had discovered or listen to Mama extolling the benefits of our luxurious surroundings. I wanted to simply be alone with my own thoughts.

Lying on the canopy bed's rose silk bedspread as twilight set in, I felt a light breeze float in the open window, and I turned my head toward it, watching the lace curtains flutter slightly. Far from feeling sleepy, every part of me seemed alive and attuned to my surroundings, which were so different from my room in our London house. No shabby furniture or bare floors. This bedchamber was decorated with delicate furniture, from a Regency-style writing desk to the chaise lounge at the foot of the bed, and adorned with a gold and white floral carpet covering almost the entire floor. A lady's room—lovely yet functional.

What would it be like to live here?

Far away from the dreariness of Highgate Penitentiary and the Sisters of Mercy Convent.

A twinge of guilt nagged at me when I realized how quickly I had forgotten Evelyn and all of the young women who so desperately needed our care at the convent school. I had taken on my work there willingly and was proud of what I had accomplished, but did I not deserve my own life filled with love and light?

Certainly, I had my poetry and my family, but I could see how the rest of my days would unfold in the years ahead, doing good works, catering to Mama's ailments, and feeling the weight of age creeping in. William would wed, of course, at some point in the future, and Dante Gabriel would find a new passionate attachment to inspire his art; but I would remain as I was now: static and alone, caught in the web of spinsterhood or a loveless marriage, moving neither forward nor backward. An endless banality.

Turning my face to the pillow, I closed my eyes.

I would not accept that fate.

★ ★ ★

The next morning, I awoke with a new sense of purpose that seemed to be reflected in the weather as the sun broke through the clouds of the previous day and caused the sky to turn a clear azure blue, a fitting radiance to reflect what had occurred yesterday and honor my happy task ahead. I chose to wear the figured Indian muslin day dress, flaxen-colored and trimmed with red ribbon and fringe along the double skirt. Simple yet stylish and so typical of Aunt Charlotte's taste. It would be a memorable day because Signor Pecora had agreed to escort me to the Biblioteca Capitolare to return the Dante book and fulfill Papa's request.

Lingering in my bedroom, I held the small copy of *The Divine Comedy* in my hands for the last time, tracing the worn leather and large ridges on the spine. The book had survived almost five hundred years and would now be preserved in a manner that might allow it another five centuries of existence. Opening the cover, I imagined all the hands that had turned its hand-sewn pages, savoring the thick, brown-edged paper, and absorbing the ornate ink script. I could see why Papa had not been able to part with it, because the volume itself was a work of art. But now it would be going home.

I closed the cover and carefully placed it in the pocket of my skirt.

After a light breakfast with Mama, I excused myself before William appeared since, if he knew where I was going, he would undoubtedly want to accompany us to see the ancient manuscripts housed at the biblioteca. He would then ply me with questions about how Papa came to possess the volume and why I had not shared the information with him, and so forth. No, I would follow Papa's wishes and keep the knowledge of this task private between my father's old friend and me.

When I reached the large front hall, Signor Pecora was already waiting, impeccably attired in dark navy trousers and matching frock coat over a high-collared white shirt. He seemed to be leaning rather heavily on his walking stick today as he moved forward, but still maintained an elegant air. For an instant, an image of Papa rose up in my thoughts, bent over his desk in his usual shabby clothing, untidy hair falling into his face, and reading glasses perched aslant on the bridge of his nose. *Dear Papa.* He never cared much for what he deemed superficial aspects of his appearance, but sometimes I had to admit that it was pleasant to focus on other things beyond the world of the mind.

"Are you ready, signorina?"

I nodded, slipping the Dante book out of my pocket and handing it to him with a little reluctance. "I am afraid that Papa scribbled in the margins on some of the pages, the annotations I mentioned to you, so I hope the director does not think ill of him. He would not deliberately try to deface such a precious item; it is just that—"

"He felt he was deciphering the poem?" Signor Pecora finished for me as he wrapped the book in a piece of blue silk; then he extended his elbow for me to take his arm. As I did so, he added, "Perhaps Gabriele never told you why he developed those theories: he thought because Dante was persecuted and driven out of Florence that he coded messages into his poetry against the Church authorities who were so threatened by his *Divine Comedy.* Personally, I never doubted the *possibility*, but I never really thought it was . . . essential to understand the poem."

Nor did anyone else.

As we exited the palazzo, I responded in a wistful tone, "Truly, I wish he had not shared those ideas with a larger audience as he did in London. As I mentioned, they were not well received."

"Do not worry, Signorina Rossetti, your father's legacy has been solidified in Italy as a patriot and a revolutionary; it is how he will be remembered here."

"And that is how I shall honor him in my heart, as well." At least I would try to see him in that way, once I no longer had the book to remind me of Papa's obsessions.

"It is only a short distance to the Capitolare, but I seem to be feeling my age today and would prefer to take the carriage." He gestured toward the same gilded carriage we had taken from the Como train station to the lake. "I know you would probably enjoy walking more, but perhaps you could indulge me."

"Certainly, and it is a treat to travel in such comfort."

Once we were settled inside, facing each other from opposite seats, the carriage began to move forward slowly along the avenue of elegant palazzos, and I marveled at the variety of vivid frescos painted on the exteriors of every dwelling. "My brother, Dante Gabriel, would love how art is embodied in the Verona architecture; it is like living in a painting."

"I saw some of his work when I was in London. It was quite impressive. He uses colors and textures in very unusual ways, almost medieval."

I smiled. "He would love to hear you say that. He and his 'brotherhood' of fellow artists even founded a movement to paint in a way they believed went back to an era before the Renaissance when painters were inspired by myths, legendary lovers, and spiritual bonds—not real life. Arthur and Guinevere. Hamlet and Ophelia. And, of course, Dante and Beatrice. No matter what is around my brother, his mind is always transforming it into a fantasized version of reality."

"To live in the world of imagination is to touch the divine," he observed.

"It has made his life . . . interesting, to say the least, but I suppose he was destined to have that fate since Papa named him after the great poet himself."

"I cannot say I blame him, because parents often want their children to have the kind of life they desired to live themselves, and Gabriele would want nothing more for his offspring than to find success as a poet and artist. Every man sees himself in his son."

Turning back to Signor Pecora, I searched his lined face and thought I saw a shadow of regret lurking in his eyes. "You speak as a father, I assume."

"Sì." He stared out the window with a blank gaze. "I wished for Angelo to have a joyful youth and never experience the kind of poverty I grew up with in Vasto. I married into the Menigatti family—it was a love match with my darling Delfina—and, while her parents initially objected to our union since I was a penniless suitor, they eventually relented because we were determined to wed. La mia bellissima moglie, my beautiful wife. We were very happy. And my wife's wealth was able to provide everything that I could have wanted for my son, including a fine education at the University of Padua."

"He was most fortunate."

Signor Pecora's mouth tightened. "But then he became involved in the revolution, and I spent my days and nights worrying that he might never come home again. Make no mistake, I admired what Garibaldi and Cavour were trying to do, but I wanted my son to take no part in the conflict. I had tried to shield him from the unrest in the country, but his friends from the university filled his mind with the fervor of patriotism, and he could not resist joining them, the Fratelli d'Italia, whom you saw at the statue unveiling in Milan. Certainly, I was proud of Angelo's courage and commitment to the Risorgimento, but he experienced horrors on the battlefield that I never wanted him to endure, and he lost so many friends. Those wounds never heal. *That* I never wanted for him. I had seen it all when I was a student in Naples, and it changes a man for the rest of his days."

The heaviness of his words seemed to shift the mood of our trip with a tinge of melancholy. "But perhaps it gave him a depth and gravity that he might not have otherwise known, a kind of transformation that sees into the heart of what is truly of value to humanity."

He sighed deeply. "I see he has won you over already with his stories of the great struggle for liberty in Italia, just as your father did, but there is a huge price to be paid for such aspirations. Sacrifice and death. Though I celebrated that day in Milan with everyone, I was secretly rejoicing that Angelo returned alive and would carry on as the last descendant of his beloved mother's family. I would see him become a father himself and fill our palazzo with the life and laughter of his own children."

I too want that future for him . . . with me.

But I could not say that because I was not certain with whom he envisioned Angelo sharing that life. Almost afraid to hear it, I quickly changed the subject. "Have you learned anything from the Como police about the attack on me?"

"I did and intended to share it with you this morning. I received a note late yesterday from the inspector looking into the case, and he believes yours was a random assault, someone who wanted to steal your jewelry. Apparently, there have been a series of similar incidents against British tourists recently, and the police intend to start patrolling the area more aggressively."

"Then it is unlikely that Fabiano has reappeared to threaten me?"

"I think so, but I intend to remain vigilant nonetheless."
He raised his chin, his expression brightening again. "Enough
talk of such depressing things, my dear. This day deserves the
sweet satisfaction of being able to carry out the final wishes of
my old friend. And you will be most impressed with the Biblioteca Capitolare. It was originally a scriptorium, a place where
churchmen would rewrite manuscripts to preserve them. Eventually, it expanded into functioning as a library where many
ancient works are now housed, including the oldest known copy
of St. Augustine's *De Civitate Dei* and, of course, many of the
writings of Gabriele's beloved Dante Alighieri."

At that moment, the carriage stopped in front of a modest-
looking building with plain sepia-toned outer walls and white-
trimmed, square windows. Compared to the elaborately frescoed
palazzos in Verona, it looked somewhat austere . . . until we
entered its inner sanctum, and I beheld the incredible collection
of ancient texts. The rich wooden shelves ringed the room from
floor to ceiling, neatly organized and catalogued with labels on
their spines. The smell of leather emanated from every corner, so
strong it seemed to have the aromatic smell of tobacco and teak.

I spun around slowly, taking in the centuries of learning
around me, and found myself at a loss for words; I could only
absorb the air and breathe in the air of the writers and poets who
had come before me. *The memoirs of the dark night of the soul, the
narratives of love, the tales of exotic adventures. I could hear all of their
voices murmuring in quiet tones.*

"I . . . I am awestruck," I stammered.

"It is rather overwhelming to see so much brilliance gathered in one place." Signor Pecora raised his walking stick and
waved it in a wide arc.

"You *must* tell William about this biblioteca, because he
would never forgive me if he found out I came here with you,

although I would prefer that you not share the reason for our visit." ˙

Signor Pecora contemplated the silk-wrapped Dante volume in his hands for a long moment. "It shall remain between the two of us. The important thing is, at the end of Gabriele's life, he wanted you to make up for his long years of keeping what did not belong to him."

"Yes." The only lingering curiosity that nagged at me was the reason Papa had made such extensive annotations on the pages of this book; he always jotted down his notes in blank journals, never on the actual volumes he used in his research. He thought that to be a type of sacrilege against the nature of the printed page. *Was it because Peppina had given him this particular book that made him violate one of his strictest scholarly rules?*

"Signorina Rossetti, you seem to be hesitating. Would you like to wait?"

I touched the silk fabric that covered the small volume in Signor Pecora's grasp, not quite ready yet to fully let go of seeing the last book that Papa had held before he died. But I knew it was not mine to keep. "If you would please give it to the director yourself while I remain here? I am not sure I can do it."

"It will be my honor." He bowed his head and moved slowly toward a small open door at the far end of the room and disappeared inside. A few minutes later, he emerged again with a satisfied expression. "It is done, and the director was absolutely delighted to have the book restored to the Dante collection; he assured me that it would be displayed prominently with the other hand-printed editions. Your father would be overjoyed to know you carried out his last wishes."

I gave a brief nod, but for some reason, rather than being relieved at fulfilling my father's dying wish, I felt a bit forlorn. At least I still had the pendant.

"Signorina, I know this has not been easy for you, but you can now be at peace that you have shown the kind of resolve that would make Gabriele proud. And you have my eternal gratitude for allowing me to be a part of this day." He assisted me back to the carriage, and as we set out for the palazzo once more, he said, "My son has arranged for a small party this evening to honor your family and introduce some of his friends to you, and it might be just the right kind of gathering to lift your mood." He leaned forward and patted my hand. "Angelo thinks very highly of you."

"As I do of him."

In fact, I love him.

A lone church bell rang out in the distance, and I gave a brief prayer that my feelings were, in fact, returned. It seemed so, from our interlude at Juliet's tomb, but . . . could I be certain when we had only recently become acquainted? We were hardly young and impetuous like Shakespeare's doomed lovers, but still, love did not need weeks or months to present itself; it could be a flash of recognition that one's soulmate had appeared within the blink of eye, could it not?

The bell ceased ringing.

Afterwards, we passed the rest of our short journey in silence, and upon our arrival, I retired to my room for the afternoon, simultaneously pensive from the day's events and excited at the prospect of being with Angelo at such a festive event. Was I being fickle to Papa's memory? Then I remembered his oft-repeated advice to me:

Ah, Christina, the fresh violets open at dawn and roses are nurtured by the earliest breezes. Do not wait for life and love to come you . . . I never did, and have no regrets.

Did he mean Peppina? Mama? Or perhaps both?

No matter. He would have wanted me to put the somber feelings behind me and follow my heart, just as he had, fearlessly and passionately.

And I would.

* * *

Hours later, as I laid out my green evening dress on the bed, I marveled at its beauty. It was the most elegant piece of clothing I had ever owned, its shimmering material made of summer silk, not heavy, but light and lustrous, decorated with black velvet accents, including ones in the shape of roses along the bertha's neckline. How unusual that Aunt Charlotte had chosen black embellishments as a contrast to the green silk, but perhaps it was to complement my dark hair.

I lifted it gently, gathered my perfume and Crème Celeste, and started for Mama's room to complete my toilette, when I heard a soft knock on my door. As I opened it, I saw a very young maid, wearing an apron, with her red hair tucked into a white cap, standing there with a shy smile. I greeted her in Italian, and she responded, explaining that she had come to help me dress and prepare for the small evening gathering. I raised my hand to decline, not used to such luxuries, but she remained in place, explaining that she could not leave because Signor Angelo had insisted.

How dear of him.

A tiny glow lit inside of me and I swung the door open wide, then closed it behind her.

"Mi chiamo Elena." She moved toward the bed and gazed down at the dress, then turned, ready to assist me.

For the next hour, Elena not only helped me into the gown, arranging the bertha and fluffing out the skirt folds; she had me sit at a dressing table and fixed my hair in a chignon at the nape with a few long curls around my face. Then she placed a band of tiny fresh flowers across the crown of my head. When she was finished, I stared at myself in the oval mirror, not recognizing the image before me. A woman certainly beyond her youthful days, but now radiating a second bloom that seemed to shine like the blazing color at sunset—smooth olive skin and sparkling eyes. I felt beautiful and alive in a way I had not in a very long time.

> Shall a woman exalt her face
> Because it gives her delight?

I had once written those lines about vanity, but now I wanted to feel that exaltation, if only for a short time. If that made me vain, then so be it.

I had one last item to complete my toilette.

Elena fastened the chain of Peppina's pendant around my neck, the little basket trinket settling in the middle of the black velvet rose on my bodice. It looked as if it had been made to be worn with this dress.

"Grazie, Elena," I said as I began to rise, but she motioned for me to stay still. She brought over a small satin box and opened the lid for me to see the contents. I gasped when I saw what lay inside: a pair of exquisite drop earrings with gold filagree and small green stones.

"Signor Angelo wanted you to have them because he thought they would complement your necklace; they belonged to his mother," she explained in Italian.

"I . . . cannot accept such a precious gift—"

She simply stared at me in the mirror until I nodded slowly.

As she placed them on my ears, I realized they did, indeed, seem to match the pendant. Both delicate and pretty. Of course, I could not keep the earrings since, if they belonged to Angelo's mother, they would be quite valuable, but for tonight, I would pretend that my pendant was also just as priceless and that both pieces were mine.

Then I noticed a small religious medal in the box.

"That is the *Madonna della Corona*," Elena said, adjusting the neckline of my dress slightly. "Signora Pecora always said it was because of the Madonna that her earrings were recovered; they were a family heirloom that had been lost for decades and were restored to the Menigattis in the sanctuary not far from Verona."

I touched the stones. "How remarkable."

"And this letter came for you today." Elena set an envelope on the dressing table, then quietly let herself out of the room. I hesitated. Was it another threatening letter? I reached for it and exhaled in relief when I spied the British postmark. It was from Dante Gabriel. Unbidden, his figure rose up behind me, lounging on the bed as he had the evening before my departure, concentrating on completing his sketch.

If only he could see me now; he would not be able to resist capturing my image.

I opened the envelope, sliding out the single sheet of paper with several paragraphs that conveyed a complete change in my brother's mood.

Red House
Bexleyheath, England

My Dear Christina,

I am so glad you urged me to visit the Morrises at Red House. After less than a week of being here, I am no longer moping about, dejected and paranoid, thinking someone was following me. In fact, I feel quite renewed. In spite of the cold rooms and smoking chimneys, I have come to like "The Towers of Topsy" (my new name for the house) with William and Jane. I take walks, sit in the cherry orchard, and design new wallpaper for their daughters' room. It is quite idyllic.

And I am creating art again, some of my best work, inspired by Jane. Her face looks as if it has stepped out of a legend. Not Guinevere, but Persephone—the embodiment of spring and rebirth. A symbol of my new life. I have done only sketches of her thus far, but I can see in my mind's eye the paintings which will follow and I am eager to start on them.

William and I are also talking about beginning a company that will be devoted to creating furniture and curtains and wall-paper, all handmade to counter the growth of mass-reproduced garbage, creating homes that are centers of living art. Perhaps it is a pipe dream, but it makes for pleasant discussion. On another topic, I anticipate you will have new verses inspired by your travels in Italy, which shall put all other aspiring poets—including me—to shame, and I shall be delighted to do the illustrations.

I hope Mama's health has improved (unlikely) and William has decided not to visit every museum in Italy (even more unlikely). But, most of all, I hope you are enjoying your new experiences abroad, unlike anything you have ever known. Embrace it all, dear sister, and I shall see you soon.

Your loving brother,
Dante Gabriel

I set the letter down on the dressing table, somewhat surprised by my brother's high spirits. But I was also heartened that he might finally be putting some of his past heartache behind him—due, in a large part, no doubt, to Jane Morris's beauty. But Dante Gabriel could not thrive without a muse, so I welcomed her presence in his orbit and vowed not to ask questions about the nature of their relationship. That was another matter for another time.

For the rest, I intended to take his advice and embrace my time in Verona. I smiled at myself in the mirror, touched the Madonna medal for luck, then went downstairs to join the party.

When I arrived in the blue and white grande salone, perhaps a dozen people were already milling about, including Mama and William, who were each enjoying a small glass of wine as they laughed and talked in Italian with a middle-aged couple. Mama looked more relaxed and animated than I had seen her in a long time. As I entered, she glanced over at me and extended a hand. I headed over and clasped her fingers briefly.

"Christina, you look lovely, my dear," she exclaimed, introducing me to the others, who greeted me and declared themselves to be longtime friends of the Menigatti family. "The atmosphere of Verona truly agrees with you."

"It does indeed, Mama."

"In fact, Christina, I have not seen you look so radiant in a long time." William sipped his wine, taking on a thoughtful expression as his eyes came to rest on the earrings. He noticed everything and knew I did not own such beautiful jewelry.

"You are making me blush with so many compliments. I think I am still experiencing the afterglow of seeing the Biblioteca Capitolare, which I believe Signor Pecora told you about, William. It is truly amazing with the depth and breadth of manuscripts housed there, and you must take time to visit it tomorrow."

William took a few moments to respond. "Yes, he mentioned it to me, and I shall certainly want to see it, but I was puzzled that you went there with him because you do not normally want to roam around old, dusty libraries."

"It was to pay homage to Papa's favorite poet, Dante, of course—apparently, he was a scholar there for several years," I said, ignoring William's frown of skepticism.

"But why would you not have asked me to come—"

"Signorina Rossetti, sei molto bella," Angelo exclaimed as he approached, his mouth curving upwards as he noted my wearing his gift. "My father has been detained with business, but he shall join us soon. In the meantime, I have someone that I would like you meet from my student days, if your family can spare you a few minutes.

"I am delighted to meet your friend," I responded and allowed him to lead me off before anyone could quibble about it, and before William could ask any more questions.

As we strolled toward the other side of the room, he murmured, "And I am so honored that you are wearing my mother's earrings; she would approve, believe me."

"It is *my* honor to wear them."

As we drifted past the other attendees, I hardly spared them a glance, being too occupied with taking in the elegant furniture and gilt-framed artwork depicting rustic and coastal scenes. Servants moved around with silver trays, featuring small delicacies and various wines, but I was not particularly hungry; I was too excited to eat anything. When we reached the far side of the room, a woman about my age stood next to a white marble fireplace; she was petite but had a determined chin and direct gaze and wore a vivid scarlet dress of moire silk.

Angelo stopped in front of her. "Signorina Christina Rossetti, I would like to introduce you to an old friend of mine: Teresa Morelli. She is a contributor to the *Corriere della Dame* and has been dying to become acquainted with you after I told her all about your renowned poetry and famous family, including your father—our great patriot."

As we greeted each other and shook hands, I commented wryly, "I think Signor Pecora is exaggerating somewhat. Certainly, Papa is revered by one and all in Italy, but my brother, Dante Gabriel, is the celebrity of the family in England—certainly not I. My poetry has found only a small audience at best."

"You are too modest, signorina," she immediately responded. "Angelo shared some of your poems with me, and I believe they are brilliant and the equal of any male poet today. In fact, I think our editor would be most grateful to include some of your work in the *Corriere* and feature you in the literary section of our journal. I know our readers would be most interested."

"I . . . I do not know what to say." Unexpected delight flooded through me.

She smiled. "Perhaps I can come by for tea sometime soon, and we can chat about the verse you might like to see included in our journal."

"That is perfect—grazie mille."

While we exchanged a few more pleasantries, Angelo had taken out a small piece of paper and was drawing something, but I could not make out its subject. Then Teresa was distracted by an older man who began to talk about Italian politics, and Angelo pocketed the sketch, quickly steering me toward the glass doors and out onto a large balcony with an impressive view of the Adige River, now dappled with the muted colors of twilight.

"I did not think you wanted to be included in a long, boring discussion of whether or not the new president of Italia has the leadership skills of Cavour. But Teresa can more than hold her own with any man."

"I believe that." Moving toward the iron rail, I leaned over and watched a small rowboat navigate the winding river. Then I looked at Angelo. "I appreciate the introduction . . . and I am truly honored by your generous gift of the earrings, but after tonight, I must return them to you."

"No, they are yours now." He leaned in closer. "And please wear them tomorrow when I take you to see the *Madonna della Corona*; it is the sanctuary where the jewelry came into my mother's possession."

It is exactly as Elena told me, but does that not make them all the more precious to his family?

I started to protest, but he interrupted, "And Mama gave them to me with strict instructions that they should go to the woman I—"

"Angelo, what are you doing out here, leaving our guests unattended?" Signor Pecora asked as he stepped onto the balcony. "It is unmannerly, to say the least. Please go inside and do your duties as a host."

He remained in place next to me. "I wanted Signorina Rossetti to see the sight of the river after the sun has set."

"Now she has seen it, you must—" Signor Pecora broke off as he transferred his regard to me, and his eyes narrowed in sudden anger. "Why is she wearing your mother's earrings? They are only to be given to the woman you intend to marry."

"But, Papa—"

"With all due respect to Signorina Rossetti, she is the impoverished daughter of a revolutionary exile—with no dowry to her name." A harsh note entered his voice that I had not heard before. "I have already spoken with you about the need to wed a woman who is your equal in both rank and wealth from a prominent Veronese family, and that is certainly not *her*." The emphasis on the last word cut through my heart like a knife, realizing in that moment that Angelo's father would never accept me as a daughter-in-law. "I have extended hospitality to the Rossetti family because of my friendship with Gabriele, but it ends when they return to England—unless you would like to leave with them; in which case I would have to cut you off entirely from your fortune."

Angelo turned mute.

And with his silence, I had my answer.

Blindly, I stumbled off the balcony and through the salon, ignoring my mother calling out my name, not stopping until I had reached my room. Locking the door behind me, I sat on the bed and slowly removed the earrings, my dream of love fading like Juliet's candle snuffed into darkness.

CHAPTER 9

MARIANNE

"If there be any that can take my place
And make you happy whom I grieve to grieve
Think not that I can grudge it . . ."
(*Monna Innominata*, Sonnet XII)

Verona, Italy
October 1947

I sat at the table in Rufina's kitchen, utterly exhausted after spending the afternoon at the Verona hospital with Professor Harrison. The image of his being struck by the car at the Piazza della Erbe flashed through my mind over and over, his body rolling over the hood and then lying there sprawled on the ground—left to die like an animal. But there was nothing I could have done to avert the accident. I had tried. By God, I had tried to get him to see the danger as it approached, but he had been too intent on making his way toward me.

Tears rolled down my cheeks and I wiped them away with the back of my hand.

I had ridden in the ambulance with him to the hospital, which had recently been rebuilt after the war, and they worked feverishly to save his life. He had a broken leg, two bruised ribs, and some internal injuries, but the doctor had caught me in the hallway and said the professor would survive. I sagged against the wall in utter relief.

One of the police officers drove me back to Rufina's, stopping briefly to pick up my bicycle near the Fontana dei Madonna Verona at the Piazza della Erbe. By the time I dragged myself into the kitchen, it was almost dark and all I could do was make a pot of coffee and heat up a bowl of soup before I collapsed at the table. The room looked a bit better than when I had first arrived, with the chipped plates replaced, the tiles cleaned, a small vase of limp yellow wildflowers on the counter. Rufina's business was clearly doing better with the influx of new partners.

As I sipped my coffee, I shifted my focus back to the three objects I had spread out on the table: the two items I had found hidden in Christina Rossetti's dresses, including the postcard from Lago di Como and the rough sketch of her, as well as the object that Professor Harrison had given to me before he passed out, a photo of the original portrait of a Menigatti ancestor wearing the three-piece emerald jewelry suite. The black and white picture was grainy and water stained, but I could still make out the Renaissance-era figure of a young woman, richly dressed, with dark hair and round cheeks, wearing a matching brooch, pendant, and earrings. Obviously, I couldn't make out the color of the stones, but the shape and size of the pieces was unmistakable.

The pendant and earrings were identical to the ones Christina wore in the sketch. For some reason Angelo Pecora had made a drawing of her wearing some of the Menigatti jewels. Professor Harrison had said the brooch had long been lost, but an English woman had been rumored to possess the pendant, the exact shape of the one that had lain on Christina's green silk evening dress.

A sudden realization dawned on me.

Perhaps the pendant had been stored away with the dress when Christina left it in the trunk . . . and Tonio had found it. He would have had access to the Fondazione, since Nico told me his cousin would occasionally help out when they started renovating the Fondazione near the end of the war; maybe Tonio simply stumbled upon the trunk and its contents while doing work in the upstairs rooms.

Was he stabbed for the emerald pendant?

Did the killer learn that the professor was closing in on the truth and try to silence him?

I sat back, suddenly wide awake. That meant the murderer could still be here and wanted to make certain that his crime would remain buried in the past. Perhaps a partisan who betrayed Tonio?

Groaning, I covered my eyes, trying to shut out the jumble of possible suspects racing through my mind. I thought I had opened a treasure trove in Christina's trunk, but instead it turned out to be a Pandora's box of hidden secrets, lies, and murder, almost costing the professor his life. Maybe it was time to simply finish the exhibit and forget about solving the mystery of why Christina had left her dresses behind; I was a costume curator, not a private investigator. And I was in a foreign country that had just suffered the trauma of fighting a world war; as Alessandro had warned me, I couldn't even begin to understand the undercurrents that still flowed, with old hatreds and vendettas.

"Marianne?" Rufina's voice pierced the quiet kitchen and I started at the sound. "Are you all right? I was at the factory and heard about Dr. Harrison's accident. Dio mio, what happened?"

Lowering my hands as she took a seat next to me and placed an arm around my shoulders, I took a deep breath, then told her everything that had happened. She gasped when I mentioned how the car had deliberately aimed for the professor and actually seemed to speed up to inflict the worst injuries possible.

"Who would want to harm an old man?" she asked incredulously.

"Someone who didn't want him to show me this photo." I tapped the black and white picture. "Little does the would-be killer know I also have this sketch of Christina wearing the pendant *and* the earrings which I found folded inside the velvet rose of her evening dress—drawn by Angelo Pecora."

Rufina stared down at the photo and the sketch as she slowly withdrew her arm. "So we now know for certain that Christina Rossetti wore some of the Menigatti jewels with her evening dress. Why would that matter?"

"Because the professor believed that the emerald in the pendant might have been the one Tonio was killed over; that's what I think motivated the attempted assassination—his murderer is afraid that somehow his identity will be revealed." I couldn't believe what I was saying, even as I heard the words coming out of my mouth: *Murderer. Assassination. Hidden identity.* "If Tonio somehow discovered the trunk, he also would have found the pendant lying atop Christina's evening dress. It would have been tempting for any man to seize it and try to sell it when people were starving and desperate at the end of the war. "

"Marianne, I think you're getting carried away—"

"No, it makes perfect sense." I stood up, grabbed the moka pot, and refilled my cup. "For some reason, Christina never wanted to see the necklace again—or the dresses. I haven't figured out *why* yet, but I think it may have something to do with Angelo Pecora, the artist who made this sketch of her."

Rufina set her hands on the table and spread her fingers across the chipped wood. "Who can say after all this time? All we can do is speculate that, whatever happened, she never wanted to look at anything that reminded her of her visit here . . ." She slowly tilted her head in my direction as I stood there, still holding the moka pot. "Are you thinking what I am?"

"A love affair that didn't work out—it's the only explanation." *Her blue-eyed phantom lover.* I moved over to the white enamel stove and set the pot down, peering out the kitchen window at the dim outlines of the courtyard outside. *I knew it.* Christina had loved and lost the man who meant everything to her—perhaps she even discarded the dresses because she too had been cast aside. A woman doesn't recover from something like that so easily, especially a poet like Christina who expressed such depth of emotion in her verse.

She had left Italy heartbroken.

And I had come to Italy to repair my broken heart. Maybe that's why I had felt a connection with Christina from the moment I saw her dresses; we were both women who had experienced such wreckage in our personal lives that we almost drowned from sorrow. I could feel it in every stitch of her clothing. Every hem. Every piece of trim. It all breathed a sense of desolation from her spirit to mine.

But she was strong enough to continue with her life through her poetry. She had survived, and so would I.

Turning around, I leaned back against the sink. "When the trunk was found after the Fondazione was damaged this past summer, did it appear to have already been rummaged through?"

Rufina flipped her palms up in uncertainty. "Alessandro called me only after Nico had found and opened the trunk. When they saw it was filled with antique dresses, they weren't sure how to handle them, nor was I, and that's when I wrote to you. To my untrained eye, the contents didn't look like they had been disturbed, but I can't say for certain—you're the expert. It's always *possible* Tonio went through the items, found the pendant, and then put the rest back in their original place. I wouldn't have known."

"If he did, he missed the earrings, or they weren't in the trunk."

"I think the latter because you and I didn't find any trace of them, unlike the indentation where the pendant had been placed. All we really know is Christina's father gave her the pendant and she was *sketched* wearing it and the earrings," she pointed out. "Otherwise, they seem to have vanished."

"I have one last dress of Christina's to examine, so maybe—"

"Not tonight," she said firmly, rising to her feet. "It's past ten o'clock and you look exhausted, so let's hold off doing anything until morning, all right? I have to admit I'm a bit tired myself. The new customers are being very nitpicky about every last detail of our contract, and they bring in their lawyers at every turn. I've been tempted to call off the whole thing off and start over again."

Feeling a twinge of guilt, I took a long look at her and noticed her mouth drooped at the corners and her eyes were ringed underneath with faint shadows. "Oh, Rufina, I've been so caught up in these unexplained mysteries about Christina, I've shut out everything else—including my best friend. I'm sorry."

She gave a dismissive little shrug. "I'm sure my business dealings will all work out in the end, but right now I'm finding it . . . difficult. Since the war destroyed most of our economy, people are wary about starting up new ventures that may take years to show a profit, and the retail industry is not an instant money-maker, to say the least. And I can't do anything that might make them even more nervous." On her way out of the kitchen, Rufina looked over her shoulder at me. "At any rate, just tread carefully, Marianne, because I don't want anything to happen to *you*."

"I promise."

And with that vow, I switched off the light and went upstairs to bed.

★   ★   ★

By morning, I was already rethinking my pledge.

I had awakened to the thought of Professor Harrison lying in a hospital bed with his ribs taped and his leg in a cast, pale and breathing heavily. He looked old and frail, and I felt responsible. I realized that if a killer was brazen enough to run him down during the busiest time of day at the Piazza della Erbe, he would likely strike again to protect his identity, so whatever I turned up while I restored the last of Christina's dresses, I couldn't share with anyone. That way, I wouldn't put anyone else at risk, least of all Rufina.

But I had to do everything I could to learn what had happened, for both Christina and Tonio.

What about Alessandro?

I had to tell him everything.

Certainly, my job was to set up textile exhibits, yet that meant delving into every article of clothing I touched with the questions of who wore it, how it fitted, and what it meant to the owner. I filled in all of the spaces between the seams with what might have been as I gave shape and form to a once living, breathing person. But this exhibit had taken that process to a new realm. I had bonded with the woman who had worn the clothing, and in an odd way, as I brought *her* back to life, I became revived as well. I had found my passion again, and how appropriate that a long-dead Victorian poet had brought those emotions back to the surface.

I had to do justice to her gift to me.

After taking a tepid shower, I donned a pair of pants and a sweater, gave my hair a quick comb, and then, before Rufina was awake to further caution me, biked my familiar route to the Fondazione. The buildings along the Via Salerno were also looking a little better as, one by one, the repairs progressed, with new windows and freshly painted exteriors. Slowly, Verona was coming back more noticeably, even in the short time I had been here.

Once I arrived at the Fondazione, I placed my bicycle in its usual spot, just inside the entrance. Then, as I headed across the marble floor to the stairs, I saw the door to Alessandro's office was closed, with a note that he would not be back until that afternoon.

A brief reprieve.

Not that I minded. I needed to prepare myself for his reaction to my news, especially the hit and run incident with Professor Harrison, knowing he would be upset, to say the least. In the meantime, I could work unimpeded while I rehearsed my confession and prepared to accept that Alessandro might fire me on the spot when he heard it. If that were the case, I would miss seeing him, sharing time together when we talked about art and history. Our chats had become very enjoyable—actually enthralling—in a way I hadn't felt since I was with my husband.

Paul.

I hadn't forgotten him, but the pain was not quite as sharp now, the grief not as engulfing, and that, too, was something new. Who would have thought that curating old clothing could be the catalyst for a kind of healing, as well? *Rufina, of course.* I had *her* to thank for bringing me to this place and this time.

My dear friend. I can never repay you.

Ascending the stairs with rapid steps, I walked into the alabaster room and halted abruptly as I caught sight of Nico placing the makeshift crinoline around the second mannequin, humming as he fastened it in the back. He looked up and grinned. "You see how much I've learned from you, Marianne? I now know how this cage-like thing works."

I stifled a laugh. "Most impressive. Let's layer the petticoats around it, and if you would help me, I think we can fit the evening dress over it. I have the stuffing for the bodice and the sleeves, so we might actually be able to finish this piece today."

We both put on cotton gloves and then lifted the dress, with Nico taking the wide skirt and I the bodice. Carefully, we slipped the garment onto the mannequin, smoothing down the folds of the skirt so they would billow out evenly over the structured hoop. Then I stood back. *Not bad.* "Once I fill out the upper half of the dress to resemble a female form, I think it's going to look even more stunning than the walking dress."

"They both look like . . . uh . . . when the lady poet wore them," he said, struggling awkwardly to express his approval from the perspective of a young man who wasn't exactly as thrilled as I was with antique attire. "Molto bella."

"Yes, quite beautiful." I picked up some of the stuffing, mostly made up of more discarded women's nylon stockings, and began to pad out the bodice just beneath the neckline, trying not to disturb the black velvet roses.

"Alessandro is out of his office this morning." Nico's grin grew wider as he made a mock prayer-like gesture. "I can finally take a *long* break. All I do is paint, paint, paint. I understand that he has a deadline, but I can't take much more. I even dream about it. Thank God it will be over soon."

"He is a bit tense with the reopening date looming," I murmured, amused at Nico's dramatic interpretation of his nightmares. "And I'm probably not much more lenient, but I have only one more dress after this one, so I won't place too many demands on you . . . which brings me to something I've been wanting to ask. When you found the trunk, did it look like it had already been opened?"

"Uh . . . I don't think so, but there was no lock on the latch, which I thought was unusual, so I could flip open the lid very easily. Those types of trunks usually had some kind of way to keep them sealed shut."

I kept stuffing and shaping the bodice to create just the right silhouette, but inside, my mind was whirling with a dozen questions. "So it might have been possible that someone found the trunk toward the end of the war and broke into it before you discovered it last summer. But who could have been up there? Weren't you and Alessandro the only ones allowed in the Fondazione's private rooms during that time, and your cousin, Tonio?"

"Sì." His eyes cut quickly to the door. "You can't tell my brother this, but Tonio didn't just do odd jobs; I think he met some his fellow partisans in the upstairs room where I found the trunk. Not too often, but I remember hearing a woman with him in several different rooms upstairs when Alessandro was gone—"

"A friend or lover?"

His chagrined expression spoke for itself.

Illicit assignations.

"I didn't want to tell my brother, since he would have thought Tonio was putting us at risk with his . . . activities." Nico fingered the lace bertha, his expression turning serious. "I don't blame him for wanting to have some privacy with a woman, but trusting anyone was dangerous then. So I suppose if Tonio *had* found something valuable in that trunk, he probably would have told her."

"Did he mention it to you?"

Nico shook his head. "I wasn't involved with the partisans beyond storing arms and ammunition for them in the cellar here, a fact I kept hidden from my brother. Alessandro made me swear that I would not join in their actual sabotage activities, and I kept my word, but that didn't mean I couldn't help them in other ways. On the other hand, Alessandro put himself in harm's way constantly, because he smuggled out all of the valuable art from the Menigatti collection to various small villages and hid them in churches; that's why there is so much left at the Fondazione. I also believe he saved people, but he would never tell me a word about it." Nico's eyes turned troubled. "To be honest, I *had* heard a rumor that my cousin found something valuable near the end of the war that he was going to trade for money and food, but he was always scavenging through the ruins, thinking he had a precious item, so it may have just been gossip."

"Then again, it may have been true this time, and the object was worth enough to murder him," I said quietly.

Nico gave a small, bitter exclamation. "People would have killed then for a pound of coffee, so who knows? I was helping some of the partisans move rifles the night he was killed, and none of them knew anything about Tonio's reputed discovery when I asked them about it later. And I couldn't tell Alessandro about my suspicions because he would have been furious that I was working with the partisans. We never spoke about Tonio's murder. We were all just trying to stay alive, so it seemed best to put it behind us. I still regret that, though. I should have been able to do something to save Tonio. I failed him."

But Alessandro knew what you were doing.

I squeezed his arm. "But you know in your heart that both you and Alessandro are true heroes."

"Few Veronese know what my brother did because he was very private about his movements during the war; he said it was safer that way for me, just in case he was caught by the Germans." Nico removed his gloves and pulled a fresh paintbrush out of his overalls pocket. "Time to go back to work . . . my brother is right: bringing up the past is depressing and pointless."

After he left, I focused again on finishing the installation of the evening dress, spending the next few hours filling out the bell-shaped arms, but my thoughts kept returning over and over to what Nico had shared with me. If Tonio had been meeting a woman upstairs during the war, even infrequently, it was very possible that they found the trunk and took the emerald pendant together. That meant at least *one* other person knew about the priceless jewel, but had she helped him or betrayed him?

And what about the earrings? Perhaps Tonio and his lover might have been searching around the other rooms upstairs to find them, and that's why Nico heard them in different parts of the building.

I looked down at the sketch of Christina Rossetti wearing the jewelry. *Where did you leave them?*

As the words echoed in my mind, I swiveled my head toward the day dress of figured India muslin lying on the table; it was the last one to be restored and needed the most mending. I hadn't examined it thoroughly yet, but the defects were not typical of the wear and tear of age. Its bright, flaxen-colored fabric had a long, vertical tear in the skirt, a torn hem, and some missing trim, suggesting, unlike the other pieces, that it had been subjected to distress when it was worn.

Had something happened to Christina when she was wearing this day dress?

I moved over to the table and patted down the bodice, but I felt nothing aside from the fabric. Then I ran my gloved hands along the top skirt where the jagged rip had cut through the material and found it had not frayed, so the dress had not been worn again after it was damaged. But there had also been no attempt to repair it. I traced the hem of the second, longer skirt and it, too, showed nothing out of the ordinary . . . until I felt something hard and round. A coin?

Quickly, I reached for my sharp-pointed seamstress scissors and gently cut three small stitches open, causing a small object to drop out onto the floor. As I scooped it up, I realized it was not a coin. It was a religious medal with a woman's face and the words Santuario Basilica Madonna della Corona. Turning it over in my palm, it looked like a typical icon from an Italian church—nothing remarkable—except that it had been sewn into the hem of Christina's dress. That meant it held some significance to her.

Why?

If only she could tell me . . .

Then I did something out of the ordinary: I picked up the dress and walked over to the large, oval mirror and held it in front of me, trying to imagine Christina wearing it. For a few moments, I could almost see her face floating above the neckline, looking as she had in that sketch, wistful and yearning . . .

Then the vision gradually faded as I sensed someone standing behind me.

Alessandro.

"I thought the first rule of every costume historian was not to ever wear a piece of antique clothing," he said, staring at me in the wavy glass of the mirror, the image of the two of us appearing almost as if we had stepped back into Christina's world in an illusion of the past. Blurry and romantic.

"I . . I was not going to try it on. I just wanted to see what the dress might look like on a real person for a change and not a stuffed mannequin." I started to lower it, but Alessandro grasped my arms to hold me in place.

"Any man would find you beautiful wearing it." His eyes darkened in the reflection, but not with desire. "Did you know that your name, Marianne, means 'the star of the sea' in Italian; it guides men to grace and salvation. But in your case, it seems to be the opposite: *you're* the Fata Morgana you're always talking about, luring men like Rupert Harrison into making near-fatal mistakes."

He found out.

"I dropped by the hospital this morning and had an interesting conversation with the professor." Alessandro released me and stepped back. "The poor, injured man was barely conscious, but he managed to tell me everything, including how he was trying to connect Christina Rossetti's emerald pendant to Tonio's murder. My question is why, after I specifically asked you to avoid poking and prying into anything connected with my cousin's death, you went behind my back and did it anyway." He paused. "You lied to me, Marianne."

"I tried to tell you yesterday, but you were in your office with the banker and I didn't want to interrupt. Then I decided to share it with you this afternoon when you returned, but . . . I was too late." Turning, I set the dress on the table and faced Alessandro, whose features had assumed that same hard, remote expression he had worn the first day I met him. "If you would give me a chance to explain—"

"I don't need to know anything else beyond the fact that your 'research' into the past seems to have brought a killer out again, and the professor has already almost paid with his life for your meddlesome inquiries."

"But if Tonio's murderer is still in Verona, he should be brought to justice," I pressed. "Why would you not want that?"

He knocked over the empty mannequin, cursing in a stream of rapid Italian. "You don't care about anything except these stupid dresses, and I'm officially ending your part in the reopening of the Fondazione. I want you out of here now, and take all of those pieces of old clothing with you."

"No." I seized the lapels of his jacket and refused to release him when he tried to push me away. "Why don't you want to learn what happened? It would finally lay Tonio to rest and bring some peace to you. It just doesn't make sense to me—"

"I won't tell you again. Parti ora!"

"I'm not leaving until you tell me the truth." I clutched him even tighter.

He clamped his mouth in a thin line for several minutes.

"Alessandro? I'm asking you as someone who . . . cares about you."

There, I had said it, and the words hung between us, an offering from the heart, waiting for him to respond.

Minutes passed, and still he said nothing.

"All right." He exhaled deeply, and I felt some of his anger dissipate. "It's because I suspect Nico might have been connected to Tonio's death."

"What?"

"You must understand that I can't lose my brother. If I knew for certain he was responsible, even in a small way, I couldn't make the choice between doing the right thing and telling the police or lying to protect him. It would be too painful, so I have said nothing for two years. Evil things happened as the war was ending, and Tonio's death was one of them. It was forgotten . . . until you started digging around. Not knowing the truth was better."

"But it festered, a wound that never healed between the two of you."

He looked down briefly.

"And you're wrong about Nico," I cleared my throat. "Because he told me today that he was with his partisan friends planning a mission the night Tonio died, but he was afraid to tell you that because you were so adamant about his not being associated with them. Your brother isn't a killer, not then and not now." Searching Alessandro's face, I added, "You need to exorcise your cousin's ghost or it will haunt you forever."

A brittle silence descended on both of us as I let my arms fall away, all emotion spent.

Finally, I spoke up, "I have one other thing to share: your brother told me that a woman used to meet Tonio here in the upstairs rooms, and I think she may be part of it—trying to cover her tracks because the professor and I were getting close to figuring everything out, including the location of the missing earrings." I pressed the medal in his palm. "It was hidden in the hem of the muslin skirt."

Frowning, he held it up and murmured, "*Madonna della Corona.*"

"What does that mean?"

"It's the name of a sanctuary not far from Verona, an old church built into the side of Mount Baldo, about an hour's drive north from here. Do you think she went there? It's difficult to access and would've been a hard journey for a woman at that time."

That explained the damaged condition of the dress.

"Yes." I had a feeling of absolute clarity that it held the key to Christina's lost earrings. "I know there's so much left unsaid between us, and we might never be able to move past my deception, but for now I'm asking you to trust me and take me to the sanctuary. *Please.*"

At that moment, Rufina strolled into the room, looking casually elegant in her best wool trousers and silk top. "May I come with you?"

"Of course," I responded readily. "I'll fill you in on my discovery along the way—"

She pulled out a gun and shot Alessandro; he grunted in pain and slumped to the floor, his blood spreading slowly in a scarlet pool across the white marble.

My hand went to my mouth, too shocked to scream.

"Marianne, it will just be the two of us on this little jaunt." Rufina smiled.

CHAPTER 10

CHRISTINA

"If I could not trust mine own self with your
fate
Shall I not trust it in God's hand?"
(Monna Innominata, Sonnet XIII)

Verona, Italy
1 June 1865

I awoke from a night that provided me with neither sleep nor
rest—just an endless wait for the dawn.

And when it came, I felt only a numb awareness of my
surroundings.

Strolling toward the window, I spied the sun just beginning
to creep above the horizon, spreading a slanted light across the
city. A stark reveal of the day to come. Glancing at the dressing table where the earrings lay in the silk-lined case, they
evoked little delight in me, only distasteful memories of what
had occurred at the party yesterday evening when Signor Pecora
had insulted my father and made it very clear that his son and I

had no possibility of a future together. Angelo was already destined to marry a wealthy young woman from one of the finest families in Verona, and we would be parted forever.

It was almost more than I could bear.

I could not imagine returning to London with its gray dreariness, plodding along every day to Highgate Penitentiary where I worked with the Sisters of Mercy, returning home every night to Mama and William's desultory conversation. The only relief coming from Dante Gabriel's visits, but those often ended badly with some type of family disagreement. I could escape all of that by marrying Charles Cayley, but would my situation really improve since I did not love him?

I loved Angelo.

But I would be barred from a life with him—living in a jail of loneliness as I had once written.

The door was shut. I looked between
Its iron bars; and saw it lie,
My garden . . .
It had been mine, and it was lost.

Sighing, I moved back to the vanity where the earrings lay in the open box. I knew I had to return them, but, set out next to my pendant, they looked like they belonged together—a matched set—and it would be hard to give them back to Angelo. Then I looked closer. Indeed, they did appear to be part of a suite with similar stones and gold filagree work. *It must be my imagination . . .*

Just then I heard a sharp knock, and an envelope slipped soundlessly under my door. Instantly, I retrieved it and tore open the seal to find the sketch that Angelo must have done of me at the party; it was only a charcoal outline but, somehow, it captured the magic of the evening. I held it to my heart as my spirits soared. At least I knew he had felt it too. Then I realized a folded note was also tucked inside the envelope. As I scanned the lines, my spirits lifted with each word:

Dear Signorina Rossetti,

I apologize for my father's behavior last night; it was unforgiveable. But nothing has changed in my attachment to you. If you feel the same, please meet me downstairs at 9:00 o'clock when I shall have a carriage awaiting to take us to the Santuario where I would like to ask you a very important question. Please wear the earrings. I understand if Papa's cruel words altered your regard for me, but I pray they have not.

Ti amo,
Angelo

Tears of happiness stung my eyes. Of course, my feelings were unchanged, no matter what his father had said. I would meet Angelo and then let destiny take its course. No tentativeness. No fear. No hesitation. Wherever fate took us, we would be together. All was *not* lost. Then I glanced at the porcelain mantel clock. I had only one hour.

I reached for the bell to ring for Elena to assist me in donning my India muslin day dress, when I heard another knock at my door, followed by my mother's unannounced entrance into my room. She was attired in her usual black crepe and carried a china cup and saucer. "I thought you might like morning tea, Christina. Your brother has already taken off to see the biblioteca and left me quite alone, so there is time for an uninterrupted mother/daughter chat."

"Thank you, Mama." Hoping that it would be short and she would leave directly afterwards, I noted with some dismay that she seated herself on the settee at the end of the bed and patted the space next to her, appearing ready to settle in for some time. Reluctantly, I sat down and took the cup of tea from her, anticipating a rather unpleasant conversation.

"I have not seen you very often during the last few days," she observed. "I assume that is because you have been enjoying the company of Signor Pecora's son."

"Yes, he has been showing me the sights in Verona: the Roman arena, the Castelvecchio, the tomb of Juliet—"

"Christina, I hope you have not misconstrued his . . . hospitality, since it appears his father is not completely happy that the two of you have spent so much time together. I am sure Angelo was simply being a good host, but since we will be leaving in a few days for Brescia, it is unwise to become too attached to him." She seemed to be tiptoeing with her words as if she were treading over tiny stones.

Setting the untouched cup aside, I cleared my throat. "Mama, I see no point in being coy. I . . . I have come to care deeply for Angelo."

My mother took in a quick, sharp breath. "But you are barely acquainted with him, and his father is obviously against a union between the two of you."

"None of that matters," I said firmly. "We have to follow our hearts' desire, just as you and Papa did."

"That was different. My father, Gaetano, did not oppose the match."

"But you loved Papa and would have married him anyway."

She did not respond for a few long moments. "Gabriele was a mature man of forty-two when we met, and I was in my late twenties with my marriage prospects dwindling, so when he began to pay court and then asked my father for permission to marry me, I did not hesitate to accept his offer. But neither Gabriele nor I had any real financial prospects, so that barrier did not divide us. Certainly, I knew he had probably loved other women, perhaps even very deeply, but that was before he met me, so it did not matter either."

So she did suspect there was a Peppina in my father's youth.

"I did not have any qualms that it was the sensible thing to do, and I came to love your father, with all of his eccentricities. I wanted a life full of art and literature and children, and we had that together, beyond my expectations."

"Oh, Mama, our household created beautiful childhood memories for me, and I am most grateful for all of those experiences, but I want to choose my own way now."

"That is not an easy path for a woman, as I know from experience. In my younger days, I turned down more 'prosaic' suitors and, eventually, wed a headstrong, penniless poet in your father, and even with my family's support, you know how difficult it has been to maintain any kind of financial stability. A constant, grinding struggle. If you and Angelo married, his father would no doubt disinherit him, so you would be facing similar challenges." Her voice held a note of concern. "Much as I wanted all of my children to be inspired by your father's love of poetry and art, I now wish there had been a little less intellect in the family, so as to allow for a little more common sense. We might have avoided some of the hardships. And if you have your own children, they must be fed and clothed, which will put even more of a strain on your relationship. It is the unvarnished reality, my dear daughter."

I knew everything she said to be true, but I did not care.

"But I want the kind of love that Dante Gabriel has felt, the scorching, raw emotion that fires the heart," I protested. "And it is not just my feelings for Angelo that draw me to Verona. It is a sense that I could have a different kind of life here: free and untrammeled by all of the conventions that seem to constrict every inclination that I have to push beyond a 'proper' woman. I could be a working poet in Italy since there are many women here who write for the *Corriere delle Dame*, like the one I met last night, and it is considered quite respectable. That kind of independence stirs my creative soul."

"It is different for men, like it or not. Dante Gabriel has the liberty to live and love, move on and love again, but women are left picking up the shattered pieces of the aftermath. You and Dante Gabriel are my 'storms,' but *you* have learned to tame your temper; sadly, he has not—to his detriment." She leaned her head on my shoulder. "Enjoy your time with Angelo, but when we return to London, you should accept Mr. Cayley's offer when he makes it. It is the sensible thing to do."

"Yes, it is."

She tipped her glance to the side. "And you have no intention of doing it."

"No."

"Well, I thought it was worth a try." She patted my cheek, rose from the settee, and picked up the India muslin frock. "Shall we get you dressed then?"

My Mama—ever the pragmatist.

In less than an hour, I had completed my toilette, with her assistance, complementing the outfit with the pendant and earrings, and made my way down the stairs where Angelo awaited. As I approached him and extended my hand, he kissed it and led me to the carriage outside.

I have made my decision and will not look back.

★   ★   ★

As the carriage rolled out of Verona on a road along the Adige River, neither of us spoke for nearly half an hour. In truth, I still had not quite accepted the import of what I was doing. I did not know what it would lead to or how it would end, but I trusted in the power of our feelings for each other. That was the only thing that mattered. As the landscape grew more mountainous, I finally prompted, "Tell me about the sanctuary."

"The Santuario Madonna della Corona. It is built on the side of the Mount Baldo slope, part rock and part shrine for centuries, then it became a church dedicated to Our Lady of Corona, Our Lady of the Crown. It is a bit of a challenging route, but when we arrive, you will understand why I wanted to take you there."

The Madonna della Corona.

Something clicked in my mind. "But how extraordinary . . . there was a tiny medal to her in the earring box you gave me yesterday."

"Not at all." He smiled. "My mother kept it with the jewelry because the sanctuary was a beloved place to her; it was where she and my father first met, and he gave her the earrings as a gift to commemorate that special day. She bought the little medal because she felt the Madonna blessed their commitment to each other in that holy spot, and it was a happy marriage. Before my mother passed away, she gave me the earrings and the medal to present to the woman I loved, so we could have a similar blessing." He threaded his fingers through mine. "It seemed appropriate to honor my mother's wish at the sanctuary when I ask you to be my wife."

Oh, yes . . . in my heart a thousand times yes.

But . . .

"Angelo, I do not think your father will ever accept me, in spite of his friendship with my Papa," I said frankly. "I am not from a wealthy family, nor do I have an aristocratic lineage—"

"You are the daughter of Gabriele Rossetti, and he was a great man," Angelo interjected. "But even that would not matter to me. All I care about is you. I know my father sounded harsh and unyielding last night, but he will come to accept our marriage once he understands that this is the course I have chosen and I will not be deterred. If not, he will be the one who breaks the bond between father and son." His features looked set and firm. "And it will be his loss, indeed."

Yet it would always be a cloud between us that he had to choose between the woman he loved or the father who raised him.

I gazed forward at the mountains ahead, my emotions mixed between joy and sadness at the prospect of Signor Pecora's ire. "He said he would disinherit you."

Angelo shrugged. "My mother left me part of her estate, so we shall not want for much. *She* came from an old Veronese family—the Menigattis—whereas my father was hardly a man of means, but she loved him and was determined to marry him. Considering all of that, it makes his obstinacy against our union somewhat . . . hypocritical, to say the least." He gave my hand a little squeeze of encouragement. "I have come through civil war and seen friends die on the battlefield and never thought those shadows would lift in my heart, until I met you. The world opened for me again like a window into a totally new life that I could not imagine."

Sweet delight rose up inside of me like a song of pure joy. *This moment of pure happiness—I never want it to end.*

The carriage jolted slightly and I realized we had started up a narrow road that curved back and forth on the side of the mountain heading toward a small hilltop village nestled among lush trees. The cloudless sky took on a sapphire hue and the air had a hint of coolness. A perfect day.

"We shall arrive in Spiazzi, the little town that lies above the sanctuary, and then walk the path down to the shrine. It is not far but angled downward. Can you manage it?"

I laughed. "Not to worry, I am quite used to walking in London and hiking around my grandfather's country home."

As we came around the last curves, I beheld the sanctuary peeking behind the craggy rocks, and I took in a sharp breath at its stunning beauty. Half hewn into the side of the mountain, the salmon-colored church seemed almost suspended from the heavens, its bell tower stretching forever upward to the divine. "I have never seen anything so breathtaking," I enthused. "How was it possible to build it on the sheer vertical slant of those rocks?"

"It is hard to say because there has always been an air of mystery that surrounds the structure; some believe monks and hermits carried the stones by hand to construct the initial shrine, but no one knows for certain," he replied. "Local legends say that a small sculpture of the *Pietà* was miraculously transported here through angelic intervention, and the shrine was then consecrated as Our Lady of Corona Sanctuary. The other story is that a feudal lord donated the *Pietà*, which seems a more likely scenario."

"But less poetic."

We exchanged amused glances.

"However it came to be, it is a testament to faith and determination," I said as the carriage halted.

"This is Spiazzi," Angelo announced, pointing at the smattering of small houses peeping out from the thick pine trees. "We must go on foot from here down a short path, but it is a little rough and uneven, so you need to be careful not to stroll too close to the edge. I shall be at your side, though, all the way."

And I shall never let you go.

He assisted me out of the carriage, instructing the driver to wait, and we moved toward a tunnel-like clearing where the trees had been cut back, barely wide enough for two people to walk arm in arm. Angelo steered me along the bumpy path, keeping a tight grip on my arm as we came upon patches of jagged stones and clumps of grass. At one rocky outgrowth, I stumbled, catching my skirt on a thorny bush, tearing the material, but he kept me from falling.

"Oh no, you tore your skirt," he said, pointing at a rip in the muslin.

"It is of no consequence; I can mend it easily." *Nothing* would stop me from seeing the sanctuary with Angelo, least of all a little mishap with my dress. We navigated the uneven path, finally emerging into a huge open area where the sanctuary stood in all its glory at the top of a flight of stone stairs. And at that moment, the bells rang out in a melodious chime that echoed around the vast peaks that stretched as far as the eye could see.

"I shall never forget this moment," I said, half to myself.

"Nor I." Angelo led me up the steps and toward the front doors decorated with a dozen square brass panels. As he pulled open the right one, we stepped inside the small, empty chapel with its high-domed ceiling and narrow interior, one side made of original mountain rock and the other of smooth stone. A single row of pews led to the altar, and we moved past them silently, until we reached the altar adorned with two marble statues of winged angels on either side. A large sculpture of the *Madonna della Corona* adorned the far wall, gazing down on us with an expression of saintly kindness, almost a benediction.

"Ti amo, Christina," he said in hushed tones. "Will you marry me?"

"Yes—with all my heart," I responded, surrounded by the beauty and love and grace of the chapel, and a sudden idea occurred to me. "Since this is the place where your father gave the earrings to your mother, perhaps we should honor the Madonna by offering them to *her.*"

"In gratitude for bringing us together. But you must keep the pendant to honor your father and *his* love for Peppina." Angelo reached over and gently removed the emerald jewels from my ears and pressed them into my palm. Then he touched his lips to mine in a soft kiss, a tender seal of our commitment to each other. *Sweet passion that speaks from the soul. My dearest one.*

Eventually, when he leaned his head back and I opened my eyes again, I noticed a niche behind him with a small painted statue of the Madonna holding her dying son in her arms; in front of them sat a tiny casket of stone. Angelo managed to slide open the lid slightly and we laid the earrings inside, sealing them up again. When we finished, he took my hand and we began to wind our way out of the chapel, our task completed. We had nothing but the future to behold, a shining new road illuminated like "a rainbow shell that paddles in a halcyon sea."

We smiled at each other and started to exit the chapel when the door suddenly swung open with a violent jerk. Signor Pecora strode in, his expression thunderous and his eyes flashing in fury as he thumped his walking stick on the floor. "What are you doing here, Angelo?" he ground out between gritted teeth. "I thought I made it crystal clear that you were to have nothing further to do with *her*?"

The contemptuous way he stressed the last word made me cringe, but Angelo kept a firm hold on my hand, facing his father with a calm demeanor. "We came here to pay respect to Mama—"

"*Silencio!*" As he came forward, he glared at me. "Where are the earrings? What have you done with them?"

Before I could answer, Angelo replied, "They are none of your concern, Papa."

"How dare you?" Signor Pecora roared, raising his hand as if he meant to strike his son. "Do you have the least idea what I have done to obtain them? I lied, betrayed friends, and deceived your mother, Delfina, about how I obtained them, all because they gave me a chance for a life with her and you. And now you simply tossed them aside? Ragazzo sciocco!"

Angelo remained unmoved. "I am not foolish, nor am I a boy. What 'deception' are you talking about, Papa?"

"I want the earrings," he repeated stubbornly. "And the pendant."

"Not until you explain."

Signor Pecora's mouth turned into a bitter sneer. "You have no idea what it is like to live in poverty, my son, and I would do anything for you to avoid that fate. I *must* have the jewels because they are part of the arrangement which I intend to make for you to marry into a family I have chosen; if you do not find a wealthy wife, our estate will be in jeopardy. Believe me when I say our financial situation is tenuous. When I met your mother, the Menigatti fortune had already dwindled, and I did everything I could to keep it going, but the situation has deteriorated."

"But you made that large donation to the Highgate Penitentiary in London," I blurted out before I could stop myself.

He grunted dismissively. "A bank loan."

"Papa, I do not understand any of this, but if we are in such dire financial straits, we can sell the palazzo," Angelo suggested.

"Never. Your mother loved her home."

I heard the older man's angry tone shift to anguish, and I felt a rush of sympathy for him. "Perhaps I should leave the two of you to discuss—"

"Please stay, cara mia," Angelo urged me. "Whatever my father has to say should be heard by both of us."

Signor Pecora clenched his walking stick with both hands. "All right, but you will not like what you hear. You know some of it from your father's letter and our conversations, Signorina Rossetti, and you know some of it from the tales I have told you over the years, Angelo; but neither of you have the whole story. I have never shared it with another living being, and I trust neither of you will, either."

We both nodded.

"It all began when I was a student in Naples with Gabriele and Fabiano. The three of us were inseparable, and truly, I considered your father my dearest friend, Signorina Rossetti. But when we became involved with the rivoluzione, the atmosphere changed overnight and became dangerous; we had to be cautious about any newcomers we allowed into our circle. Then Gabriele fell in love with Peppina, who was young and pretty but often indiscreet about our activities, putting our lives at risk." His eyes clouded over as if he could see into the past. "One night, I went to her apartment to speak with her about it, and she was with a man from Verona who said he wanted to join us, but I did not trust him. We had a scuffle and he fell, hitting his head on the sharp edge of her table. He died a few hours later, and I instructed some of our friends to throw his body into the sea. I thought that was the end of it. However, when Peppina and I went through his belongings, we found an old volume of Dante's poetry and an emerald jewelry set. It was obvious he had stolen them because of the book's Biblioteca Capitolare stamp and the Menigatti family's crest on the velvet case that contained the gems. So we decided to keep the lot . . . Gabriele and Fabiano never were aware of what transpired."

"My God, you killed a man, Papa!" Angelo exclaimed in disbelief.

"It was an accident, and those were perilous times. If I had reported it to the police, they would have executed me immediately. And I did not want to die. So Peppina hid the stolen items until we could find a way to sell them to finance the rivoluzione. But that time never came. King Ferdinand was restored to power and put a price on Gabriele's head, so we all escaped to Malta to regroup, except for Peppina, who came a few months later. When she arrived, however, she gave me only the brooch and the earrings to raise money for our cause; she wanted to keep the rest for herself. I acquiesced. But then the rivoluzione collapsed and the cause we had believed in was no more." He looked down briefly and shook his head. "At that point, Gabriele began to talk incessantly of emigrating to England, but Peppina did not want that future, so their relationship soured and she grew more despressed by the day until, sadly, she threw herself off a bluff. I assumed the book and pendant were swallowed up in the dark waters with her. Afterwards, Gabriele sailed for England, and Fabiano disappeared, so I was left friendless and alone. I decided to sell the brooch to present myself as a man of means, traveling to Verona to restore the earrings to the Menigatti family, hoping for a reward and certainily never intending to reveal how I acquired them. And I received a pearl beyond price, my son—your mother."

Angelo made a guttural sound of disgust. "But your marriage was built on a lie."

"I never regretted it," he said firmly. "In fact, when we met here at the sanctuary, it was love at first sight, and I gave the earrings to *her* before I even met her parents. They were so overjoyed at the restoration of even part of their priceless jewelry set, they agreed for us to wed, even though I was not from a noble family. You see, their estate was heavily in debt even then . . . which brings me to you."

As he turned to me, I squared my shoulders in readiness for what would follow.

"I always believed the pendant and the Dante book lay at the bottom of the sea, but I was wrong. A few months ago,

Fabiano contacted me because he was quite ill and wanted to see me before he died; he had been living under an assumed name in Venice all these years with a wife and family. He confirmed everything that your father related to you in his letter, Signorina Rossetti, including the fact that Peppina left him the pendant and Dante book before she committed suicide. I was shocked." He tapped his cane for emphasis. "After Fabiano left, I realized that the pendant might still be within my grasp."

A gradual realization dawned on me. "You did not meet my Aunt Charlotte by chance in London, did you?"

"No, I traveled there to ingratiate myself to your family and learn the whereabouts of the jewel," he said without a trace of remorse. "But to my delight, you had already arranged to travel to Italy with it, having no idea of its value, so I had my chance at last to acquire the last piece of the Menigatti jewels. All I had to do was simply take it from you, but that proved a bit more difficult than I anticipated. I sent you the threatening note about Gabriele being a traitor, then hired a man to rob you at Lake Como, thinking I could blame them both on Fabiano. But the robbery attempt went awry, so I then asked your family to stay with us in Verona, pretending to assist you with returning the Dante book while I found a way to take back the jewel. A perfect plan. Except that I did not anticipate my son would fall in love with you."

"Papa, *why* did you do such things?"

"My son, I need both the earrings and the pendant as part of that bargain with the family in Verona who are willing to bestow a large dowry on their daughter to acquire the Menigatti lineage—if she receives the jewelry. And you must marry into wealth or your mother's legacy will turn to dust."

"Mama would not want me to wed someone I did not love— ever." Angelo pulled me away from his father and hurried me toward the door. "And you are nothing more than a common criminal."

As we moved past Signor Pecora, he sprang at me, reaching wildly for the pendant, but Angelo knocked him aside with a slap across the face. We then hurried out of the chapel with his father in pursuit, shouting, "My son, listen to me—"

"I never want to see you again," Angelo muttered as we started to descend the stairs. When we had almost made it down, I felt his father's breath on my neck; he was right behind us. I looked over my shoulder and saw he had raised his walking stick to hit me, and, in a panic, I yelled out Angelo's name. He seized his father's arm and they wrestled for the cane until Signor Pecora let go, but when he did, Angelo lost his balance on the bottom step and tipped backwards toward the cliff's edge.

Frantically, I grabbed at his jacket, trying to keep him from falling, and our eyes locked together in that moment, frozen in love and fear . . . then he slipped away. I heard a long, anguished scream that grew more and more faint—and finally, nothing.

Oh God, no!

I sank to my knees, sobbing wildly until I collapsed, crushed and beaten, to the ground.

CHAPTER 11

MARIANNE

"Youth gone, and beauty gone if ever there
Dwelt beauty in so poor a face as this;
Youth gone and beauty, what remains of bliss?"
(*Monna Innominata*, Sonnet XIV)

Verona, Italy
October 1947

I knelt down next to Alessandro, ripped open his shirt, and was alarmed to see the red patch of blood expanding across the lower part of his torso. Turning to Rufina in total bafflement and disbelief, I exclaimed, "Have you totally lost your mind?"

"It's only a flesh wound." Rufina said with a shrug. "I know how to handle a gun, and I can assure you he won't die, unless you don't agree to drive me to the *Madonna della Corona*. Then, unfortunately, I will have to fire again, right through his heart." She aimed the barrel at Alessandro's chest.

"No!" I tried to shield him with my body.

Still conscious, he tried to push me away, but his arms had grown weak. "Just do what she wants . . . I'll be fine."

Quickly, I went over to one of the mannequins and tore off a large section of the petticoat under the silk evening dress, folded it into a square, and pressed it against his side; then I lifted his hand to cover it and apply pressure to stanch the blood flow. As I watched his face turn pale, I felt tears roll down my cheeks. "I can't just leave you."

I heard Rufina clear her throat. "I'm waiting."

"Don't worry." Alessandro managed a slight smile as he clamped the improvised bandage in place. "I have survived much worse injuries."

Torn between screaming for help and fearing that Rufina would follow through on her threat, I leaned down and pressed my lips to his briefly. "Don't you dare die on me. Nico will be here soon—"

"I'm afraid not," Rufina cut in. "I sent him to the other side of Verona to buy more paint, so that should keep him busy for about an hour, enough time for Marianne and I to drive to the sanctuary and complete our task."

As I stared down at Alessandro, his words flashed through my mind: *Nico never carries money, so every time I send him on an errand, he's back in ten minutes to pick up cash that he forgot.*

He gave an imperceptible nod, as if he could read my thoughts.

Rufina seized my arm and yanked me to my feet. "I hate to interrupt this touching scene, but we need to move along. My car is parked on the street out front, and if you say or do anything to draw attention to us, I will shoot you and come back to finish him off." She nudged me with the gun. "Let's go."

Taking one last look at Alessandro, I allowed her to propel me out of the room and down the stairs. When we emerged outside, the street was empty, except for Rufina's small car with the engine still running. "You take the steering wheel, and remember, I will have the gun on you the entire time."

I shuddered, and not just from her warning; a strong wind was sweeping in from the north with a hard, biting chill. Having no choice, I did as Rufina directed, and she slid into the passenger seat, watching my every movement. I shifted the car into gear and jammed down the pedal, causing the car to lurch forward.

"Just drive normally. We don't want the police to pull us over, for your sake," she warned, tapping the iron gun barrel against my ribs. "Go to the end of the street and make a left turn; it will take us along the Adige River and out of the city. Then we'll head north toward Spiazza, which is the closest village to the sanctuary, and from there, a narrow lane leads to the chapel. It shouldn't take more than fifty minutes."

Complying with her directions, I tried to focus on the road to keep calm, but my breath was coming in short, staccato gasps and my hands were sweating as I clutched the wheel. *What has happened to my dear, old friend? This woman is a stranger.* "Rufina, we've known each other for fifteen years and shared our innermost thoughts and dreams . . . you were even the maid of honor at my wedding. I don't understand any of this."

"Of course not. You think I'm the same young student you knew in Boston, but I am not. The war changed everyone, including me. You have no idea what I had to do to survive," she scoffed in a harsh tone. "While you were safe in America, I had to see my country destroyed, learn to scavenge for food and the most basic necessities, and lost all sense of dignity and pride and honor. I told you I was glad my parents did not live to see the war, but I'm more grateful that they didn't live to witness my shame."

For a moment, I felt a twinge of sympathy, remembering the Rufina I once knew—laughing and lighthearted—always looking for the next exciting adventure. "They would still love you, and I'm the last person to judge your behavior during the war, but this . . . you *shot* Alessandro and have forced me at gunpoint to help you accomplish some kind of criminal act. That is *not* the Rufina I once knew."

"She died, bit by bit, starting the first time she had to sell her body for food."

"Oh, Rufina, I am so sorry . . ." I halted, not knowing what else to say as I steered the car toward the rising mountains ahead. "But I'm pleading with you to forget about this craziness, let me turn the car around so we can tend to Alessandro and sort things out—"

She laughed. "That's the one thing I didn't plan on: that you and he would grow so close. I never dreamed that you'd ever get over Paul, or Alessandro would set aside his bitterness over Tonio's death, but I guess there is always a wild card in every scheme. Not that I mind. You can have him."

As Rufina spoke, I realized gradually that I had been duped by my old friend; she had written those letters to cajole me into coming to Verona as part of some kind of elaborate plan to achieve a heinous end. "I want to know the truth: Why did you ask me to help with the costume exhibit?"

"Do you remember our first student exhibit when you chose a damaged seventeenth-century dress to put on display?" she said, pausing for me to nod. "You worked for weeks to find the exact type of lace that would have been attached to its neckline, researching catalogues, poring over old documents, and calling every antique clothing store in New England until you found a matching piece. But you did it, and you brought that same dogged determination to every job you took on. So I figured you would do the same thing with Christina Rossetti's lost dresses, especially after reading her father's last letter to her. You wouldn't be able to resist the lure of figuring out why her dresses had been hidden away in Verona, and I would finally get what I wanted: the Menigatti emerald earrings . . . you see, *I* was the one who found her dresses with Tonio."

"What?" Blinking in surprise, I didn't notice the car had drifted to the right until one wheel hit the unpaved side; instantly, I corrected my course. "I thought the trunk was discovered only last summer—"

"We found it two years ago." She directed me onto a one-lane road that had a steeper incline, then leaned back against the seat. "Tonio and I were partisans and would meet at the Fondazione, at first to share information; then our relationship became more intimate. I liked him—truthfully. But we were desperate for money and decided to sneak around the . upstairs rooms, hoping that there might be some piece of valuable Menigatti art that Alessandro had overlooked when he hid the collection in the countryside. But we turned up nothing until Tonio discovered the trunk. Before we even opened it, I spied the initials and realized it had belonged to Christina Rossetti."

"But how did you know that?"

"My grandmother, Elena, had worked for Giovanni Pecora from the time she was fifteen, and when he was old and alone on his deathbed, he was raving about how he and a woman named Peppina had killed a man over the Menigatti jewels. Apparently, he managed to acquire the brooch and earrings; he sold the former and used the latter to ingratiate himself with the family, even marrying their daughter. But Peppina took the pendant and gave it to her lover, Gabriele Rossetti, along with an antique Dante book—"

"Both of which he passed on to Christina, as he mentioned in the letter," I finished, half to myself.

"Then she brought them with her to Italy. And that's where the old man's story grew interesting because he tried to steal the pendant from Christina and would've succeeded if his son, Angelo, hadn't thwarted the plan by falling in love with our poetess. Angelo brought Christina to the Sanctuario Madonna della Corona, gave her the earrings, and proposed marriage, but Signor Pecora followed them and tried to stop the union. He fought with his son, and Angelo fell to his death. The earrings were never found. Afterwards, the old man never forgave himself for what he'd done and lived the life of a recluse, seeing and speaking to no one."

"How awful."

And that explains so much about Christina's lonely existence in England when she returned; she had lost the love of her life.

"Molto triste." She waved a hand dismissively. "My grandmother actually helped hide the trunk with Christina, who swore her to secrecy on Angelo's grave, and when she finally confessed it to me after she caught a fatal case of scarlet fever years ago, I never believed her tragic tale of the handsome blue-eyed man and his English lady love . . . right up to the moment Tonio and I found the trunk. Then I knew it was true. My grandmother hated Signor Pecora for what he'd done, but she stayed out of loyalty to the family—and Christina."

I steered the car up the deserted switchback road, imagining the horror Christina must've felt the moment when Angelo tipped over the side of the cliff, ending all of her dreams of love. The depth of her pain must have scarred her for the rest of her life.

My thoughts flashed back to Alessandro lying in a pool of his own blood. *I cannot bear to lose him as I did Paul.*

When I was close to the summit of the mountain, I caught sight of the sanctuary: a magnificent, salmon-colored church with a peaked roof and soaring bell tower, clinging to the rocky mountainside as by magic. But I couldn't take my eyes off the narrow road for more than a few seconds as I approached a sharp curve that led to a cluster of houses.

"Just keep going through the village," she directed, then pointed to a tree-lined lane. "That pathway leads to the sanctuary, and don't worry about my car—it will make it. I've been here before."

I swallowed hard but kept going, and we emerged shortly into the open, empty square in front of the church. I hit the brakes and turned off the engine, exhaling in relief. "Rufina, what did you do after you and Tonio found the trunk?"

"What do you think? We scoured through it, read Gabriele Rossetti's letter, and found the pendant on top of the silk evening dress. The emerald wasn't large, but it was quite valuable, so we decided to sell it. Tonio wanted to use the money to help the partisans, but I wanted us to split the proceeds so I could use my half to start over somewhere after the war ended. He wouldn't listen and took the pendant a week later to meet with a buyer. When I showed up instead and demanded the jewel, he refused." She reached for the car door handle, keeping the gun aimed at me. "I didn't mean to kill him; he came at me right at the moment I pulled out the knife. It was an accident, and I regretted it, but nevertheless, I sold the emerald and stashed the money away."

"You left him to die," I said, aghast at her callousness. Where was the dear friend I once knew who couldn't bear to see an animal run over in the street? Truly, she had become a vile, heartless killer.

"It was *his* fault, not mine." Rufina motioned me out of the car as she looked toward the sanctuary. "If a priest appears, say nothing because I *will* shoot you."

I believed her.

As I slid out from behind the wheel, I scanned the surround-ings and realized there was no escape route since the sanctuary was carved into the side of a vertical cliff and surrounded by mountain peaks on all sides. I would have to go along with her madness. At the last minute, I reached inside my bag for Paul's precious Murano glass compass. *Guide me one last time.*

Rufina shoved me toward a steep flight of stairs that led to the chapel. "You go ahead of me, but don't try anything stupid."

Slowly, I ascended the steps, my mind racing to think of a way to disarm her, but I came up with nothing. When we reached the church with its Gothic façade, I turned to try and reason with her one more time and noted a flash of silver on the winding road below. *Could it be Alessandro's Alfa Romeo?* Rufina started to follow my glance, and I quickly spoke up to distract her. "But you weren't content with only the pendant; you wanted the earrings, too."

"Why not? I deserved them both." She kept her eyes on me. "I went through Christina's dresses several times, searched every room at the Fondazione, and even came here to the sanctuary twice; but I couldn't uncover where Christina had hidden the earrings. It nagged at me day and night. Then the trunk was revealed when the Fondazione's walls were damaged in those summer rains, and I came up with the idea of asking you to set up the exhibit, thinking you might succeed where I failed. And you did, along with Professor Harrison. I'm sorry I had to steal a car and run him down once he found out about the Menigatti jewels, but I couldn't allow him to ruin my plans." She frowned in mock regret. "All of my talk about meeting with vendors to start up the family factory again was mere fabrication. I intend to leave Verona once I have the earrings to add to my proceeds from the pendant and start my new life abroad."

"But Rufina—"

"Go inside—now!"

I pivoted on my heel and moved in a daze toward the large, brass-paneled doors. For a few seconds, I thought I saw the hazy figure of a dark-haired woman in a long dress hovering at the entrance to the chapel, then disappear inside. Shaking my head to clear my vision, I struggled to contain my anxiety, but it was becoming more and more difficult as Rufina prodded me repeatedly with the gun.

Once we entered the chapel, I scanned the craggy rocks of one interior wall, and the closed doors beneath the archways on the other side. There was no way out. I clutched Paul's compass to protect me, sensing that I now stood in the very place where Christina had on the day she came here with Angelo.

"So, where are the earrings?" she demanded.

"I told you, I don't know; I just had a feeling when I found the *Madonna della Corona* medal sewn inside the hem of the last dress that it had something to do with them, but it was only a hunch—"

"And yet this was the last place Christina visited wearing the pendant and earrings." Her eyes darted from the high-domed ceiling to the stained-glass windows. "They have to be here somewhere, so figure it out as if your life depended on it. Because it does."

Just pretend to look around until help arrives . . . and pray it will be soon.

Slowly, I walked toward the altar, which was flanked by two marble statues of winged angels, and thought I heard the whispering sound of a hem sweeping across the floor. It seemed to be leading me on. Along the way, I spied small niches with various statues of saints and peered through archways with stone carvings of biblical scenes, but nothing seemed like a place where jewels could be hidden. When I reached the large statue of the *Madonna of the Crown* with its arms stretched forward, I tilted my head up toward her benevolent gaze of devotion and grace, but it held no answer to the whereabouts of the earrings.

I turned in defeat. "The earrings could be in a hundred different places—"

"Find them!" Rufina screamed.

"I can't help you."

Her eyes narrowed and she aimed the gun at my chest . . . then I began to tremble. *But I would not give her the satisfaction of seeing me beg for my life.*

Instead, I threw the compass at her, right at the moment the front door slammed open with a loud bang and Nico appeared, shouting something in Italian as he rushed at her. Taken aback as the glass compass shattered at her feet, she faltered and blindly swung the gun in Nico's direction as Alessandro rushed in from under one of the arches and shoved her sideways, causing her to drop the gun. She spewed curses at both of them and tried to claw at Alessandro's face, but Nico seized her in a tight grip, not letting go as she yelled and kicked at him. Then two policemen appeared, placed Rufina in handcuffs, and dragged her away.

My heart bursting with relief, I ran toward Alessandro and then stopped abruptly as I saw the bandages wrapped around his torso where his shirt hung open. "You're alive . . . I was so worried."

Grinning, Nico slipped an arm around his brother. "It will take a lot more than a slight wound to kill Alessandro."

"She murdered Tonio," I blurted out, along with the rest of her evil plot. "I never would've believed that Rufina would be capable of such horrible things . . ."

"Nor I," Alessandro said in a grim voice.

My legs almost gave out at that point as reality set in, and they both guided me to one of the pews. I took several deep inhalations with my eyes closed for a short while until I had steadied my breathing again. Vaguely, I heard the brothers murmuring together, and then Nico patted my shoulder before he left.

Alessandro took a seat next to me. "He's going to inform the police of what you just told us and bring my car up here, but I'm afraid he'll have to drive you back to Verona while I go with the police. I'm still too dizzy to take the wheel . . . and you should not be alone at Rufina's villa right now. Please stay with us."

I leaned my head on his shoulder briefly in acceptance.

We sat in the quiet of the chapel, side by side, until I heard the bells in the tower above ring out a sweet-sounding harmony.

"Do you really think Christina hid the earrings here?" Alessandro asked.

"I am certain she did." In my mind's eye, I saw Christina and Angelo hovering near a small niche in the rough rocky side of the church, and I led Alessandro toward the painted statue of the Madonna holding the Christ child; at its base lay a small stone casket. "They placed them in there to honor their love."

Alessandro reached out to open the lid, but stopped. "Then that's where they should remain."

We smiled at each other and left the casket untouched.

For love's sake.

★ ★ ★

Two weeks later, Alessandro and I stood together inside the alabaster room, greeting people as they strolled in to see the Christina Rossetti clothing display, now titled "The *Monna Innominata*." It seemed a more fitting theme than the one I had originally conceived since the woman and poet I had discovered was the subject of this exhibit—not her father—and, as she wished, her life story here would remain hidden, except for her dresses. Her family members were referenced only on a lineage map which I had placed near the door, and there was no mention of Angelo Pecora anywhere. I had given Gabriele Rossetti's letter and the artifacts which I had found sewn inside Christina's garments to Professor Harrison for safekeeping with the promise he would keep them secret.

And, in fact, nothing else besides the dresses seemed necessary for the exhibit to create a powerful impression of Christina Rossetti; they illuminated her time in Italy, arranged in slightly different poses on one side of the room behind velvet ropes, with a description of each fabric and design, as well as the type of occasion during which they would've been worn. The vivid textile colors glowed against the white background. Across from the dresses, however, I did include large posters with Christina's fourteen sonnets hung in a perfect row on the wall, with a glass case positioned in front, holding several antique books of her poetry which Nico had located.

We decided *not* to seek out her father's Dante book at the Biblioteca Capitolare, agreeing that it, too, should remain in obscurity.

I was content with those decisions.

It was only the second day of the exhibit, but I was already overjoyed with its success, in spite of all of the trauma connected with Rufina's vile schemes. I still recoiled inside when I dwelled on it, my emotions raw and bruised.

Alessandro must have read my thoughts because his arm slipped around my waist. "She's in jail now and cannot harm anyone again."

Savoring his tender and reassuring gesture, I closed my eyes momentarily in relief. "It's difficult to believe all of that happened."

Or that I sensed Christina's presence that day at the Madonna della Corona.

"Rufina lost her way during the darkness of the war years and couldn't make it back to the light . . . I too will mourn losing the woman I knew from my youth." Then his voice hardened slightly. "But she has to pay the price for Tonio's murder, whether it was accidental or not, and for her other crimes against Professor Harrison and you—thankfully, Rupert is on the mend."

"She used me like a pawn."

"Ah, but if she hadn't asked you to come to Verona, I would never have met you and found happiness again, especially since you've decided to stay and work at the Fondazione," he whispered in my ear. "You saved me from the fate of a bitter, lonely old man—thinking my brother was a killer—and thank you for not telling him about my suspicions; he would have been very hurt."

I gazed up at his face, lit with warmth and passion. "We saved each other. Like repairing a damaged dress, I now see it's in how we mend the hurt and accept our flaws that we find the real beauty again in the world." Paul was the one who first told me that, and I would never forget it or him, even though his compass was gone. But I had the strength now to let my heart guide me forward.

"Sì—vera belleza."

"Maybe you'll even start painting again," I prompted, straightening my Schiaparelli scarf.

"Perhaps."

A local Veronese couple came forward to chat with Alessandro, complimenting him on the reopening, and he introduced me as the museum's new textile curator. I beamed at their enthusiastic reaction and promise of support for future exhibits. *This was my home now.* As they moved off, I transferred my focus to where Nico had positioned himself next to the crowning glory of the display: the charcoal sketch of Christina Rossetti, which I had seen in her biography, drawn by Dante Gabriel the day before she left for Italy; it held the position of honor on an easel at the far end of the room. Her artist brother had caught that moment of longing and expectation in her face, anticipating the trip to Italy, not knowing the great love and great tragedy that awaited.

A moment caught in time.

"You never guessed that I was picking up Christina's portrait that day we went to Padua," Alessandro teased. "But I had already contacted a private collector connected to the university who bought the piece years ago; he was most generous to loan it to us."

"I'm relieved *now* since Rufina never contacted anyone in London to donate Pre-Raphaelite art, and frankly, I would have been very surprised *then* . . . especially because I thought you truly didn't respect my work," I confessed.

"On the contrary, I admire it, and you, beyond all reason."

His words thawed the last of the icy shell that had encased my heart after all of my loss and suffering. It would be a new day, for both of us, as it never was for Christina. "I hope she found some type of peace, if only through her verse."

"I think the poems speak for themselves," Alessandro's arm tightened around me, "in a glorious celebration of human faith and devotion, but also frailty and loss."

Leaning into his embrace, I exhaled in a bittersweet sigh of agreement. When Christina scrawled Fata Morgana across her father's letter, she knew her "blue-eyed phantom" was dead and gone. Nothing would bring him back to her.

But, at least, I can give her this exhibition to pay tribute to her as a woman and poet.

Never to be forgotten.

EPILOGUE

Albany Street, London, England
9 July 1865

I stared out the window at the street below where people walked past our red brick house in a stream of faceless, nameless figures like silent soldiers trudging toward some unknown land. The sun managed to peep through the clouds with a watery eye, but I scarcely noticed it because its light held no warmth, no comfort for me.

Angelo was lost forever.

"Why are you always sitting there with your lap desk, not speaking or writing, but just looking off into the distance?" Dante Gabriel asked as he ambled into our parlor with a sketchbook in hand. "Every time I come by, I find you fixed in that same position, day after day. It is maddening."

I did not respond, absently running my fingers along the feather of my quill pen.

William kept his head buried in a book, and Mama concentrated on her embroidery, both remaining silent as well. Even her lapdog sat quietly next to her. They did not know the whole story of that day at the Santuario Madonna della Corona, but they understood enough to accept that I did not wish to discuss it.

But Dante Gabriel was another matter altogether; he knew something was amiss from the day we returned and obviously wanted our family to bring it out into the open. Today, he seemed especially anxious, pacing in nervous agitation, talking endlessly about his last stay with the Morrises at Red House and how I should accompany him on his next visit because it would improve my disposition. He tried to fill up the strained atmosphere with words and more words . . . until I could barely stand it.

Fortunately, a knock at our front door downstairs ceased his endless chatter. I drew aside the lace curtain and recognized Evelyn Ashford from Highgate Penitentiary, her head twisted upwards. Instantly, I pulled back. Even though we had returned to London weeks ago, I still did not feel ready to take up my duties with the Sisters of Mercy at the convent again. I would at some time, but not yet.

It was too soon after I came to my senses on the steps of the santuario with a priest bent over me, his face wrinkled in concern.

Too soon after I informed the police that Angelo had ambled too close to the edge of the cliff and fallen accidently; I knew his father had caused his death, but I saw no point in further punishing a man who had destroyed his entire life. He would exist in his own purgatory for the rest of his days.

Too soon after I packed the pendant and Papa's letter along with my dresses—their secrets sewn inside—and instructed Elena to conceal the trunk in the Menigatti palazzo. I never wanted to see them again, but I could not bring myself to destroy the beautiful clothing and jewelry that were part of my brief time with Angelo.

Too soon after I burned the copy of the *Corriere della Dame* that he had given me; that dream died with him.

Too soon to let all of the memories surface once more and confess to Dante Gabriel what had transpired . . . and perhaps that time would never come.

"Mama, I believe Evelyn is here to speak with me," I said woodenly. "Would you mind saying that I am out of sorts?"

"Of course." She set the handiwork aside and rose from the settee, scooping up her lapdog and motioning for William to follow her, their footsteps clattering on the bare wood floor with a hollow sound; then they shut the door quietly behind them.

Once they had exited, Dante Gabriel spun on his heel and strode toward me. "For once and all, Christina, will you please explain to me what is wrong? Something took place in Italy that changed you—and not for the better—yet, for some reason, you refuse to reveal it to me. We have constantly shared our inner-most thoughts with each other, bonded as the two 'storms' of the family, so I do not understand your reticence. Even Mama and William have turned stony-faced about the trip and will not speak about it. Why?"

"Because nothing out of the ordinary happened."

"I do not believe you." He slipped a hand under my chin and tilted my face upward. "My dear sister, you have the expression of a person who has lost the one thing held most dear in life, that cherished being who brightens even the darkest corner of the soul. I know that look because I see it in the mirror every day—and, sadly, now you wear it too."

I twisted away from him. "You are being nonsensical. I am simply tired from all of our travels."

"Is it Charles then? Has he broken your heart?"

It is shattered . . . though not by him.

"No, but I have ceased all communication with Mr. Cayley. I do not intend to marry him, so there is no point in encouraging his courtship. It is finished."

Dante Gabriel stood there for a few moments, still and mute. Finally, he picked up my quill, dipped it in the inkwell, and handed it to me. "If you will not confide in me, then let your pen tell the story." He threw himself into a nearby chair, crossed his legs, and began drawing me as I set out a fresh piece of parchment paper on my lap desk. As I started to write, I felt Angelo guiding my hand, and I came alive again with the memories pouring out in a flood of rapturous creativity.

I wish I could remember that first day,
First hour, first moment of your meeting me . . .

★   ★   ★

Postscript:

After Christina Rossetti's return to London, she wrote some of her most brilliant poetry, including the *Monna Innominata* sonnet sequence, which received great critical acclaim. She remained unmarried and died on December 29, 1894, while working on her latest book of devotional verse, and was buried in the Rossetti family tomb at Highgate Cemetery. Her brother, William, somewhat cryptically commented, "Had she [Christina] henceforth lived in Italy . . . she would, I believe, have been a much happier woman than she was." Today, Christina Rossetti is considered to be one of England's finest Victorian poets.

ACKNOWLEDGMENTS

By all rights this book should have never seen the light of day. I drafted it as the world was finally emerging from the pandemic, but every step of the way toward completing this work was a new and different personal challenge, culminating in the loss of our house in Hurricane Ian. My manuscript was unfinished but, like so many other people in southwest Florida, my husband and I were struggling to find the resources to recover. But they came—in the form of the many, many people who helped us, without whom I wouldn't have been able to publish this novel. My college community at FSW extended more lifelines than I can count, including a place to live and the warmth of friendship (Wendy and Dana, and Dan and Mary Ellen, you're the best); and my writing community provided small grants for us to start up a new life (thank you, MWA, SINC, and Authors League Fund). We will be eternally grateful for your generosity and support.

On the publishing side, I would like to recognize my eternally optimistic agent, Nicole Resciniti, who is both a cheerleader and champion of my work—and just a genuinely nice person (as well as consummate professional); I'm so fortunate to have her as my creative partner. And a huge shout-out to the Crooked Lane Books team who took a chance on this novel, especially my editor, Faith Black-Ross, who guided me along in the editorial process with both wisdom and encouragement. Thanks to all of you for giving me this incredible opportunity.

On a more personal note, I have no words to express my love for my husband, Jim McLaughlin, who has been at my side during the roller-coaster of life during the last few years, always keeping the faith through the great joys we shared in Italy researching the book to the many hardships we experienced post-hurricane. He's my partner and forever friend.

Finally, I have to acknowledge the beautiful experience it has been to write about a poet with the depth and lyricism of Christina Rossetti. An intriguing yet private woman, her verse has always had the soulful ability to reach across time and inspire me, this time to new heights as a writer—and I loved every minute of trying to make her come alive as a character. Traveling to Milan and Verona to research her story and learn about the post–World War II fashion industry was just icing on the cake.